For Carol Enjoy [handwritten inscription]

LILY TORRENCE

Fred Andersen

Fred Andersen [handwritten signature]

MuseItUp Publishing
CANADA

MuseItUp Publishing
https://museituppublishing.com
Cover Art © 2013 MuseItUp Publishing
Print ISBN: 978-1-77127-888-1
eBook ISBN: 978-1-77127-481-4
First eBook Edition *January 2014

For Regina and Alfred,
who were there.

Chapter One

Los Angeles, 1943

The roar never stopped. Airplanes. Warplanes. Each one sounded like it would fly in the window. But they all went over, roaring like thunder. From the bedroom Maria could see fields. Cows. And a gully, full of weeds and trash.

Her eyes opened and it was all still there. A car door slammed outside, and shoes scraped the wood floor in the front room. Rough voices. She sat up and pushed the dark curls away from her eyes. The bottle on the dresser still had an inch in it. She poured the liquor into a glass and gulped it down, burning, and crawled awkwardly back onto the bed.

The door opened, and the big one came in. The one with the pink ears, like a rat up close. He came to the bed, and she unzipped him and unbuttoned him. His pants slid down and he crawled over her.

"You smell bad." He piled into her hard a few times. His body pressed her down. She could barely draw a breath.

"You're disgusting," he growled. "You never take a bath."

"I'm sorry." She knew better than to fall for that one. There was no bath in this place. If she said that, he would punch her in the stomach, or the face. A strong memory stirred in her. A cold morning, a wet wind off the lake. Walking by the railroad track, mittens furry inside, huge clouds of

1

steam rising from the train engines, and the men burning coal in a barrel, clapping their hands and cursing.

She did not notice when he left. Quiet all around now. Maybe the war was over. Sailors rushed into the room. Sailors in blue sailor suits and white caps. They came to rescue her. In white gloves and white belts, with white pistols, shooting all the bad men. The bad men squealed like pigs and died.

A voice called her name. *Maria. Maria.* She had been awake when the sailors came, but now she opened her eyes and wondered if the dream would ever end. It was her friend, Lily, from before, but she looked different. And she was telling her something.

"Come on. It's time to go. Hurry."

Maria stood up, and Lily put a long coat on her and led her out the door, through the front room, empty, and out into the dark. A car. Red. She sat in the seat and the car drove.

* * * *

The whole thing started long before someone planted two slugs in Marty Nuco. Few minded Nuco getting killed, but the affair threatened careers and reputations all over town.

So Lyman understood why they covered it up. But a young girl was killed, and bad people got away with extortion and murder, and it just seemed to Lyman that he was the only one left who could tell the real story.

And he thought he should tell the real story.

It began for Lyman Wilbur on a Friday in March, 1943, when he showed up at Colosseum Pictures for the first time. He parked at the street entrance in a little cul-de-sac off Santa Monica Boulevard, a block west of Crenshaw. This was the office entrance, not the studio lot, so there was no gate, no burly guard, none of that stuff you see in movies. Just an office building three stories tall and a block long, a cream stucco art nouveau temple flanked by high blank walls that disappeared into the distance.

It was a bright, quiet spring morning. As he climbed out of his old Chrysler Six, Lyman caught a whiff of corned beef and cabbage. Probably from the lunch stand on the corner.

Corned beef and cabbage was a great metaphor for Lyman's mission that day. He had come to the studio to sell out, to hand over his art, such as it was, to be pickled, boiled, and pounded till it could be cut with a fork. For this Lyman would get cabbage. Lots of cabbage. He had already sold his novel to the studio, and was about to be hired, he was pretty certain, to help rewrite it as a movie script.

Heavy, dignified bronze plates on either side of the glass double doors read COLOSSEUM PICTURES STUDIOS. He entered a spacious, silent reception lobby. Some deep leather armchairs did not look like they got sat in much. Easels displayed posters of recent Colosseum films. At a flat desk toward the back of the room sat a tall, dark-haired item whose name, according to the plaque on her desk, was April Showers. No. April *Sheffield*.

Her name didn't matter. What mattered was that she wore a sharp gray plaid suit, and a man's dark blue silk tie. She had smooth ivory skin, and her hair fell in loose, but not unstudied, waves. She had a professionally severe expression that looked like it might warm up at the right time, in the right place.

Lyman made himself stop. His habit of narrating his life like one of his Archer Daniel detective novels was something he needed to control now. And that hard-boiled style so easily slipped into self-parody.

"Have you an appointment?" The woman scarcely glanced at Lyman, because he was not the perpetually thirty-eight-year-old, rock-jawed, cat-reflexed Archer. He was the gumshoe's creator, fifty, soft and pale, in an outdated brown suit and round horn-rimmed glasses. It had been ten years since a young woman had looked at Lyman with any kind of interest, and that had been a drunken floozy in a dive saloon.

Lyman gave the businesslike demeanor right back to her. A little smile, a little nod. See how she liked *that*. "Lyman Wilbur for Mister Sheldrake."

Miss Sheffield lifted the handset of a black desk phone and punched a button. She leaned back, waiting for an answer. The short gray jacket, unbuttoned, also leaned back, and the white shirt stretched against her breasts. The thin gold pen in her hand tapped against the blotter. She spoke into the phone and replaced the handset.

"Mister Sheldrake will be here directly. Won't you please have a seat?" She smiled perfunctorily and watched Lyman until he sat.

Lyman pulled a pipe out of his jacket pocket. It already had a wad of sweet-smelling Bond Street tobacco in it. He picked at the tobacco with the butt end of a wooden match to fluff it a little.

Fear and joy competed in his mind over the turn of events in his life. His invention of private eye Archer Daniel had lifted Lyman from pulp-mag obscurity to the best seller lists, but his income remained pitifully small. Then director Max Beckerman liked *Double Down*, the first novel in the series, and convinced Colosseum Studios to buy it. That check had been the biggest Lyman ever cashed, but it barely covered his debts. To get ahead, he needed this job. Writing in an office, however, with other people, would be a big change for him, and Lyman had long ago realized that he was a creature of solitude and routine.

Striking the match on a smoking stand next to his chair, Lyman began drawing and puffing, and a cloud of smoke rose above him. Miss Sheffield did not approve, he inferred from the minute change in the curve of her pale, swan-like neck. Well, the hell with her and the hell with doubts. The die was already cast. He looked as good as he could look and felt as good as he could feel. He was here to go to work.

Lyman reviewed the movie posters on the easels, each under its own spotlight. *My First Divorce*, starring Claire Howard; *Paid in Blood*, with Edmond Glover; *WAC Attack*, featuring Hi-Ho Henshaw. Life as presented by Hollywood was glamorous, grimacing and pie-eyed. Looming dangerously close to Miss Sheffield, a red-eyed gorilla from *Jungle Rage* seemed almost to be bursting out of the poster to pounce on her. She appeared unconcerned.

A door in the back of the room opened and a man appeared.

"Mister Wilbur? Fred Sheldrake." The man advanced toward Lyman and extended his hand. "Welcome." The producer looked the part. Bald dome, insincere smile, chalk-stripe suit, preceded by six inches of cigar.

"We're real excited about doing *Double Down*." Sheldrake ushered Lyman back through the rear door and into a hallway. "Normally we don't hire the book's author to work on the screenplay. It's hard to ask you to murder yer own child."

"Yes, even Abraham had trouble doing that."

Sheldrake cut him a sideways glance. "Oh—over at Metro."

Now it was Lyman's turn to be confused, but he already felt buoyed by the producer's infectious confidence.

The cigar waggled. "But Max insisted. And what Max wants—he loves that detective character of yours, with all the tough cracks— whaddaya call him?"

"Archer Daniel," said Lyman.

"Yeah, Daniel. We are thinking of Edmond Glover for the role, so you know we're taking this seriously. First class all the way."

"They say he's brilliant."

"Who? Max?" Sheldrake chuckled. "Yeah, we're all brilliant. Now you're brilliant, too."

Sheldrake skipped up a flight of stairs, beckoning Lyman to follow. "Here we are, the writer's ward, er, wing."

They walked through a long hall of stained mahogany doors. A single typewriter tapped in one of the rooms, but otherwise the whole floor seemed deserted.

Some of the doors had name plaques screwed to them. On others, the name was printed on a card tacked to the door: an unsubtle indicator of status, Lyman assumed. Just past another set of stairs, the door at the end of the hallway had the name "Max Beckerman" engraved and firmly affixed.

Sheldrake rapped once on the door and pushed it open. "This is his office. Your office."

Lyman followed him in. In the middle of the room, a trim, short man with a crew cut sat in a swivel chair behind a desk, jacket off, one cordovan shoe propped up, speaking into the mouthpiece of a Dictaphone machine in German-accented English. He glanced at his visitors and kept talking.

While Max finished his memo, Lyman surveyed the office. A half-dozen large sash windows formed the east wall, and beneath them stood a long row of well-stuffed bookshelves. A Turkish rug lay like a maroon and gold pool in the middle of the room, around which clustered the desk, a sofa, and an easy chair. Close to the door stood an antique bentwood hat tree bearing at least four hats, and an assortment of canes, crops, and umbrellas. Behind that, through an open door, Lyman could see a private bathroom. Framed art reproductions hung on the walls.

"Very nice," said Lyman.

"Best we've got," Sheldrake purred. Lyman knew from newspaper columns that Max Beckerman was a refugee from the Nazis who had come over long before the war. He was said to be a friend of glamorous stars, an art collector, wit and raconteur. And—Lyman pushed his glasses against the bridge of his nose for a better look at a small ink and watercolor on the wall. It was signed "Picasso." Not a print. He felt a definite twinge in his confidence.

Max concluded his memo. "...Und we vill meet at the theater in Westwood at seven." He smiled, and winked at Sheldrake. "Mit a kolossal schlong on it." He giggled, and hung up the microphone on the Dictaphone stand. "A little present for my secretary. She's multilingual." He sprang to his feet, still laughing.

"Here y'are," said Sheldrake. "Max, Mr. Wilbur."

"Mister Wilbur, a great pleasure!"

Lyman extended his hand, a little reluctantly. Had he heard that right? *Colossal...* What kind of man made jokes like that to a lady, secretary or not? And why did the word multilingual sound profane when this guy said it? "The pleasure is mine, Mr. Beckerman."

Max grabbed Lyman's hand and pumped it enthusiastically.

Lyman decided he'd better get over being offended. This was Hollywood, where normal behavior did not apply. And he really needed this job.

"Okay," said Sheldrake. He gave a half salute and left.

* * * *

"Please—" Max directed his guest to the couch, and Wilbur settled into it somewhat tentatively, as if he didn't feel like he really belonged there. Max wasn't completely sure on that point himself. Hiring this guy was a gamble.

"People are usually disappointed that I'm not a tough guy." Wilbur's teeth clacked softly on his pipe. "An ex-cop or something. If I was a tough guy I'd be in North Africa right now. Which I am obviously not."

"They don't want us old men. So we make good movies. That's how we help." Max wondered if this guy was going to hold the German accent against him. He wouldn't be the first. "But I know what you mean. People can get funny ideas. The best movie I ever wrote was about Park Avenue millionaires."

"I loved that movie," said Wilbur.

"Thank you very much." Max liked that one, too. "But I have not only never lived on Park Avenue, but when I got here in thirty-three, I slept on a friend's couch. I could speak only twenty words of English."

"Incredible." Wilbur smiled and made a siphoning noise on his pipe.

He was about what Max had expected. Not that different from Max's previous writing partner, Gil Gladstone. Both of them big and soft, with the prissy overtones of Eastern prep schools. But this guy wrote from darkened streets, from saloons and tenements. He seemed to have an affinity for goons and fairies and dangerous dames. Gil had always clung to the phony veneer of class. Good taste. That was why Max had sought a new partner.

The phone on the desk rang, and Max hopped up to get it.

"Mister Beckerman?" said the receptionist. "Miss Boynton is on her way up."

It was unexpected, but perfect. Max had several reasons for wanting to see Deborah Boynton. Personal and professional. As he hung up the phone, he quickly scanned through his appointment book for the rest of his day. For once the page was mostly blank.

Wilbur had moved over to the gas grate, and stood studying a photograph on the narrow mantel. In an apparent attempt at chattiness, he pointed at the picture. "Isn't that Deborah Boynton?"

"Yes, as a matter of fact." The coincidence was too perfect not to be scripted. A real-life meet-cute. "And as a matter of further fact, that is our Chloe." Max watched for a reaction. "At least, that's who I want. What do you think?"

Wilbur stuck his pipe in his mouth, and then pulled it out. "Deborah Boynton in our...your...in this picture? Oh my, yes!"

"Yes, and as it happens, I just got a call from downstairs."

* * * *

Lyman watched, mystified, as Max stepped to the door and opened it with a flourish and a slight bow.

In walked the woman from the photograph. Deborah Boynton. One of the biggest stars in Hollywood, as movie magazines like to say. Or somebody says it—Lyman felt a little unusual, and decided to keep his hand on the mantel, to stop the shiver trying to wiggle up his spine.

Deborah Boynton smiled. "Hello, Max."

"Hello, Debs." Max embraced her, and kissed her near the corner of her mouth.

She was surprisingly petite, wearing a simple but very pretty peach-colored dress of a fabric that seemed to float just above her skin. A necklace of white and black coral stones circled her throat. She was hatless, and her hair, swirling up in front like the prow of a ship, was darker than Lyman remembered it from the movies.

"Well, my dear, this is a pleasure for early on a workaday morning!" Max said with a teasing formality.

"I'm on vacation now, but I came in to see Mr. Corvus." Deborah gave Max a pat on the arm, and hitched up the purse that hung off her shoulder. Lyman remembered that Harry Corvus was the emperor of the studio.

"So I wanted to drop in," she said. "It's been too long."

"Indeed it has!" Max glowed. He waved a hand toward Lyman. "May I introduce. Deborah, Lyman Wilbur."

Lyman detached himself from the mantel and tried a step. Deborah grasped his fingers in her gloved hand and gave them a friendly squeeze. "Hello!" She smiled. "It's so nice to meet you."

"The pleasure is mine." Lyman's mind swirled, seeking something intelligent to send to his mouth. "Mister Beckerman just told me you will be in this picture."

Max interrupted. "Mr. Wilbur is here for his first day. He is the author of *Double Down*, the detective melodrama I believe I told you about."

"Yes, of course!" Deborah smiled again. "Am I to be in it?" She pulled off one of her gloves.

"Well, dear, it would be perfect for you. But you haff, I imagine, the final word." Max touched Deborah's elbow and guided her toward the sitting area in the center of the room, gesturing for Lyman to follow. Deborah settled in the stuffed chair, pulled off her other glove, and stacked purse and gloves on the cushion next to her.

"I haff not the final word, as you well know," Deborah mocked him merrily. "But I could speak to Mister Corvus."

Max took a seat on the couch, almost knee to knee with her. Lyman did not know what to do with himself, so he perched on the edge of the desk.

Max glanced at him. "Mister Wilbur is the leading writer of the hard-boiled school, a graduate of it, you might say."

Lyman felt his face burn. "Oh, well."

"Yes, actually, I am a big fan of yours," said Deborah. "I've read four of your novels. How many are there?"

Lyman laughed. *If I'd been wearing a fedora I would have pushed it back with my thumb.* "Four."

Deborah's eyes twinkled. "Then I guess I'm caught up! I read three hundred books a year, but not a lot of mysteries. So many writers come to Hollywood and have a bad experience. I hope that won't happen to you."

"I've only come to Hollywood in a sense," said Lyman. "I've lived in L.A. for a long time."

"Of course, that's the setting of all your books."

Lyman was impressed. She really had read them.

Max clapped his hands. "Yes, my dear. Please do mention to Harry that it would be very nice to have you as Chloe. But don't think for a moment that I don't know who the Queen of Hearts in this studio is."

Lyman stared at Max. He seemed to be playing a German butler—in fact, Lyman realized, it was the comic butler from the Park Avenue movie they had just been talking about.

Deborah stood up. "Well, I'm overdue."

"Yes, we're hard at work here." Max rose with her and touched her elbow. "But meet us at Lucey's for a drink at five."

"No, I'm back to the ranch after my errands. I don't hang around unless I'm at the Canteen. That means so much to the servicemen." It took Lyman a moment to realize she was referring to the Hollywood Canteen, the free recreation club for servicemen. Many of the biggest stars volunteered there.

Deborah headed for the door, putting on her gloves and slinging her purse strap over her shoulder. She flashed her teeth at Lyman. "Mister Wilbur, a pleasure!"

Then she was off, with Max trying to catch up, out the door and down the hall. Lyman heard Max say, "How am I to see you when you are all the time snoozling young soldiers?"

When Max returned a few minutes later, Lyman said, "She seems very nice."

Max tossed himself into the desk chair so that it rolled a little and rotated a quarter turn. "She is the best friend I have in this town, and I mean men, women, *relatifs*. But tough! Ach! From Brooklyn, the Irish slums. Had the worst childhood one could imagine. Orphaned. Abandoned. Eating garbage. Food thrown away, you know? Now she raises horses just to soak up the extra money."

The afterimage of Deborah's parting smile lingered in Lyman's vision. "That's quite a distraction, having movie stars just drop in like that."

"No. It never happens. Especially with Deborah Boynton. She wants something. But what, I have no idea. I want something, too." Max let out a short bark of a laugh, so that Lyman would know exactly what he wanted: Deborah Boynton naked on a half shell. "I talked her into meeting us for a drink."

Lyman knew this moment would come. "Oh, I don't drink."

But Max's train of thought had already left the station. "Nah, me neither. Two scotch sodas and I get a headache. Oh—" He blinked at Lyman. "You mean you really don't drink."

The thirst, the tickle, the memory of booze tried to rise up from somewhere between Lyman's heart, stomach, and spine. "Yes. No." Lyman forced the most self-assured smile he could manage. It was a hope, a curse, a lie. But for now it stood.

* * * *

"G'bye, Daddy."

Marty Nuco opened his eyes. The cutest seven-year-old girl in the world smiled at him, inches from his face, her eyes glistening with love. The two older kids stood right behind her, all waiting for his kiss to send them off to school. He sat up in bed and pressed his lips onto the top of each head in turn. The boy's hair smelled like a dusty dog. The three ran out of the room, and the sound of their laughter gradually merged with the morning song of the birds outside. Janet would lead them to the car, and then take them down the hill to the Glen Rock Academy. He went back to sleep.

Two hours later, having showered, shaved and after-shaved, Marty walked into the kitchen dressed in a light-gray wool crepe suit, a white linen shirt and maroon silk tie. He knew he was an impressive package, well-built, handsome, natural blond hair—and charming, with his Georgia accent that conveyed, he was sure, both manliness and cultivation. The perfect image for the most successful talent agent in Hollywood.

Usually Janet would have returned to have breakfast with him, but today she had gone somewhere, and the cook brought him barely-poached eggs, ham and fried potatoes, and a square of cornbread. The *Times* lay untouched on the table, and he opened it. Leisurely. He had no reason to leave the house before eleven o'clock.

The war news was good and bad. The U.S. and Britain lost seventy-one planes in a massive bombing raid on Germany, but they had done serious damage to the Focke-Wulf aircraft plant in Bremen, and had also hit factories in Pilsen and Mannheim. The Allies had begun to encircle Axis forces in Tunisia, but American casualties had passed five thousand in the campaign.

A little deeper in the paper he saw a story about a crackdown on B-girls in downtown Los Angeles bars, and the paper also saw fit to editorialize on the subject. "B-girls are wheedling parodies of singers and dancers whose real job is to get patrons to buy them colored water which is paid for as whiskey," the writer intoned. "The sordid impudence of the B-girls leads to doping and robbing and graver crimes."

This story disturbed Marty. He did not like to get involved with the routine business of the girls, but he thought he had best check in on that. He left the paper and the dirty dishes on the table, took his cup of coffee with him and walked outside. His money, handkerchief, fountain pen and pencil set were all in their proper pockets. His watch was on his wrist, and his sunglasses and keys would be waiting for him in the car.

He walked to the garage, his mind already full of the appointments and conversations he knew would fill his day. The garage was set off to the side of the house behind blue-green juniper bushes. The big overhead door had been left open when Janet left. He set his empty coffee cup on a bench, and slid into the Capri-blue 1942 Lincoln Continental Cabriolet. The factory that used to make these now built tanks.

When he slammed the car door, the hood popped up a couple of inches, as if it had not been properly latched. Marty had already inserted the key in the ignition and was about to turn it when his hand leapt backward as if from an electric jolt. He stared at the key, and the starter button, and his heart pounded so hard he thought he might pass out right there.

In his mind he saw another car. A grainy picture in the newspaper from when, 1938? You couldn't even tell what kind of car, it was so twisted and split open from the bomb. That had been downtown talking. The bosses. *And they did that to a cop. They would do it to me.*

He quietly pulled the latch on the door and eased himself out of the car, leaving the door open. He backed away slowly, then turned and trotted out of the garage, giddy at his escape.

They would kill me for it. It was the first time it had really struck him. *Why buy me off? Just eliminate me.* He didn't run the girls, but he got a cut of everything they made, in exchange for his influence and connections in the movie studios, which he used to help downtown keep charge of the movie unions.

But he knew that some in the mob thought he cost too much, and returned too little. Marty thought about Sylvie—the toad he'd made rich. Sylvie worked for downtown. And Sylvie knew how much the whole thing depended on Nuco. He knew who buttered the bread. So if downtown was looking to cut him out, it probably wouldn't be Sylvan Koch who did the deed. But the downtown mob had all kinds of ways.

Already Nuco's fear had begun to subside, replaced by a low blue flame of anger and contempt. Under the handsome facade, the silken tones, he was Tobacco Road, Huey Long, Ty Cobb. Tough. Ruthless. A gladiator. He had ducked the blow, and they would not catch him flatfooted again.

He went into the back yard. Tony was there, working on a flowerbed.

"Hiya, Tony."

"Good morning, sir." Tony stopped working and stood.

"Good morning. You done anything on the car this morning?"

"On the car? No sir."

"Under the hood? Check the oil? Or maybe last night?"

Tony smiled, unconcerned. "No. No."

"Well, I want you to pull it out and give it a quick wash."

"Fine sir. Later on I will clean up this flower bed as the señora asked."

"'At'll be fine. Chop-chop, just a quick one. You're Filipino, right?"

If Tony found this an odd question, he did not show it. He nodded, then turned and walked toward the garage, wiping his hands on a rag.

Of course Tony wasn't Italian, or Jewish. But he was the person who could have easily rigged the car. Marty stood there on the lawn, glancing agitatedly around him, trying to sort it all out. The house was a Tudor revival, and had the front door set in a turret with a pointed roof like a witch's hat. It reminded him that no place was safe. Anyone could be gotten to.

But what if Tony was not working for them? Then the thing would go off right *here*. The publicity from that, in a top-shelf Beverly Hills neighborhood. That would be worse than killing him. He started to run to catch Tony, but he heard the car door slam and he froze. He stood, holding his breath. The twitter of birds, the whine of a truck gearing down a hill somewhere nearby.

The starter turned. The engine purred, and the car backed out of the garage. Marty's breathing resumed. He trotted to the driveway.

Apparently he could trust Tony. Apparently no one wanted to kill him. Today. But he had been alerted now. He would be careful.

Tony already had a bucket out.

"Fuhget it, son. Gotta go." Marty got in, pushed the starter, and was about to pull away when he noticed the hood was still loose. He pointed to the hood, and Tony stepped over and pushed it down. Just as he did Marty screamed wildly, "No! No!" *The bomb is rigged to the hood! To the goddamn hood!*

The hood snapped shut. Tony stared at him. The moment of panic had made Marty's hands shake and his stomach churn. Tony collected the washing stuff and headed to the garage. Marty slapped his cheek, and patted his hair back into place. He drove away. Birds. A woman with a baby carriage.

He went to The Embers, on Venice Boulevard. It was a new kind of place—a cocktail lounge, they called it. Not a saloon, not a cafe, but a dark, quiet, windowless retreat from whatever was pursuing, a nightclub for the daytime, a hotel bar without the hotel. Marty parked in the alley and walked in the back door. A half-dozen morning drinkers sat at the bar, and three pretty but bored-looking girls chatted at a corner table.

He went back out and down the alley to the rear door of Sylvan Real Estate. In the small, cluttered room Sylvie sat at a desk, looking at a ledger. Marty sank down on the couch by the wall. He looked at the other man, whose face hovered over the ledger as if he was sniffing it. Koch had dark, oily hair he combed straight back from a low hairline. A white shirt billowed out around his waist below the short workman's jacket he wore, like cream oozing out of a cream puff.

"Any girl drinks," said Marty, "She buys her own. You see the paper?"

"Nah." The man did not look up from the ledger.

"B-girl crackdown coming. Mostly downtown, but."

Koch glanced at him. "We don't do that. We're class. That's skid-row shit."

"I know," said Marty. "But I don't want to give anybody an excuse."

"Yeah, no shit."

"Just make sure they're not pickin' up pin money that way. The bartenders are always in on it."

"Yeah that would be stupid. And we got some real dumbasses workin'..." Koch coughed once, clearing his throat. "Workin' for us." He gave Marty an appraising look. "Say, you okay?"

Marty smiled. "Fit as a fiddle."

"And ready to fuck," said Sylvan Koch.

* * * *

Ted Hardy sat with his wife, Ruth, in the restaurant. The same restaurant as every day, just across from the hotel and next door to the theater. Some of the troupe were finishing dinner, but Ted and Ruth were just ordering. They didn't have to be at the theater for another two hours. Ted was the star. Without him, there was no show. But nobody worried about Ted Hardy anymore. It had been a long time since anybody had.

Ted was a rock. And he and Ruth stuck to the pre-performance routine like a train to a track. Dinner would be unhurried, and Ted would finish off with coffee and cigarettes. An hour before curtain, he would walk the short distance to the theater and get into his costume, which, other than his character's battered fedora, was almost indistinguishable from his street clothes. His makeup took ten minutes. Then he would sit with Ruth, calm and quiet, maybe do a few lines of a crossword puzzle. And then he would go out and be warmly funny night after night. Which was, of course, much harder than he made it look. That's why he was a star.

It didn't matter what theater it was, or what city it was, big or small, east or west, Ted Hardy delivered. He had been touring with *My Friend Turnip* off and on for almost three years.

Ruth tapped the menu. "Tomato juice?"

"Sure," said Ted.

Ted Hardy was a rock, or rather, he had become a rock, with the help and support of Ruth.

The waiter appeared, and Ruth was all business. Part of Ted's reward for doing six or more performances a week was that Ruth handled everything. "How's the lamb?" she asked.

"It's the best thing we have on the menu," the waiter enthused. He was also the owner. His name was Henry.

"Wonderful!"

Ted hadn't even looked at the menu. "And for Mr. Hardy? The baked —"

"Haddock, yes, with asparagus. No potatoes."

Henry nodded. Ted stuck to routine. It wasn't superstition, even though he was on a winning streak. It was just the way he did things now.

"They do have turnips," said Ruth.

"Yes, and they've had turnips every night for two weeks. Thanks for not mentioning it until now."

"Well." Ruth gave him a coy smile. "I'm known for my self-control."

The waiter smiled and took the menus. "So, Mr. Hardy, you are leaving us soon?"

"Yep. Off to L.A. We're doing a war-bond appearance in Sacramento on Monday, and opening in Los Angeles on Thursday."

"I know it will be a hit there too," said Henry.

"It's a good play. It's been very good to me."

"You're terrific in it."

"Thanks, but I'm playing second banana to a vegetable. And lucky to be doing it." It was a stock line Ted used, but opening in Los Angeles was going to be different for him. Ted had become a solid citizen, maybe even a great American, but when he left Hollywood, ten years ago, he was a different man.

It was 1934 when he divorced Deborah Boynton and gave up the fight for custody of their son. When he was tarred and feathered and run out of Hollywood on a rail, his once-promising showbiz career in tatters. In the following years, her career ascended on gossamer wings, while Ted toured the cesspools of the east coast, doing vaudeville, state fairs and bit parts in dated melodramas, enduring the looks and whispered questions. Ted Hardy? Didn't he used to be in *movies*?

Then he'd found Ruth, and the turnip, and his life had changed. So opening next week in Los Angeles, as the star of a sought-after comedy, was going to be a moment to savor.

* * * *

Deborah had insisted Max meet her at the Polo Lounge, which she called a much tonier place than Lucey's. Max wondered about that new word. *Tonier*. No German cognate. Was there such a word in Française? *Tonnerre, tonnelier*?

Max found her in one of the green banquettes in the shaded end of the room, half behind a planter. It was a spot much favored by Hollywood people who wanted to be glimpsed, but not stared at. Most of the gawkers at the moment were at the other end of the room, watching a va-voomy starlet shove her cleavage in the face of a well-known red-nosed comic actor.

Deborah had added a smart black-and-gray peaked hat to her ensemble. Max felt the hat sort of loomed above him if he got too close to her. That was, he reflected, no doubt its purpose.

Max ordered a scotch and soda. "Herr Wilbur won't be joining us. I sent him home with a couple of screenplays to study. By the way—" Max handed her a book. "He sent this. I think he keeps a box of them in his trunk."

"*Double Down*. How nice." Deborah opened it and read the inscription. "'To Deborah Boynton, with the very best wishes, Lyman Wilbur.' So you've got yourself a new partner."

"Just for this picture."

"Really? Then what?"

There was a burst of laughter from the bar area. A distinctive Philadelphia drawl cut through it, followed by another round of scandalized laughter.

"I don't know." Max sighed. "Gil went home to wrote a story about a dog for a boy's magazine. Or maybe it was the other way around. I don't know that I trust him around either group."

"Stop it." But she laughed. "He's married, and he's a gentleman." She looked down at the book, reading the first page. "Yes, I remember this."

Max fixed his eyes on hers. "Let's can the shop talk, shall we? I would rather talk about what I can do for you."

Deborah closed the book. "Well. There might be one thing. Not for me, but I would consider it a favor."

"What?"

"There's a young lady I am helping." Deborah took a sip of her martini. She had downed about a quarter inch of it in twenty minutes.

"One of your stray kittens." Max knew of her penchant for helping sad cases. Young actresses who needed a break. Hoboes who needed a meal. She even rescued the occasional broken-down horse, and retired it to her ranch.

"She's a dancer, a Mexican girl from the east side. Her name is Lily. Very lovely, sweet, good manners, and all that." Deborah gave his fingers a little squeeze with her gloved hand. "And I can see something in her."

Max leaned a little closer. Just a little. A soupçon. "Something?" he purred. "Something of the young Violet Murphy?"

"Violet Dunphy. *Murphy* I might have kept. Lily's a wonderful dancer."

"Like you."

"And works like a horse."

"Again, like you."

Deborah laughed. "Stop it! She's had a couple of chorus parts. Tall. Blonde. She has a quality."

Max swirled his whiskey. "I thought you said she was Mexican."

"She had a little help with the hair. The point is, she doesn't look Mexican, or act it."

Max looked at the book on the table. "Actually, there's a blonde baby in this thing. The one with the jewel in her..." He pointed at Deborah's stomach.

Deborah blinked. "Oh, yeah, belly button. I remember that." She set the book on the banquette next to her, and in the process, put her shoulder more in Max's path. "If you could just take a look at her."

"Certainly I can look, though I doubt her belly button can compare to yours. So. Are *you* interested in this film? Chloe is a great part."

"I've got a reputation to think about." She looked very dubious. "My character has to have a heart."

"You've done tough roles."

"But you do such great comedies. Let's do one of those. There's a war on. People want to laugh and sigh and look at beautiful stars in beautiful clothes."

Max knew very well how obsessive Deborah was about her career and her image. She had been a big star in the early thirties, doing weepies and some pretty good melodramas. When those movies went out of style, so did she. And she got some bad press about a divorce. Suddenly the execs at her own studio wouldn't give her a decent role. But then the problem husband disappeared, and she clawed and maneuvered her way back until she established herself as one of the best of the sophisticated-type comediennes.

Those dark days of hers had coincided with Max's desperate beginnings. He had done some things back then that he'd been trying to forget ever since. Just as she had, just as anyone would do when it's a question of survival.

Max took her hand again. "My dear, I will take care of you. You know that. Let's not worry about it now." He leaned close to her ear. He was going to give this another try. "I have a bigger problem—why I can never see you."

"You're a married man." She pulled her hand away and clamped it on the stem of her glass.

"A technicality. Virginia is a child. Probably a mistake. We don't truly live together as husband and wife anymore."

"Nevertheless, you are. Husband and wife."

"Bah!" Max dismissed the idea. "We are conveniently arranged, that's all." He looked at the table for a visual aid. "Like a napkin in a napkin ring."

Deborah sighed. "Max, we know each other much too well for this sort of folderol. Get yourself a starlet, take her to a hotel, take off her clothes. Then you and I will get along fine. Like an olive and an onion." She plucked the toothpick out of her drink, and held it above the glass. A green olive and a pearl onion were speared on it, dripping cold, glistening liquor.

Max laughed, genuinely pleased. Deborah played the game so well. But he would have her. He knew the rumors about her and her co-stars. Yes, and her directors. Inside that castle of control, she was just neurotic enough to assume the traits of her character. And in *Double Down*, if he could convince her to do it, she would be playing a strong woman who falls for a stronger man. That was the only way to get to Deborah Boynton, as well. Be stronger than she was.

After she finally finished her martini, Max walked her out. They would always be friends, no matter what else they were. She took his arm, and he said something witty about a couple coming in who looked strikingly like Mussolini and Hitler—Hitler being the man.

* * * *

Lily had been sitting in the parking lot of the hotel for a while, in the red Plymouth roadster, thoughtlessly trickling the tips of her fingers along the hard circle of the steering wheel. She had told herself two dozen times to leave, had even started the car twice, and then shut it off.

In a turmoil of indecision, she stared at the reflection of her eyes and cheeks in the car mirror. All her life people had told Lily she was pretty, and she believed them, but it didn't mean anything. Her mother had disappeared when she was still the center of Lily's world. Her father had abandoned his three children to move in with a widow and *her* children. Lily had been raised by an aunt, her father's sister. She had spent her high school years sleeping in a porch built onto a house on a street that might as well have been in a Mexican mining town, it was so removed from the rest of Los Angeles, or even America.

She had grown tall, and undeniably beautiful. Large, dark eyes, high, classical cheekbones, a strong nose that stopped just short of being Indian, and thick, wavy hair, lately dyed honey-blonde.

She gazed at the hotel entrance, where a doorman stood in a glade of banana trees and palm fronds. A car drove past, the top halves of its headlights blacked out.

Beauty was her way to be somebody, but it was not enough. That was why Lily had cried and begged her aunt and worked at anything to pay for dancing lessons, and why she sang in choirs, and acted in plays, and even learned to play an abandoned accordion she found in the closet.

And after untellable struggles, she had been chosen by God, it seemed, to live in the household of the glamorous Deborah Boynton. Yet this wonderful opportunity had plunged Lily into constant despair. She did not know why she had been chosen, or what her role was. In fact, all the other residents of the house, except Deborah's uncle and son, were servants, or, anyway, employees. Although Lily understood that Deborah intended to help her with her career, Deborah hadn't done anything except get her a couple of extra roles, and suggest Lily begin dance training again, with a teacher she knew. But you couldn't be idle at Deborah's house, so she helped with the chores. And waited.

Lily feared that Deborah had had a change of heart about her, and she wondered what wrong move, wrong word, wrong facial expression had done her in.

There was another explanation, of course—that Deborah had found out something awful about her. And there was plenty to find out.

Lily's anxiety had doubled this morning, when Deborah, with a rare day off, had mentioned she was going into town to see her old friend Max Beckerman about a role—not for herself, but for a young protégée of hers. But she did not say it was for Lily. Deborah's matter-of-fact manner had not encouraged questions, or even comment.

So was Lily in competition with someone else for something? And if so, for what? Having deduced that Deborah's first stop would be the studio, Lily had driven there to wait. She'd seen the big Buick go in the gate, and followed it when it came out an hour later—to lunch, to three different shops, and then here to the Polo Lounge. Where now she sat wondering, not daring to go in.

She did not want to think about what Deborah was doing in there, but she couldn't stop thinking about it. Her toe wagged against the brake pedal. Was it all about to end before it began? Had Deborah found out about Lily's past, about the things she had done to survive, about how she had sold herself in the most shameful way?

Then, finally, she saw Deborah walking out with a man, arm in arm, sparkling, radiating glamour and sexual magnetism. The man was short, energetic, waving his hands as he talked. A type Lily knew all too well. Full of it, and on the make. One of those self-proclaimed geniuses that infested Hollywood.

And Deborah. So elegant, so simple, so relaxed. What an ass Lily had been to come here! It accomplished nothing, for there was nothing to be done, nothing to be learned.

The short man walked Deborah to the curb, where Emery, Deborah's chauffeur, waited with the big Buick. The man opened the car door for her, and Deborah stepped in, laughing. The man leaned in there for a long time, kissing her, anyone could tell. Then he came up for air, smiling. He closed the door, and as the car pulled away he patted the back fender as if it were her ass.

Lily Torrence, born Lily Torres, watched the short man walk back into the bar. Whistling. The arrogant prick. Her mission had been foolish, but the anger and fear she felt would not be wasted. She was going to do whatever she had to do to stick with Deborah. She would become what she had to become. That was all.

* * * *

Max really just went in for one more drink, and then he was going to a poker game. He sat at the bar. "Give me a weak Macallan and soda."

The bartender nodded.

The girl came in and stood there looking lost. Tall, with long, blonde hair and big knockers. She approached the bar, close enough to Max that he caught a whiff of perfume as she leaned toward the bartender.

"Please," she said. "My car won't start, and my friends already left."

The bartender gave her a sympathetic smile. "I could call you a cab?"

Max raised himself up from the barstool. "Perhaps I could assist you."

Max ordered champagne for her and helped her drink it. He suggested they go somewhere to eat, she asked if she could stop at her apartment. She said her name was Gloria, but by this time she could have told him anything, because by this time his lust was in charge and wanted very badly to be introduced to her. So of course they could go to the apartment. Taking a chance, Max reached for her when the door was closed, and she responded. They never did get to dinner.

Happy as he was, Max figured the meeting was probably not a chance encounter. He happened to mention Deborah Boynton, and the girl got all excited and wanted to know everything about Deborah Boynton. He indulged her for a while, in afterglow. Then the girl fell asleep and he left.

Chapter Two

Deborah Boynton lived way out in the San Fernando Valley at a crossroads called Zelzah. The first time Lily Torrence went out there, she turned around before she reached it, not believing there could be any houses farther down the road.

She had met Deborah at the Hollywood Canteen, a recreation center run by the movie industry for the thousands of servicemen gathered in Southern California to train and ship off to the Pacific war. Deborah went there at least once a week, performing, shaking hands, and signing autographs for the soldiers and sailors, who seemed thrilled to see a glamour queen like Deborah involved in the sorts of simple theatrical things they might have done themselves back in their hometown high school.

Lily also went to the Canteen as often as possible—to clear tables and wash dishes for a dollar a night. And to try to meet someone who could get her an acting or dancing job. One night Deborah noticed her, and struck up a conversation. Lily had gone there on the streetcar, and Deborah gave her a ride home. Lily told the star selected details about her life, and Deborah seemed to approve of Lily's level-headed sort of ambition. They met at the Canteen several more times, and talked on the phone. A few weeks later Deborah invited Lily to come stay at her ranch, and got her the first movie part she had had in almost a year.

The house seemed to Lily like a Mexican hacienda in a movie, all stucco and tile, long verandas shaded by bougainvillea. The ranch was a big place, with almond and citrus groves and large pastures. On the pastureland, Deborah had built a riding ring and stables. She hired a trainer and raised Quarter Horses and Thoroughbreds as a business proposition, and because she loved horse racing. "But I don't get emotionally involved with the animals," Deborah said. "Any more than I do with the almonds."

Lily knew some of this from a magazine article she had read during her most miserable time. The article had given her hope when her dream of stardom and happiness flickered and sputtered and almost died.

Now that she was here she could see the reality. The den had gleaming flagstone floors and knotty pine paneling on the walls and ceiling. The living room was long and wide enough to play baseball in, if you wanted to. Islands of furniture were planted here and there in the gray-white carpeted expanse, and the fireplace rose like a rocky cliff at one end of the room.

The place was run by Deborah's Uncle Buck and his wife, Moira. Buck was an uncle in name only, a distant relation of Deborah through her sister's marriage. "Jes' an ol' country boy from West Harrisburg," Buck called himself. He and Moira had met in a circus, where he trained animals, and she was a magician's assistant. Deborah also had a son, away at boarding school.

Deborah and Moira sometimes joshed Buck about his tendency to pick up strays, that is, people with hard-luck stories, to work on the ranch. But Deborah had no room to laugh, because Lily was her stray, and there had obviously been others before her.

They had a custom at Deborah's house. Meals were served for all the staff and hands in a large dining room off the back of the kitchen. Buck and Moira would preside, and Deborah often attended, as she would tonight.

Two hours before dinner on this Saturday, Lily and Moira were helping Adella, the Austrian cook. The beef had been braised and the vegetables added for beef stew. The aroma of baking bread filled the kitchen, and Lily stirred the batter for a chocolate cake, sneaking licks off her finger. The phone rang, and Moira answered. After listening for a moment, she asked

Lily to go tell Deborah that Mister Nuco was on the line. Lily found Deborah in the den, reading, and delivered the message.

Lily desperately needed to hear what Deborah said, and she had a stroke of luck. Deborah picked up the phone extension, and reached for her pack of Marlboro red-tips. It was empty.

"Fine, fine. What do you know?" she said into the phone, holding her hand up to Lily and making a V with two fingers. "Yes, but right now I don't mind the taxes so much. The government needs it."

Lily hurried into the kitchen, got a pack of cigarettes out of the carton in the cupboard, and took it back. As she entered the den she slowed down.

"Glen is fine, except for being in the middle of the Pacific Ocean." Lily could hear the insect buzz coming from the receiver pressed to Deborah's ear. With a fingernail Lily pulled up the foil next to the tax stamp and tore off a square, revealing the first six cigarettes, tightly packed. She hit the pack against her knuckle to dislodge a cigarette, pulled it out, and handed it to Deborah. Even in that insect buzz from the phone, Lily heard the southern drawl and the soothing confidence of Marty Nuco's voice, and it made her skin crawl.

"No, he's not due for any kind of rotation home, that I know of." Deborah's end of the conversation was clear and direct, as always. "Unless he gets wounded—and don't you dare get him wounded."

Lily couldn't stand there anymore without seeming to eavesdrop, so she walked away, but lingered just outside the doorway. Even from there she could hear the zz-zz-zz of Nuco's laughter coming through the phone. "Not if he showed up tomorrow," Deborah said, curtly. "Not hypothetically, or any other way."

Even though she had only been in the house a few weeks, Lily knew they were talking about Glen Spangler, one of the handsomest leading men in movies. His friendship with Deborah had blossomed into romance when he enlisted in the Navy, and, eschewing any kind of show-horse role, he went onto a cruiser as a radioman. That's what Louella Parsons said, anyway. *When Deborah saw him in his dress uniform, and saw the seriousness of his commitment, she realized he was a man who could not just play the hero, but could be one, in the worst possible circumstances.*

Deborah had told Lily that story was largely a product of Louella's imagination, though it couldn't be denied Deborah had had some kind of relationship with Spangler in the past.

But Lily was listening for something else: any sign that Nuco was talking about her. Because anything Marty Nuco had to say about her to Deborah was sure to be very bad. The world knew Marty Nuco as one of the most successful talent agents in Hollywood. Lily knew him a different way, as a man who could destroy her.

The conversation ended, and Lily went back to the kitchen. As far as she could tell, her name had not come up. She was fairly confident Nuco did not know of her relationship with Deborah, just as she had not known, until a few minutes ago, of Deborah's connection to Nuco. But if Nuco was Deborah's agent, if they talked on the phone regularly, Lily could not take any chances. She had to take care of that situation right away.

Tonight, if possible. She made a couple of phone calls, and tracked down her cousin. He would help her out, and he would keep quiet.

* * * *

It was Saturday night, so Lyman knew the smell came from the Greeks down the hall. Lamb, or maybe mutton. Anyway, sheep. The spicy aroma filled the apartment building, as if they roasted the animal on a spit in the middle of the living room. The whole family would be there, and when you talked about that family, you were talking about a whole family.

The music would start soon. Zithers. Bouzoukis. Bazookas, for all Lyman knew. It would not be blaringly loud, but certain notes on those instruments made Lyman's fillings hum.

When they could, he would take Tina to a movie on Saturday night. But tonight she was just back from three days in the hospital. She lay on the davenport, struggling to breathe, her face pale as water, her hair coming out of its pins. To all the world, an old woman with a frayed quilt pulled tight around her. But Lyman remembered her as the vibrant, charming savior of his soul, and he still saw her unmistakable beauty and dignity, even on the worst of days.

Lyman sat at the desk nearby—actually just a kitchen table pushed into a corner of the parlor. Besides the parlor, the apartment consisted of a bedroom, a kitchen and a small dining alcove. Not much, altogether.

"I don't mind them having a party." Lyman laid down the script he'd been studying. "I don't even mind them being Greek."

"Sure you do." Tina gulped a big breath. "I don't care. Let them have fun. It's better than listening to the radio. And when you get ready for bed you'll pound on the wall and they'll settle down."

Lyman smiled, despite his irritation. "But I'm trying to work."

"Well, maybe you should..." A racking cough interrupted her. The emphysema had been slowly choking his dear Bettina for at least five years, but some days were definitely worse than others. Her thin frame shook with the effort.

"Anyway, we'll be leaving them soon," she gasped.

"Yes, we will be getting out of this dump. I promise you that." Lyman had not yet signed a contract or gotten hard details about money. The money for the movie rights to *Double Down* was almost gone. The salary from the studio would be the thing that would begin to put them ahead.

Tina's attack had subsided, and she lay back. "Come talk to me." She crooked her index finger.

Lyman snapped off the gooseneck lamp on the table and slid the dinette chair closer to the sofa. "We'll get our furniture back."

"Thank God for that. I didn't think I'd ever see it again." Her voice trembled.

"Nine years." That's how long most of their furniture had been in storage at the Move-Rite on Western Avenue. It seemed incredible. He ticked off former addresses. "Big Bear. Hemet. Garden Grove."

"Lincoln Park. That was the worst. Much worse than this."

Lyman leaned toward her. "Wherever we could live for almost free. You've been more than patient, my love."

"It'll be worth it," Tina laid her hand on his arm, where the starched white cuff folded back. "It's your dream."

"Someone said that the Hollywood studios are the greatest collection of artisans in one place since they built the great cathedrals of Europe. That's hard to believe."

"I can't believe you met Deborah Boynton." Tina sighed.

"I can't either." Lyman still felt a little giddy about that. "You'll get to meet her, too. I hope."

"I don't care about that. Just promise to tell me about what goes on there."

Lyman grasped her hand tenderly. When they married in '22, he was an up-and-coming businessman, and she was the duchess of a group of Old Los Angeles semi-bohemians with money. They shared a love of literature, art, and bootleg liquor. By 1934, everything had been lost but their marriage and his thirst. It had been a long, slow scratch since then. But she had never wavered from him, and he would not have lasted a day without her.

"There really will be money, won't there?" Her question echoed all the disappointments she had endured.

"Yes, there will, at least for a few months. And a lot of it. This is the movies, not publishing." Lyman had thought that having his books published by a big New York house would assure his income. He was wrong. It paid a little more than the penny-a-word he'd gotten for his stories in *Nightshade*, the pulp mag where he'd learned his craft, but it still did not pay very much. "And if I do a good job, maybe they'll give me more work."

"I know you'll do a good job." Tina smiled hopefully.

The only light in the room came from the small lamp on the sideboard in the dining alcove. In the shadows she looked the same to Lyman as she always had. Beautiful. So beautiful that no one seemed to notice that she was forty-three when they got married. After all, he was twenty-nine then, not exactly a hobbledehoy.

But there could be no doubt that one of the nicest things that money could do for them now would be to ease her decline, to slightly veil it from his eyes, and perhaps from her own.

Tina pushed herself up. "Well, I'm going to bed. Will you come?"

"Just shortly. I want to hear the war news. And I have to bang on the wall."

She cleared her throat softly. "You've worked hard today."

"Really just doodling." Lyman had been reading the old scripts Max gave him. "Just made a few notes."

"A few notes." She shook her head, smiling. "They're going to love you."

Lyman gave her a hand up, and she stood gathering herself for a moment.

"My book they love. Myself may be another story. After all, Max Beckerman and his ex-partner were actually called 'Hollywood's Happiest Couple' in some movie mag."

"What happened to them?"

"I guess they got a divorce."

Tina smiled, and almost chuckled. She tried to avoid laughing, poor thing, because that could lead to a coughing attack.

* * * *

A high, gray fog rolled into Westwood early Saturday evening, bringing with it a clammy warmth. Max parked the car and walked with his wife the half block up Broxton Avenue. Virginia looked absolutely gorgeous this evening, seemingly born in azurite satin, her chestnut hair pulled back, the total effect making her dark blue eyes even more arresting.

The marquee of the Toltec Theater glowed brightly under the lowering damp: PREVIEW TONIGHT STARRING EDMOND GLOVER.

Virginia pointed to the sign. "What about the blackout?"

"They took off the restrictions for nighttime businesses."

"Nighttime businesses?"

"Theaters. Restaurants. That sort. They said they were losing customers. I don't think the Japs will be flying over anytime soon." Max smiled easily. He sometimes wondered if Virginia ever read a newspaper. But today had been a good day, and that was not a given with her. Despite what he might say under the influence of lust to Deborah or another potential conquest, Max loved his wife more deeply than he had ever loved anyone. She also drove him crazier than anyone else.

"I could find this place by the popcorn smell." Virginia inhaled prettily through her nose. "We've been here before."

"I've had good luck here before."

The Toltec was what the studio marketers called a nabe—a neighborhood theater—with a good cross-section audience. College students, aircraft workers, housewives. After they watched the picture these people would fill out cards to tell Max and the producer and the marketing department how they liked it.

Virginia smiled at him. "You're superstitious."

"There's nothing wrong with that. If this crowd likes it, it's done. No new scenes. No re-edits." Max was also superstitious about Virginia. It could be discouraging with her. It could seem hopeless. And then she would surprise him with her tenderness, her understanding, her brilliance, and it made his love for her burst out all over again.

And today had been a good day.

A nearly full house watched the new picture. The moviemakers and their dates sat in the last row. Fred Sheldrake, who produced it, was there with a girl no one knew who spent the entire movie with her head lying on his shoulder, so Max had a constant uneasy feeling of sitting next to a decapitated body. Virginia sat on Max's other side like someone who had actually come to watch a movie. Gil Gladstone, co-writer, came alone, except for his usual self-importance. Marty Nuco, the talent agent, was with one of his clients, Toni Leeds, a dark-haired, porcelain-skinned ingénue who had the second female lead. Nuco was the agent of some of the biggest stars in Hollywood, including Edmond Glover, the star of this film.

Glover would not be putting in an appearance tonight, *Gott sei Dank!* Max had had a tough time directing Glover, who turned out to be as surly and paranoid as his reputation had foretold. It wore on Max. That was no way to live. He was almost sorry they'd put Glover in the picture.

Almost. Not quite.

Because the audience was going for it. And what they were mostly going for was Glover. Despite the problems, he had given a beautiful performance. Max could tell by the backs of their heads that the audience members were totally immersed in the story. Glover played a French resistance fighter, but the audience didn't give a hoot about that. They had come to see Edmond Glover: tough, intelligent, and soulful. And they were getting what they wanted.

Then there was a burp.

At a key moment near the climax of the picture, a Gestapo officer stood over Glover holding a pistol, snarling. They were on a dock in Marseilles at night, in the fog.

Along with everything else, Glover was great in action scenes. He punched with authority and pulled the trigger with no regrets. In this scene on the dock, he slumped against a crate, beat up, woozy, almost done for.

The German in the black leather coat mocked him, and democracy. "You know it is over. Your American allies are far away, and quite indifferent to your fate."

Glover struggled to stand, hooking his arm over the top of the crate to pull himself up. A reverse camera angle showed that the crate was actually full of fish. Unseen by the Nazi, Glover gripped something inside the crate. Tense music filled the theater, almost unheard by the engrossed audience —that stinking Nazi!

Suddenly Glover whirled, and socked the Gestapo agent in the face with a two-foot-long fish. The villain staggered back and Glover knocked the gun from his hand. They struggled along the dock in a furious fight.

But it was no good. Once the viewers realized he'd hit the guy with a fish—it took a few seconds—they emitted a burst of surprised giggles. Now they were hearing the music, which sounded much too obvious, and the action of the fight seemed like re-processed slapstick. A man in the audience yelled, "Holy Mackerel!" and another wave of titters rose up. Max found himself sinking down in his seat.

Sheldrake separated himself from his young paramour and tapped Max on the arm. The two of them stood up and sidled out to the lobby, followed by Gil Gladstone.

"I told you that goddamn fish idea..." Gladstone hissed at Max as the three men gathered in front of a dark red banquette in the corner of the empty room.

"Don't *glower*, Gilbert!" Max grumped. "So back we go to your grappling hook." To the empty lobby he announced, "I still hate hitting a guy with a grappling hook." Behind the concession counter, the popcorn machine applauded politely.

Sheldrake spoke around his cigar. "As long as yer re-shooting scenes with Edmond, there's that scene in the cafe where his toupee slipped or something."

Max laughed. "In a pig's eye, use Edmond Glover! I wouldn't make a VD training film with that son of a bitch now. I'll use a stand-in to swing the hook." At one point during filming, Glover had called Max a Nazi. Pretty funny, considering Max was a German Jew.

An usherette in a lumpy green uniform opened the doors on either side of the snack stand, and people began to come into the lobby, where they stood around, or queued up for refreshments. Virginia emerged, with Sheldrake's blonde, and sat on the banquette behind the three men.

Max looked at Sheldrake. "Why aren't they leaving?"

The producer shrugged. "Double feature."

Virginia tugged on the bottom of Max's jacket. "Look..."

Max glanced down at her, and turned to where she pointed. The crowd seemed to swirl to the other side of the lobby, and Toni Leeds stepped out of the manager's office, smiling brightly, shaking hands, signing things. She froze for a moment as a flashbulb went off, then resumed her slow progress across the carpet.

Marty Nuco walked beside the actress, watching, directing traffic. A big blond type in a blue merino suit, he towered over Toni and her fans,.

The small throng made its way out on to the sidewalk, where Nuco opened the door of a waiting car for Miss Leeds. The car drove away, and the crowd began to file back into the theater.

Nuco also walked into the lobby, and joined Max's group. He nodded to the two women, who had stood to watch the scene. "Ladies."

Gil Gladstone smiled at Nuco, and Sheldrake waggled his cigar, both men uncharacteristically deferential. Max tapped Nuco's shoulder with all the caution he'd show to a large reptile. "Lovely choreography with Toni. But no limousine?"

"No." Nuco smiled. "She's not a limousine yet, just a late-model Cadillac sedan. She's still in the shopgirl-with-a-heart-of-gold phase of her career." Nuco spoke with a sort of patrician southern accent. *Shawpgull. Ca-ree-uh.*

Virginia leaned to Max's ear. "Darling, if you are going to be a while, get me a cab, will you?"

Max felt disappointed. He knew she hated movie shop-talk. Nevertheless, he thought they had made plans. "Do you not wish to go to The Mocambo?"

"No, just home."

"You take the car, then."

"All right, dear. Don't be too late." Virginia flashed a smile to the group, kissed Max's cheek, and walked away. Max ruefully watched her go.

Sheldrake had chewed the mouth end of his cigar into a soggy rope. Now he lit the dry end with a gold lighter. "Nice job by Glover," he puffed at Nuco.

Nuco's Georgia gentility disappeared. "Since this morning I no longer represent the cocksuckah."

"Oh, you don't say?" Max wondered what this was about. "You dropped him?"

"No, he fired me. Accused me of having cahnul relations with his seventeen-year-old daughter."

Max took great pride in his cynicism, but this shocked him. "That's disgusting."

"You ever seen his daughter?" Nuco chuckled malevolently. "He *accused* me. I never touched her. Never been in a room alone with her."

"Well, it sure sounds like Edmond."

"He'll hire me back tomorrow. And I've still got a few clients."

That was certainly true. Nuco had the best stable of talent in town. Big stars. And young actors and actresses and writers on the rise. Some people wondered how he did it. Max had a real good idea, and it was not a pretty picture.

Nuco turned to Sheldrake, whose girlfriend had him in a lascivious embrace. "By the way, honey, how old are you?"

"She's twenty-three, aren't you, Phoebe?" Sheldrake gave her a squeeze.

"Certen-mont." The girl giggled. "Twenty-three if I'm a day."

* * * *

It was the scene where the cop and the doctor argue with him over who has the right to confiscate the magic turnip. And Ted Hardy—as Lloyd Schlenk—agreeably supports both sides. The doctor thinks the turnip can move a person instantly through time, and the cop thinks it can move a person instantly through space. They're both right, Lloyd points out, or at least as right as each other.

It was the third act of the last night in San Francisco. Ted liked what he was doing out there. It was smooth tonight, and the audience was warm and engaged, the ideal response to this play. The Assistant Director watched from a chair in the left wing, unusually relaxed. And for some reason he kept drawing Ted's eye. Not by any action. He mostly seemed to be daydreaming, gazing about five feet over the actor's head.

DOCTOR: I'm afraid the situation's changed since this afternoon. I urge you to give this up.

COP: Don't tell me your troubles.

LLOYD: Say, that's not a bad idea. What are your troubles?

COP: It's a terrible idea. We're bogged down in pointless argument. We've got to do something.

LLOYD: It may be a hopeless argument, but it's far from pointless. The argument is the point.

DOCTOR: He's got an argument there.

The doctor points, and Lloyd's eyes follow the gesture all the way to the butler, who is just walking up carrying a tray with four glasses of champagne.

It was a reliable laugh, and one of Ted's favorite lines in the show, because it had no line. He sold it totally with expression and timing.

The laugh came on cue. The A.D. with the dark dreamy eyes met Ted's glance and smiled. Ted suppressed a little sputter of joy.

The butler held out the tray and each man took a glass. Then the butler took one. Frequent drinking was a motif of the show. Lloyd was sozzled most of the time, though he didn't show it. Ted, on the other hand, when he was drinking, had shown it all too well. Angry, always looking for a fight or a piece of tail. He would even proposition a cigarette girl right in front of Deborah, and she would have to pretend it was a joke. Yes it was Deborah who had borne the brunt, and, to tell the truth, she was the only one in Hollywood he really wanted to impress.

Though there was one person he wanted to kill.

* * * *

Marty Nuco slowed the car, and turned off Crescent Heights Boulevard onto a smaller street near Carthay Square.

It was a dark, quiet neighborhood of two- and three-story apartment houses, with outside staircases and verandas, tile roofs and earth-toned stucco walls. Hidden away, safe, old but classy. Marty spotted the Packard coupe parked by the closed garage behind the corner apartment, saw her dark shape in the driver's seat, and the red dot of a lit cigarette.

Marty parked his car on the opposite side of the street. He walked over to the Packard and opened the door. She grabbed his hand and stood. Her keys jangled when she dropped them into her purse. Her high heels tocked on the gravelly, uneven pavement. He led her up the five steps to the side door of the apartment, and let them in. Once inside, in the dark kitchen, he pulled her to him, and they pressed half-open mouths.

Virginia Beckerman pulled herself more tightly to him. "I've been missing you. I've been dying."

He gazed into her dark, endless eyes, and anger seized him. She whimpered as he pulled both of them down to their knees. "No, honey!"

He released her and she remained kneeling, unmoving, head bowed. "What is it?"

"*It* is that Max has you, and I never will. I could crush him, or kill him, but he would still have you. The only thing I want."

She looked up at him. Willing to give him everything, yet utterly untouchable. "I'll get a divorce."

"But I won't." Marty could not stand to see her, or think of her, because he could not ultimately have her, and he could not rid himself of her. It wasn't one thing that prevented them from being together. It was everything. He could not fight for her, he could not strike at Max, because then he would lose her. He could not divorce his wife, he could not be separated from his kids, who were his hope and treasure. He could not even be seen with Virginia in public, because that would make her a target, a lever his enemies could use against him.

He helped her up, remorse swelling in him.

She circled his neck with her arms, her gaze steady, fearless. "Fix me a drink. You may never own me. But you have me now."

* * * *

Two hours after dinner, Lily went into the deserted kitchen and found a sharp steak knife. She wrapped it in a thick cloth napkin and put it in the pocket of her long coat. Then she made a phone call. She didn't exactly sneak out—she had her own car, and nobody was a prisoner at Deborah's —but she didn't tell anyone where she was going, either.

She drove to the apartment and took the elevator to the fourth floor. There was no one to be seen in the hallway. Apartment 412 was an unintended gift from a former lover, a producer at RKO who'd paid a year's lease in advance and then been drafted. A very valuable gift, considering the wartime shortage of apartments. It had been her own hideout, and now it was a hideout again.

When the elevator opened, she crossed the hall and let herself in. Maria stood frozen in the kitchenette off to the left, holding a tea kettle upside down over the sink, her face all circles of anxiety under a dark halo of ringlets.

"Just me," Lily chirped.

"Oh God!" Maria set the kettle down and leaned weakly against the sink. "You gave me a fright."

"I had the lock changed, remember?"

"I know, but, well." Tears welled in Maria's eyes.

"I know." Lily embraced her. "I know. How are you doing?"

"I still get scared. And lonesome. I'm afraid to go out."

Lily led Maria into the living room. The apartment was just off Sunset, north of downtown. The living room window looked down on the flat, gray roof of a drugstore, and a small triangle of the street out front, with no other tall buildings nearby. That sense of being hidden from view made it feel safe, at least to Lily. "I know it's scary. But I did it, Maria, and so can you. You've got your whole life to live."

"But what if they find us?"

"If they find us we'll negotiate." Lily had brought her here to keep hidden until she was ready to go home. Lily came by almost every day, bringing groceries and whatever small items were needed, and some clothes. They were about the same age and the same size, though Lily was taller. "You're still better off."

Maria sighed, and sank down on the sofa. She pouted. "I miss my sailors."

Still standing by the window, Lily looked out at the night to hide her astonishment. "You're not serious."

"I know, I'm so stupid!" Maria smiled sheepishly. "And I'm so grateful to you for getting me out. But...I like sailors."

"Oh, Maria!" Lily laughed, but more in amazement than anything else. She herself could barely stand to talk about her nights of horror. What she had given up freely seemed worse than what she'd been forced to do.

"Me, I got no ambition. I just want to have a good time. Without screwing my brains out." Maria giggled. "I'm twenty-one now. I want to live."

Lily sat on the couch next to her. "I want you to know, I'm going to see Koch tonight."

Maria's expression changed instantly. She sat straight up. "No, you're not."

"I'm not telling him about you. I'm not that brave. It's something I have to get settled, my own situation. I thought I could disappear, but obviously, if I'm going to make it in movies, I'm going to be seen."

"Oh, I know you'll make it." Maria's eye's shone. "You're so beautiful, and talented."

"How do you know I'm talented?" Lily was touched. "You've never seen me in anything."

"I just know." Maria sagged back on the couch, trying to blink the tears out of her eyes.

"Why are you crying?"

"I don't know. How did you get mixed up in this?"

Lily fished a handkerchief out of her handbag and handed it to Maria. "They have a talent agency. I saw the ad in the paper one day when I was on the streetcar. Isn't that how they hooked you?"

Maria shook her head.

"They sent me to acting classes, and auditions. The classes weren't very good, and the auditions were phony, I think. It took me a while to figure out what was going on. But then I fell in love with Marty, and for a while I didn't care if it was a lie."

"Who's that?"

"Marty Nuco? He's an agent. He's very big. He could have gotten me big roles."

"But instead," Maria said, "He took advantage of you."

"How'd it happen to you?"

"I got knocked up." Maria had squeezed the damp hankie into a ball and held it tightly in her fist. "In San Diego. A sailor. His friend took me to an abortionist. When I woke up I was in a hotel. Somehow I never got out. They gave me money, food, plenty to drink, and reefer. And I was a long way from home."

"But you're so sweet. So innocent."

"Innocent?" Maria snorted. "I was smokin' and drinkin' when I was twelve. I've made love to men, boys, women and girls. Every way you can."

"No, what I mean is, you care about people. You cared about me when I needed a friend."

"We all hate it." Maria rolled the ball of the handkerchief between her hands. "We hate it in different ways."

* * * *

By eleven o'clock, Lily was on Venice Boulevard, driving slowly past The Embers. She was very familiar with the place, in a way that twisted her stomach into a knot.

A few doors down from the bar stood a row of shops and offices, including the office of Sylvan Real Estate. The big front window was dark, but what could be seen from the street meant nothing.

At the end of the block she turned the car into the small parking lot of an all-night hamburger stand. Her cousin Yaqui stood in front, languidly smoking under the Mission Orange sign, very skinny and very young, his foot on the parking block. She motioned, and he came over and let himself in on the passenger side.

"A new Plymouth."

Lily shook his hand. "*Como estas?*"

He nodded. "Okay. Where'd you get a new Plymouth?"

"It's not new. It's a thirty-eight. I bought it. I made a little money."

"Very nice." He looked around the inside of the car. "Very nice."

"How's my aunt?"

"She's good. You don't come around much. She moved to Avenue 35. Eagle Rock. Great neighborhood. You should come by."

"I heard she moved. You living there?"

"Yeah. So what's the caper?"

"I need to talk to someone. And I just want you there. Nothing's going to happen. But I'll feel safer."

"Okay. I got this." He pulled something out of the pocket of his gabardine jacket and showed it to her. A gun.

"Shit!" Lily cursed. "That doesn't make me feel safer. Put it away."

He wiggled it around. It was ugly, like a black china bulldog. "Hey, I've got it if we need it. You don't tell me nothin' so I assume we're not dealin' with Father Clancy."

"No. Put it away."

He stuck it back in his pocket.

Lily drove the car through the parking lot to the alley, and back behind the row of offices. Koch's office appeared deserted from this side as well.

No light shone in the two small windows on either side of the door, and there were no cars around. She pointed. "That's where I'll be." A little farther down the alley turned, and she parked in the shadows there. "Stay here and watch. If I need you I'll just come out, or I'll yell."

"You sure about it?"

"Yeah. There won't be any trouble. I'm going to go inside and wait. Don't know when he'll show up. Here." She gave him the car keys.

A small porch protected the rear door of the office, and on one of the posts supporting it hung a tin thermometer that advertised Carrier Air Conditioning: Weather Makers to the World.

The girls sometimes gabbed about that little thermometer, because, they said, a spare key to the office lived in a slot in the back of it. No one had ever done anything about it, of course. They were scared to death of him. But that's what they said. Still, Lily was almost surprised when she swung the bottom of the thermometer out and found the key there.

The girls did not know much else about Koch. He worked for gangsters. If you called him *Mr. Cock* instead of *Mr. Coke*, you might get slapped. The real estate office was just a front. His real business was the Sylvan School of Acting, the talent agency that had lured in Lily, and plenty of other girls. A contract was signed, lessons were given, introductions were made. Then for each girl came a day when they were called in and presented with the bill for all that, and the contract pulled out, and the clause shown to them in which they agreed to pay for everything. The poorest and weakest went into one of Koch's houses. Others became bar girls, or call girls. And a very few found themselves doing special favors for Marty Nuco.

Even though his first name was Sylvester, the school was named Sylvan. Maybe that was supposed to sound classier. But the man himself was a slob who could barely be bothered to get a haircut or a shoeshine. Where Koch went after work—whether he had a family, a friend, or ate raw meat and slept on a rug—no one knew. The girls said he drove himself to a doorman building on Wilshire, got out, and disappeared inside. A colored man would park the car in the basement garage, and bring it out when he was ready to leave. Or so they said.

Lily unlocked the door and poked her head inside. She stepped in, and stood for a while with her back to the door, daring herself not to turn around and run. Her idea was that she would catch him off guard, and make a deal with him. She was willing to buy her way out, in exchange for silence. She had been one of the girls, but that couldn't be allowed to stop her now.

Her eyes adjusted to the dim room, lit only by the traces of light that filtered through the curtains. She made out a desk, a file cabinet behind it on the right, and on the left, a battered couch along the wall, a serape thrown over its back. A heavy coffee table sat in front of the couch, covered with newspapers, ashtrays, and candy wrappers.

Lily lowered herself uneasily onto the couch. It was chilly, so she kicked off her shoes, pulled up her legs, and pulled the serape over herself. She waited, alert but calm.

Around midnight, the curtains in the windows glowed, and the murmur of a big, smooth engine trembled in the air for a moment. A car door opened and closed, and a few seconds later the office door opened.

"It's cold in here," Lily said.

Koch did not seem surprised to see her.

"I need to talk to you."

He walked around the desk and switched on the brass lamp that stood there. "Ah, yes. The dancer. You disappeared on us."

"Huh!" Indignation burst out of Lily. She pulled the serape a little tighter around her. "I know how much you miss me. Well, I don't miss you."

Koch shrugged and sat down. "Don't forget, we trained you. Dancing lessons, acting lessons. Quite an investment."

"I'm out now, and I'm staying out."

Koch smiled an evil grin. "Your kind come here thinking you're something special because you sang 'Mary Hadda Little Lamb' in the church basement. Yeah, you're special. Every one of the hundred of you that show up every day are special."

"All I ever wanted was an even chance."

Koch shook his head. "We gave you the chance. The training, connections into the studios. If you didn't make it, that's your personal problem. You don't look good any more. My advice, lay off the booze."

While he talked, Lily stared across at his face, green and greasy in the harsh glow of the desk lamp. She said, "Connections? Really? You turned me over to Marty Nuco so I could be one of his fringe benefits. I was always up for a part, if I would only take care of the producer, the star. I never got the part, but one of Marty's clients always did."

Koch grinned. "You got the shaft. What they say, lit'rilly. So what. It's the system, kid. You got to buy your way in."

Anger snapped through Lily like a whip. "Yeah, I heard that routine before," she said, as evenly as she could. "I wasn't headed anywhere but the ashcan."

Koch slid a short, thick cigar out of his shirt pocket and snapped a match with his thumbnail. "And then you disappeared."

"That's right, but I'm back in town now. I've got a chance now. But only if you and Nuco cooperate."

"Why should we cooperate with you?" He puffed the cigar to life.

"Because I know a few things I could use against you."

Koch barked a laugh. "Go ahead."

"I'm willing to buy my way out."

He exhaled a thick cloud of smoke. "You have money?"

Lily shrugged. "Not now, but..."

"Then *shut* your goddamn mouth." He slammed his fist on the desk, causing the lamp to bounce.

Lily's heart jumped, but she couldn't let him see fear. "I came to you tonight because I thought I could reason with you. I know Marty will listen to you. I'm going to make it in movies, and then I'll be one of his clients and give him his ten percent, or whatever he gets. And then I will pay you very well. But I have to know you're not going to sabotage me. You keep my secrets, and I'll keep yours."

Koch stared icicles at her. "At least you understand who works for who. I don't ask him to do something, I tell him." He sat back in his chair. "Yeah, I made him, too. Marty Nuco was a smooth-talking punk who wanted to be a Hollywood big shot. Those are almost as easy to come by as sluts who want to be stars. So we let him be a big shot. Live in his paper-doll house. But *here* is where the strings get pulled."

"I know that. That's why I'm talking to you." Lily did not really know who was the boss in this scheme. But she knew she couldn't talk to Marty Nuco. He had a hold on her that she did not want to test.

"Yes, you'll deal with me." Koch stood up. He was an ugly but powerful man. "And I find your offer to be unacceptable. You're not going to be in movies. You're not going anywhere. I've made an investment in you. I have to have a return, and the only asset you've got is your pussy."

She still huddled under the blanket, with her feet pulled up. Koch came around the desk, and leaned over her.

"Besides, bargaining with whores? Well, I think you can see how that would never end once it got started."

Lily was afraid, but she would not let him say that. "I told you, I'm not one."

"No," he said. "You got that wrong, too." His right arm made a short piston stroke and his fist crashed into the side of her jaw.

It stunned Lily. Koch slapped her and mashed his hand into her throat, choking her. She tried to push him away, but his grip was like iron. She went limp. The blanket flew away. He let go of her and stood smirking as he unbuckled his belt. His trousers dropped. He did not remove his jacket. Lily sobbed and shook her head, pleading with him.

Koch crawled on top of her, yanking her coat and skirt up, prying her legs open with a knee. He ground his face into hers in a crude farce of kissing. Although physically engaged in struggling with him, Lily was detached from the moment. *You think you're taking something from me?* she screamed silently. *Big deal!*

But even farther inside than that, her plan had commenced. If it was to be rape, she knew he would not kill her, and she was ready to deal with that herself. Yaqui would not be needed. Her struggle did not lessen, but became another kind of urgency. His hand rubbed the crotch of her panties. She groaned, a sound she knew could be taken as either protest or pleasure.

Koch smiled, hearing what he wanted to hear. "You bitches are all the same," he growled. "You fight it and fight it, but you know you..."

He was almost there, but suddenly he reared back. Lily held the point of the steak knife against the flesh of his throat. A thin trickle of black blood flowed into his collar. They stayed frozen like that for a moment, him rearing back, her reaching up.

"Do you know who is the greatest general of Mexico?" she gasped.

"Christ a might!" He tried to escape by rolling off the couch onto the floor, but he banged the back of his head hard on the edge of the coffee table, and she rolled right on top of him, kicking her knee into his gut as hard as she could. The tip of the knife still pushed into the soft place between his windpipe and his jawbone.

"Do not move again, *pendejo*, or you'll be dead."

He lay his head back on the floor, gasping for air.

"Who was the greatest general of Mexico?" she hissed.

She could see his mind working like you can see a steam engine working. "Pancho whatsisname?"

"No, *puto*. It was General Obregón. Alvaro Obregón. He was the toughest, meanest cold-hearted son of a bitch that ever lived. And do you know who I am?"

"No," he whispered, his eyes wild. He was more afraid of this crazy talk than he was of the knife.

"I am his daughter. The bastard daughter of the meanest son bitch that ever lived. And I will cut off your dick and cook it in a tamale if I ever see you or hear from you again."

With one last thrust of her knee into his belly, she stood up. He lay there, panting, pale, and sweaty, staring up at her. She hurried out the door, and trotted away, really afraid now for the first time. The lights of the car went on, and Yaqui drove up. She waved her hand to let him know she was all right.

"Where's your shoes?"

She slid in. "Just go. Don't need the shoes."

Yaqui put his foot into it. As the car roared down the alley, Lily turned back. Koch stumbled out into the alley, looking at them. It was too dark to tell for sure, but he might have raised his arm. There might have been a gun in his hand. A second later the car veered out of the alley onto the street, and away.

"Did you get it settled?"

Lily let out a breath. She tried not to shiver. "I put a knife in his throat."

Yaqui laughed for a second, but only a second.

"Not all the way. Just to let him know I'm a little crazy, a little dangerous."

Yaqui chuckled again. "You? Dangerous?"

For once she wasn't going to apologize. "That's right."

Chapter Three

Monday morning, Max awoke feeling light and jolly. One of the few men in Hollywood allowed to both write and direct, Max's writing days started later and ran longer than shooting days, which were limited by budgets and union rules. Max dressed in tan slacks and a white linen shirt with a cadet-gray sweater-vest over it, collar open, no tie.

He walked from the bathroom into the bedroom and opened the curtains to look out upon an exquisite California garden, where vines tumbled down from tall trees into flower beds and a rock-lined pond. The soft light from the window washed with loving gentleness over the slim reefer of Virginia, still wrapped in sheets, watching him contentedly.

Max bent down to kiss her soft, full lips. "Adiós, chérie."

"Auf Wiedersehen, mon amour." They both smiled at the pet endearments.

Max went out the front door of his house, putting on a buttermilk-yellow panama, and eased into the cold leather seat of his Bugatti roadster for the short, pleasant trip from the Hollywood Hills to the studio.

After a brief weekend respite, the laborers and artisans had returned to the stages and outdoor sets, the shops, warehouses, dressing rooms and offices of Colosseum Pictures. Showgirls were being feathered, war heroes were having wounds and mascara applied. The string section of the studio orchestra would already be warming up in the rehearsal hall. As

Max drove down the narrow street to his reserved parking place behind Soundstage Six, he passed carpenters putting the finishing touches on a replica of the Roman Coliseum not much larger than a studio mogul's daughter's wedding cake. He entered the office building through the transcription room, where secretaries furiously typed the lengthy memos Benzedrine-crazed producers had dictated over the weekend, making a pleasing mechanical clatter.

Max certainly had not forgotten that Lyman Wilbur would be working with him today, but it struck him unpleasantly somehow to see this large, owl-like creature perched on the couch in a tweed suit more suitable for a small town banker than a creator of witty fables for the dream factory of Hollywood. But, Max reflected, that was what he wanted from Wilbur. Cheap suits. Ugly spectacles. All would be fine. Compared to directing, writing was like eating pudding. All he had to do was establish the routine.

Max stopped at the hat tree, took off the panama, and replaced it with a green Tyrolean with a badger brush. He noticed Lyman watching him. "This hat I wear specially for writing." He clamped it over his crew cut. "It's good luck. This hat wrote lines for Greta Garbo."

Lyman smiled, but seemed distracted. He sucked noisily on his pipe. So Max's first *mot* had been wasted. Was the man some sort of grassweed?

"Well, then." Max headed for the desk, where a pile of memos had already collected in the in-box. The sun shone in the row of windows along the wall, lighting the room with a pleasant morning glow. He glanced at a few of the memos, all perfectly typed on the Colosseum Pictures pink half-page memo form. *Hayseed*, he realized, was the word he had meant. Was the man some sort of hayseed? "How was your weekend?"

"Productive." Lyman stood and handed him a sheaf of papers, about thirty pages, neatly typed. "I didn't nearly finish, of course, but I would call it a good start."

"*Was ist das?*" Max looked at the gift. "*Double Down*. Act One, Scene One." He read a few lines, then riffled through the pages, stopping here and there. He read out loud: "'Camera follows Archer into the office. The ice-cool blonde eyes him. Close up of her thin, gold pencil tapping the desk indolently.'" He looked at Lyman. "You read the screenplays I gave you?"

"Yes, I—"

Max cut him off. "Mister Wilbur, a screenplay is not something you throw together over a weekend."

Lyman smiled, and his pipe clicked between his teeth. "Of course. I—"

"And camera movements are not dictated by a beginner writer to a director." Max could hear his voice rise. He adopted a friendly, teacherly tone instead. "We will work together on writing this picture. You will help me turn this admirably flavorful novel you wrote into a usable set of dialogues. He says, she says. That is all, and it is enough."

Lyman blinked at him for a long moment. "Naturally, I expected there would be revisions."

"Revisions!" For just a moment, Max considered throwing Lyman's papers at his puffy, offended face, and just dropping the whole project. Instead, he fanned the pages at the blue cloud Lyman's pipe had already created above their heads. He dropped the sheaf on the desk, picked up a steno pad and handed it to Lyman. "Read this," he said. Lyman began to read. "Out loud," Max instructed.

Lyman scowled at him, but obeyed. "'This is a tennis court, sunny day. Jack is playing tennis with a woman. On the next court, Jill is playing tennis with a man. Jack's opponent hits a long crosscourt shot that he has to run almost into the next court to return. At the same time, Jill hits a long crosscourt shot in the opposite direction. Both shots are returned into the wrong court, and the two men pass each other so Jack is now playing Jill.'"

Lyman shrugged and looked up, obviously not impressed. Max explained. "It's called a 'meet-cute.' I've written a hundred of them, and this is one of the best. It's how you get Jack and Jill together with some panache at the start of a picture. That's what I wrote this weekend." That was not literally true, but Max wanted to make a point.

Lyman sighed and stood up. "This was all a mistake."

"No. Please sit." Max raised his hand and Lyman hesitated, then sank back to the couch. "I did not say it's how you start this movie! It's just a little exercise I do to get the juices flowing. Writing a movie is slow and tedious. Ideas are dreamed up and dropped by the dozen. How long did it take you to write your novel—this one, *Double Down*?"

"Well over a year. There were interruptions, a lot of rewriting."

"But of course!" Max purred at him. "There you sat, writing, thinking, mulling, contemplating the bust of Pangborn. Re-writing, re-re-writing! The end result? A thing of beauty! The eye just rolls down the pages of your book. Even the white spaces are well done. But there are no white spaces in a movie. There is the dance of smoke from a cigarette against a woman's flawless skin, the crash of fist into jaw. This movie may take six months to write, but when it is done it'll flow across the screen like champagne!"

"Six months!" Lyman's mouth dropped open.

"The only difference is, you will be getting a thousand a week to do it, and we will be doing it together." Max walked down the row of windows and began throwing them open. "Now, it is a beautiful, hazy California morning. I am going to teach you everything you are capable of learning about movie writing." He turned to Lyman and launched his second *mot* of the day. "Which may not be much."

* * * *

Now Lyman knew about the money. It was shocking. A new Chevrolet every week. But he did not have it yet, and at the moment he was not sure he even wanted it. He wasn't flat broke, he'd be fine. He did not need to take any bilge water from a sawed-off Bismarck.

Lyman had lived in England as a youth and trained there during the war. He had fought in France and visited Holland and Germany, and he was familiar with the sort of Continental arrogance Max evidently ate for breakfast. Lyman would not have it. He could walk out of here after half an hour and never look back.

But for some reason, when Max said sit, Lyman sat. Not some reason —he knew the reason. It was the hope that lay in a dumpy apartment near Hancock Park, struggling to breathe, lying in a rented bed beside a rented lamp. Bettina had been his sun and his support through all the tough years. And it had been the draining of her very life.

So, fine. *Très bien*. He sat for his wife. He would batten the hatches. For Tina he could put up with this little arsenheimer long enough to bring home a few Chevrolets.

* * * *

Deborah did not insist that the workers at the ranch be unmarried, but in most cases, she did not allow their families to live there. Most of the men were older anyway, or crippled somehow—otherwise they would be in the service. A couple of them were stable boys, smallish, sunbaked ex-jockeys. But Lily noticed one, a younger man, sleek, almost chubby, with a square face that creased into an easy smile.

"You're the new fellow, aren't you?" Buck asked him at dinner. Lily knew he was about to get a grilling.

"Yes, sir, Joseph Dujanovic."

"Dujah...what is that, Polish?"

"Nah," interrupted Adella, the cook. "Serbian. Like Princip."

"Yes, Ma'am, exactly right. I sure appreciate the meal, ma'am."

"Address your thanks to Madame," Adella nodded toward Deborah. "If you don't know, these meals are free."

"Yes, ma'am." Joseph nodded deferentially. "Thank you."

"We give you a lot," said Deborah. "But we also expect a lot."

"So don't try to take advantage," said Buck's wife Moira. "No sin goes unpunished." She said it kiddingly, and the new man smiled. He did not seem particularly aware that a movie star passed him the basket of rolls. But then, Deborah didn't act like a star. Here, she was first of all the boss-lady. And no one, not even the most miserable laborer, could pull the poor-mouth act on her. "I grew up in Holy Socks parish," she would tell them with a twinkle. "Myrtle Avenue. Brooklyn. A sixth floor walk up with no stairs."

Later in the evening Lily was in her room, lying on top of the bed, somewhat absently shaping her nails. The radio on the nightstand played soft romantic music, but Lily was thinking hard thoughts. She, too, had grown up poor, and though she might not have been as desperately poor as Deborah, she was just as determined to get to the bright side of the tracks. But she was not one to beg. She would earn everything she got.

Maybe Deborah saw that. Maybe that was their connection. And she was a dancer, like Deborah, and a talent, rather than just a cute kid. She was tall, strong and graceful, with Chinese cheekbones, as she called them. The camera loved those cheekbones, everyone told her so.

The room where she lay now was so far and away the best place she had ever slept that it only made her more determined not to lose it. Someone, probably Moira, had put fresh cut flowers on the little table by the window, and the brocade bedspread she lay on seemed to be woven with strands of gold. She could not let this be taken from her, and greed or envy had nothing to do with it. Lily worked hard at every part of life, and had proven to herself, even if no one else saw it, that she would do literally anything to succeed. Sometimes she made bad decisions—she had been nineteen when she signed up with the Sylvan School, and a few months older when she let Marty Nuco turn her out, as she saw it now, giving in to the advances of a studio investor.

She had gone to Koch to negotiate, rather than Nuco, because she thought she knew how to deal with him. She had no idea how to deal with Marty Nuco, because she both hated and loved him with such fire. Of course, it had gone badly. She should have known better than to try to talk to a whoremaster, and because she had humiliated Koch, she knew that he would never be satisfied now until he destroyed her. She had thought for a moment of pushing the knife into his throat and killing him, but she was grateful now that God or luck had stopped her. Whatever happened, she did not want a man's life on her conscience.

But now both Nuco and Koch had reason to come after her. And as long as she remained an anonymous actress, they could easily do it. Only fame and power could protect her, and Deborah was the key to that. Lily would do whatever she could to gain the star's confidence and influence.

She mulled these ideas over, looking at them from different angles, testing them against different actions she could take.

There was a tap on the door, and Deborah stuck her head in. "Hi."

"Hi," Lily said, locking her plans away into a hidden place in her mind.

Deborah smiled. "How are you?"

"Oh, fine, fine. Just doing some thinking."

"They're playing cards in the dining room."

"Oh," said Lily. "I'm not much for cards." She knew about the card game. But she still felt uncomfortable with the others. She had come here to be an actress, not a cook.

Deborah sat in the barrel chair next to the nightstand. She held a tall, frosted glass. Lily knew there would only be water in there.

"Well, I have a little bit of news. I spoke to some people at the studio when I went in on Friday. I got a call back today. There's a part for you."

Lily's heart pounded. She could feel a blush burning her face.

Deborah held her hands up in a stop sign. "It's not big. It's a chorus part. A backstage murder mystery. But they said there's two production numbers that you could be in."

"Oh gosh!"

"That starts right away. Maybe Wednesday. I've got a phone number—"

"Oh, Deborah!" Lily swung her legs out of bed and reached across to hug Deborah. "Oh, thank you so much."

"Now, it's just a door. How far it goes depends mostly on you."

"Oh, I know, I know."

"Which is not to say—if you want my advice?"

"Oh, yes, please."

"Don't come on pushy. That shows fear, not confidence. Your job right now is to look natural when the camera finds you, and stay out of the way. I know that's hard, because you want to show them everything you can do. But it's better to let the audience find you, to think, who is that girl. Besides, there are going to be more parts for you. I've got a few more peaches in the pantry."

"Deborah, I'm so grateful! When you said you were going to see about a role for someone, well, I guess I assumed, well." Lily recalled her fear and greed and pride on the day she had followed Deborah around. And her tryst with the German guy, just trying to find out. She felt ashamed. "I guess I assumed you were talking about someone else."

Deborah took Lily's hand. "Now, who else would that be? I admit, I was being coy. I didn't want to say anything too soon."

"You said your protégée, and I didn't—"

"You're it, sweetie. There's no one else." Deborah took a drink of the cold water. "Now, being on film, that's not like anything else. An inch looks like a mile. I think you have something, a spark, an honesty, and they'll see it. The audience. It's almost scary. All those professionals at work, every trick in the book, but the audience still knows things these men don't know. And if you've got something, the crowd'll see it. I don't mean pretty eyes or a nice figure, I mean something deeper. Good or bad, they'll see it."

"Oh, come on." Lily was fascinated. Deborah rarely talked about her career or her work. "Like they can see through you? You're kidding me."

Deborah set her drink on a magazine that lay next to the lamp. "I don't mean they can read your mind or see your soul. God knows, some of the blackest hearts in the world have sold themselves like lunch meat, but movie crowds have an ear for false notes. That's why Joan Crawford could play Norma Shearer, but not vice versa."

Lily was surprised. "Because she's a better actress?"

"No, because she is totally devoted to Joan Crawford, the star who was created for the audience, but also by the audience. She becomes whatever she thinks the audience wants, and the audience appreciates that devotion."

"Just like you!"

"No," said Deborah. "There are things I won't do. Things I wouldn't try."

Lily tried to put into words the complicated feelings she had for Deborah. It wasn't easy. "I like that you are, I don't know, independent?"

"Independent?"

"At least from men. In your pictures, you don't throw yourself at them, they come to you." Lily hoped that she sounded sincere, not fawning. She really did admire Deborah.

"Hmmm. Really?"

"Don't forget, I was part of the crowd. Still am. And you're like that in real life. You are independent. You have a career, a house, a family, but... you know."

"But no man." Deborah smiled. "No. Not now. Not for a while. But I was married once. I gave it everything I had."

"You wouldn't let him make you get married." Lily tried not to say it, but it just spilled out.

"Who? Do what?"

"That agent man."

Deborah seemed surprised. "That was a private call."

"I'm sorry. I didn't mean to pry. It was Marty Nuco, wasn't it?"

"Do you know him?"

"Oh, no!" Lily protested. "Just the name. But isn't that what agents and studio executives do? Make you marry someone just for appearances? Just so they can control you? You're so wonderful to me."

Deborah's flash of anger seemed to die away. "Oh, sweetie, don't worry about me." She patted Lily's arm. "I might get married again, or I might not. Maybe when this war is all over, and the good ones come home."

"Like Glen Spangler?"

"No, not him." Deborah took a sip of water.

"Is it because of him? That he's...not interested?"

"No, not the way you mean. Now that you're here, one thing you should never do is play the gossip game. Others will do it, but don't you."

"Sorry," said Lily.

Deborah paused. The ice cubes in her glass settled themselves as if getting ready for a bedtime story. "You will hear rumors about everyone, and they're all vicious or unbelievable—that's why they get passed around. No, Glen doesn't go for men. No men for Glen. He likes women, but only as accessories. Being his wife would be a full time job."

"I didn't, don't, think he was..." Lily stammered. "I mean, like you say, the audience can tell—they know something's missing. I didn't get that feeling with him."

"How about me?" Deborah said. "Ever get that feeling of something missing?"

Lily was surprised by the question. "No, I don't think so. I've seen you do lots of different things, comedy, drama, and I ate it up." She was thinking, *she couldn't mean that.*

"That's one reason I live out here," Deborah said. "I stay off the party circuit. I don't care about rumors in the company town but I do care about *them*. The audience. In that way I guess I am a little bit of a slave to my image. My personal life is not going to interfere with that rapport. I'm no Elysia Tisbury."

"I never heard of her."

"Exactly. She's a pretty darn good actress who never made it. Leading lady type. But the audience could tell something was missing."

They chatted on for a few minutes about a song that was on the radio. Then Deborah said goodnight and went to her room down the hall.

Lily thought for a few minutes. Deborah was so direct most of the time, but this conversation was puzzling. She got up and walked down to the kitchen to get a drink of water. Moira was in there, sitting at the kitchen table with her feet up on a chair, blowing smoke rings and playing solitaire. Lily already felt easy enough with her to ask her just about anything.

"Who's Lisa Pilsbury?"

Moira laid a black jack on a red queen. "I think it's Tisbury. Some actress. New York."

"Was she, uh, funny?"

"I don't know about that." Moira chuckled. "You mean a lez? So they say. But then they say that about every actress. Why?"

"Oh, her name came up."

"It still does, from time to time." Moira peeled off three cards. "Yeah, she was probably funny. But she couldn't keep it under wraps. No sin goes unpunished, especially the sin that dares not speak its name." A husky laugh escaped from her. "I musta heard that in a play once."

Lily nodded. She got a glass from the cupboard and turned on the tap.

"There's cold water in the icebox," said Moira.

"That's okay. This is good." Trying to find a safe subject, she said, "That new guy, at dinner—he looks pretty young and healthy. How come he's not in the—"

"Service? Ex-con." Moira frowned but she did not look up. "Buck gave him a break. I don't like it."

Chapter Four

They got down to work, and the first week passed quickly. Max wanted to talk through the whole movie before they started writing. *He could have just said that,* Lyman fumed. But perhaps Lyman had, he admitted, come off as a little too proprietary about his book. A little too much the proud papa with his Act One, Scene One.

One of their most difficult tasks was addressed immediately. Occasionally in one of Lyman's books a woman turned up naked or a man turned up pink. Private Eye Archer Daniel was never shocked at anything he saw. But the movie censors seemed to be shocked by everything.

"We haff to lose most of this scene where he goes to the big blonde's apartment." Max walked back and forth in front of the row of windows, slapping things randomly with his swagger stick. "There's about two lines in here the Hays Office will allow."

Lyman had started out on the couch, so he stayed there. "Why? There's no sex in it."

"There's no sexual *act*," said Max. "But it's dripping. There's a girl with a jewel in her navel. Ach! According to the rules, we can't even admit she *has* a navel, much less put an opal in it."

"Okay." Lyman considered. "But he has to go to the apartment to find the book on her dresser with Chloe's name in it." He scanned the scene on pages seventy-three and seventy-four of the novel. "And we have to somehow show her flirting with him, and Stanley has to beat him up."

"One thing at a time." Max stopped, holding his baton in front of him like a conductor. "Stanley can beat him up in the foyer, or on the landing..."

"*Nobody* gets thrown down the stairs," Lyman said emphatically. "That's too clichéd."

"Fine." Max whacked the back of the armchair with the stick. "He can flirt with the big blonde somewhere else. Back at the nightclub. Instead of pissing on each other, they make it a little more interesting."

Lyman didn't like it. "Nightclub scenes are inherently dishonest."

"You have all these rules," Max sputtered. "No fight on the stairs, no nightclub. But just as an example, let's say she walks up to him and says...what?"

Lyman grasped for a phrase. "Ah...ah...'What's the matter, don't you recognize me with my clothes on?'"

Max barked a laugh. "Good! Too good! If we're going to steal, let's steal from the best! Tallulah Bankhead!"

"Actually, Dorothy Parker."

"Nah. I've heard Tallulah tell the story."

Max's peremptory tone admitted no possibility that Lyman had heard the story from *Dorothy*. He hadn't, of course. He just did not like having his face rubbed in the German's name droppings.

"Here you go!" Max hit the smoking stand with his stick, making a loud *whang*. Lyman flinched. A small cloud of ashes headed for the carpet. "One: we can show a picture of her with the jewel and the navel. A painting or a photo. As long as we don't show her actual self, they will allow it, believe it or not. Two: the apartment can be the same, but they have a terrific fight and make the room hardly unrecognizable right away."

Lyman removed his glasses and rubbed a hard semi-circle around each eye. He was already tired of wrestling with Max. The mangled English made it hard to take him seriously, and his imperious attitude made it hard to disagree with him. And then you had the question of whose story it was: Lyman's because he wrote it, or Max's because the studio bought it?

Lyman's trip to England in 1918 was a bad weather crossing in an ancient mail packet that had been converted into a troop transport. The ship seemed to strain against every wave. Eventually they made it across, and Lyman never took a happier step than the one that put him on the pier at Southampton. After the first day, every moment of that trip was an intolerable strain. But he had tolerated. And his pay for that job was rather less. He would tolerate.

* * * *

Even on a difficult day at the office, Lyman quickly realized he could enjoy one reward: lunch at the writer's table of the studio commissary. The food was good, and the companionship better. The writers—Nebgen, Korngav, Ackerman, Linda Jasperson, and others—ate, played cards, smoked, gossiped and made cracks. Without exception they saw themselves as expatriates from the New York, London or Paris literary crowds. They were all witty, sophisticated and educated, yet most now wrote scripts they considered schlock: war movies, tearjerkers, crazy musicals, a sheik movie, a gangster movie, oaters. The only thing that all of these movies had in common was that in all of them, words of dialogue were considered little more than a necessary evil. Just this morning, Hunley and Hallum recounted having an entire page of dialogue reduced by a leading cowboy star—with the director's agreement—to one "Yup," one "Nope," and a "Don't bet on it."

So the writers rebelled with childish behavior. Drinking on the job was part of it. Lyman knew all about that. Drinking had ended his career in real estate in the early thirties, and he had been battling it ever since. Sobriety had given him the clarity and determination to succeed as a writer, or, looked at another way, writing had helped him stick with sobriety. He fought the temptation of alcohol every day, but the cafeteria was the one place he could meet the other writers where drinking would not be an issue, and where he could vicariously relive the high times and artsy conversations of his youth.

Lyman fought a second temptation: he felt sure that a Martian dropped into a movie studio would conclude that the chief business of the place was the pursuit of young women by old and young men. Lyman listened with fascination and disgust as the men at the table, and the two women, gabbed about the sexual endowments and proclivities of everyone from the *biggest* stars to the biggest extras. Then he went back to his office and took another sex scene out of the screenplay.

His own sex life was non-existent, and had been for so long that he had almost forgotten about it. Old-fashioned men of his age did not chase recklessly after females. If he started drinking again, he might start acting very foolish about women. Said one way, that sounded like a good thing. Said another way, it sounded very, very bad. It would be different if Tina had the option of leaving him, but she did not. She was completely dependent on him. So cheating on her would not only be immoral, it would be unconscionable.

* * * *

As Lily stood outside the apartment, she heard music. Once inside, she realized the music was the background for a radio drama. A male voice, a kind of a country voice, said, "I don't think I can help you any, Mister Dollar. It was an accident pure and simple. Miz Jeffords fell out of the loft and landed on a harrow."

There was no other sound in the apartment. Lily stepped into the living room, ready to bolt. A lamp glowed next to the couch, but no one was there. She called in a high whisper: "Maria?"

No one answered but the radio. She took another step into the room. In front of the couch, two men's shoes, black, lay comfortably askew. A tie hung over the back of the couch. Lily would not go into the bedroom. She was turning to leave when Maria came out, tying the belt on a robe.

"I didn't mean to, uh, scare you." Lily couldn't keep the sarcasm out of her voice.

Maria smiled without looking at her, not amused. "I'm not scared."

"Of course not." Lily reached over and hooked the red-and-gold striped tie with her finger. "Who is he?"

Maria wobbled a little. "He's okay."

Lily realized she was tight. "How do you know?"

"I met him at the tavern. You know, over on Exposition."

"Really? How'd you get there?"

"Walked, what else? I got no money. Even for a bus. I got bored. Nothing to do."

Lily could understand. Listening to the radio was no fun if that's all you had. "But it's dangerous."

"No, it's fine. He works at Lockheed."

"How do you know?"

"Okay, I don't. But I don't care. He bought dinner, bought a bottle. What am I supposed to do here, knit?" Maria walked over to the couch and sat down. "Come on." She patted the cushion beside her. "Come sit. It's not dangerous."

"He still in there?" Lily sat down and kicked one of the big brogans under the coffee table. "It's good, really. It means you're ready to go home."

"Or I could knit, if I had yarn. I was ragging, but I do know how to knit."

Maria's robe had fallen open around her white breasts. She pulled it closed and smiled uncertainly. "What?"

Lily knew she had been caught looking. But she had come here with a purpose. "There's something I have to ask you. It's not easy."

"Ask me anything. Except to go back to, you know." Maria slumped.

"I'll never ask you to do that." With a gentle finger Lily lifted the girl's chin and studied the pale rose skin of her face and throat. "Make love to me."

"Do you like it that way?"

Lily shrugged. "I've never done it. Never wanted to. But someone I know wants to. So in a way, it's like an acting class. You show me how a woman would like it. I mean, I know, but you know, you could show me, I don't know."

"When? Where? Now?"

"No, not now. Not with him here. I'll come back tomorrow night."

"No. I'll get rid of him." Maria's arm snaked out and around Lily, and she kissed her, lingeringly, on the cheek. She turned her head. "Johnny?" she called. "Baby?"

It all seemed very familiar to Lily, but she'd never been on this side of it before. Being the one who needed it.

Maria turned back to her, a sly smile on her face. "How about a slug?"

* * * *

The day finally arrived when the co-writers ran a sheet of paper into the Smith-Corona. Lyman was unsurprised to learn he would be the typist, but he was not unhappy about it. Typing gave him something to do besides look at, listen to, and argue with Max.

Lyman did not have to guess which aspects of himself annoyed Max. Anytime he stuck up for an idea or offered an unwelcome suggestion, Max would make "witty" comments about Lyman's English education, his alleged intellectual airs, his clothes, his taste in literature. Always with the implication that Lyman was not a real man's man, like Max. Somehow, Max's intellectual and artistic background made him sophisticated, but Lyman's own accomplishments and tastes made him a fruit.

He had learned from the other studio writers that Max's former writing partner, Gil Gladstone, was a homo, and that Max was sensitive to comments about that fact because the men spent so much time together when writing a script. But that did not keep Max from working with him for five years. Lyman wondered if maybe Max just got used to needling the other guy about being a fairy. There was no doubt that Max was a needler. Maybe the other guy just took it because he had to. Maybe if Lyman took it, he could work here for five years. But he didn't like people who picked on homos.

This particular morning, a Tuesday morning, Lyman and Max were having a wrangle about police procedure and ethics. In the novel, the cops were carefully drawn and basically decent. For the movie, Max wanted them to be thuggish bad guys. Lyman would not give in.

Lyman had spent a number of hours talking to cops and District Attorneys when he was a pulp writer, picking their brains for operational details of law enforcement, and probing their psyches for dark impulses.

"Just for the dynamics of the story," he told Max. "If everyone is evil, it loses its impact. Contrast is what we need. Juxtaposition." Lyman was standing by the window, looking through his copy of *Double Down* for a description of the chief detective. "I know cops. They are basically decent, just not always very smart."

Max was pacing a circle between the desk and the door, irritable, waving a Malacca cane. "But we don't have time to make these cops realistic. If this story is based on the corruption of the cops, then they are all corrupt." Max gave the desk a loud whap with the cane, and threw himself into the stuffed chair. He squinted up into the strong sun coming through the windows. "Jesus!" he barked. "Shut those blinds!"

Lyman, annoyed to begin with, had been startled by the slap of the cane on the desk. "Call your Chinese houseboy," he growled.

"Huh? What are you talking about?"

Lyman boiled over. "You do not address me in that fashion! Ever!"

"Why, you blue-nosed prima donna son of a bitch!" Max spat out the words. "I want you to tell me who wrote *Double Down* becoss it couldn't possibly have been you, you tight-assed..."

Lyman threw the book at him as hard as he could, and missed by three feet. He pulled himself up to the full five-foot-ten-and-three-quarter-inches of his shabby dignity and announced, "I bid you sweet fuck all." He held his hand under his chin and wiggled his fingers in farewell.

Lyman left the office, went down the stairs, and exited the building at full stride, muttering to himself, his eyes burning a channel through the asphalt of the studio street. Turning a corner, he almost ran down a young woman who was walking slowly, looking at a book.

"Excuse me!" Lyman puffed at the top of her head as he stumbled around her. She looked up, but it took him a moment to recognize her. It may have been the wisp of perfume he caught that triggered his memory. It was the receptionist from his first day. He had seen her since then, but only at a distance, at the studio commissary. "Oh, hello," he said.

I looked at her. A puff of breeze blew a few strands of dark hair across her eyes, and she combed them back with her fingers. When I met her in the lobby that first day, her hair had looked coal-black. Here in the sunlight it had a reddish tone, but still it was very dark, like Bordeaux wine in candlelight.

"Pardon me," she apologized. "I shouldn't read while I'm walking. It's gotten me in trouble before."

Lyman glanced at the book in her hand. It was one of those new twenty-five-cent pocket books. *The Good Earth.* "No, my fault entirely," he said. "You don't remember me, but you let me in the first day. I work here now. Or I did until a couple of minutes ago."

"Oh yes. I am glad you got the job, and sorry you lost it." She was amused. That was good.

"I can't seem to get along with the director, or my co-writer." Before she could be confused, he clarified. "They are the same person. I believe he—or they—may be an escaped trunk murderer." Reaching up to doff his hat, he realized he had left it behind. "Lyman Wilbur, script monkey," he said, touching his forehead in a kind of salute.

"April Sheffield."

Lyman noticed that they were walking toward the commissary, and he smelled fried chicken. "Are you going to lunch? May I walk with you?"

"Of course."

She was just being polite, Lyman knew, but he did not care. He had forgotten about this young woman, who had made such a strong impression on him that first day. He recalled how he had promised himself he was going to *enjoy* his time at the studio.

"Early for lunch," he opined.

"I start at seven thirty."

"Have you worked here long, at the studio?"

"Six years," April said. "I went to college for a year, then..."

Because Max and all the ways he hated him were much on Lyman's mind, he could not help but think about the way Max talked to his lovers on the office phone. "Pardon me for being personal, but are you married? I'm not asking for the usual reason."

"What's the usual reason?"

"Well," Lyman replied. "As a sort of come-on. If you say yes, they take one approach, and if you say no..."

"Who are you talking about?"

"Men," said Lyman. "Especially men at this studio, whose main preoccupation is...well..."

"Sex? I've heard of it." She obviously thought it was funny.

"Sometimes I wonder if it's that, or just the challenge of tricking young girls into..."

A small, sweet laugh escaped her. "But girls play the game as well. If it ends with a wedding, we won."

They arrived at the cafeteria, where the early shift was funneling in. "Well," said Lyman. "Enjoy your lunch."

April was already turning away. "G'bye."

He continued on. Meeting April Sheffield had caused a plan to form in his head. A solution. There would be no lunch at the writer's table for him today. Lyman felt much too alive, too exposed, for empty cleverness. He walked slowly now, his head up, listening, seeing, breathing in the air, the aromas. And not wearing a hat.

He knew where he was going, and he savored the trip. For eight years he had been sober, serious, isolated, and disciplined. Tina and a couple of cats and the craft of writing had been his whole world inside a garden gate. He had accomplished a great deal, he knew, but now he was on a larger field and he had run into an obstacle in Max Beckerman that he could neither move nor crack. And April Sheffield at that moment had literally changed his direction.

Lyman Wilbur is dead! Long live Lyman Wilbur!

At the studio gate, he smiled at the Central Casting cop and kept walking. Across the street and a block from the gate, Lucey's rose like an enchanted villa guarded by a row of ratty palm trees. Tan stucco, tile roof, dark shutters, the whole Mediterranean blather. Lucey's had fine food, they said, but Lyman was not after a meal.

He strode through the foyer, and headed for the gloom of the bar and the mist of spilled beer, bitters, sliced oranges, and dead cigars that saturated the room. Behind him, the restaurant rattled with the routine preparations for the lunch crowd, but the bar was quiet. He thought about how April Sheffield's pale skin and dark hair looked in the sunlight, and how she would look in the midday shadows here, on the stool next to him. Lyman knew that he was an old man to her, flabby, angry, impotent. What she did not know was that he had looked at her with the same hopeful, hurting, eyes he had at twenty-five.

A bartender approached.

"I'll have a rye and water, please." Lyman smiled, already feeling the warmth. "Make it a double. I'm meeting an old friend."

When the glass was placed before him on its little white coaster he studied it for a moment, teetering on the ledge Then he stepped off.

* * * *

Her car was not in the garage when Max arrived home. He walked through the house turning lights on. The breakfast dishes still sat in the sink, and a half-empty quart of milk stood on the drainboard. He touched it. Room temperature. He put the milk in the fridge, saying to himself, "This is some wife I got."

In the den he flipped on another light. Paintings by Constable, Mu Ch'i and Jawlensky looked down on Virginia's slippers, scattered newspapers, and an ashtray that overflowed with butts, balled-up Kleenex and orange peels. He stopped at the bar in the corner of the room and poured a slug of cognac into a heavy crystal Old Fashioned glass.

"Virginia!" he shouted. "*Sweetheart!*" Max drained the drink. It had not been a good day. He had an asshole at work who was impossible to work with, and a wife at home he could not live with. He stood there staring into the large antique mirror on the opposite wall. He hefted the heavy glass and almost flung it at his image. "Nah," he intoned. "That mirror is Louis Quinze. But these glasses are only Marshall Petain." He walked out onto the patio and flung the glass at the barbecue fireplace that he had never used. The glass shattered, but Max got no satisfaction from it.

She really wasn't worth it, he told himself. Spoiled, indolent, venal, corrupt. When they met, Virginia painted—not without talent. But she had not picked up a brush in the last two years. They had tried to have children. Now they rarely tried. She was beautiful, utterly charming, but above all, elusive. That was the quality that made her so entrancing. Just when Max thought he had her nailed down, committed, she would give him one of those smiles, and Max would know he had been suckered in some mysterious way.

But she had never been untrue to him. Max really believed that. Not out of virtue, but just lack of interest.

The phone rang, and he walked into the house and picked it up.

"Max!" It was Virginia, of course.

"Where are you?"

"At Collins' service. I had a flat?" She sounded impatient, but Max was in no mood to concede anything.

"Oh. Where were you, so late?"

"It isn't late, or it wasn't when I first called you, about a half hour ago. Bridge with Mary Lou. Where were *you*?"

Max muttered something.

"Did you say meshuggah?" Her scorn leapt from the phone earpiece. "Don't you be meshugga-ing me, sweetheart!"

She still had not been untrue to him, as far as he knew, but even that gave him no satisfaction.

* * * *

Because of her inexperience, Lily wanted Deborah to lead. This meant letting herself be seduced. Deborah seemed in no hurry during hours of talk that led from the cozy den, where a fire crackled, to the settee in the bedroom.

The older woman seemed shy at first, but an occasional word or look of encouragement from Lily kept things rolling. Once they were in bed, Deborah's inhibitions disappeared. She whispered, "If I seem shameless, it's only what I learned in hotels on the road. From the ladies of the chorus." By then Lily's heart burned with its own lust for Deborah—not sexual, but proprietary lust.

Now she was content, thinking of the Bible verse, "Blessed are the lowly, for they shall inherit the land." Lily lay with Deborah in her arms, still feeling the thrill of the seduction. They were in Deborah's huge bed —a featherbed. It felt like lying on a cloud.

The bedroom reflected Deborah's true personality. Bookshelves lined two walls. One was filled with knickknacks, delicate vases, teapots, dolls, artificial flowers, and jeweled eggs. The other set of shelves held hundreds of books, scattered figurines and music boxes. On the top of the dresser stood dozens of framed photographs of Deborah, her family, and friends. Glancing around, Lily again had that feeling of the rightness of it all. Of belonging.

She was going to be with Deborah a long time.

"I love you," Lily whispered.

"Oh, don't say that," came the lazy reply.

"I have to. I want to."

Deborah stirred and stretched. "I love you, too. But you know how it is." Lily heard a warning.

"No, how is it?"

"Oh, come on." Deborah sat up.

"No, *amorcito*, how is it?" Lily thought Deborah was now going to explain that their love had to be hidden behind closed doors, how she must be very discreet, and so forth. She did not mind such restrictions.

Deborah smoothed sheets over herself. "It's a cold, cruel world out there. Let's be happy here and now and not worry about tomorrow."

"Nothing bad will happen tomorrow," said Lily.

Deborah rolled away from her.

"What is it?"

"I'm getting married," Deborah murmured.

"What!"

"We'll announce it soon."

"Who we?" Lily was stunned. Who are you...Oh, no. That *pinche joto*. Spangler."

"Oh, stop."

"You let Nuco talk you into it!" She arched over Deborah. "You gave him that power!" Nuco! He clawed at Lily's happiness like a rabid dog! Now he was even in the bedroom with her. "How could you? You told me that guy wasn't for you, and I *know* you don't love him, because I know what love is."

"Everyone knows what love is." Deborah looked up at her, sad and composed. "It doesn't last, or mean anything. Like this here. It'll disappear." She reached up and lightly smoothed the hair at Lily's temple.

"Oh no it won't," Lily smiled. "I'm not going anywhere."

Deborah fixed her with a cold, dark-eyed stare. "Don't tell me that," she purred. "Don't make me regret that I let you in my bed. That doesn't give you any say in my life. Be nice, stay calm, and we can have a nice little...affair."

"Okay, okay! I just meant that my feelings for you are real, and I know that you're only doing this because that Nuco said to. What do you care what he says?"

Deborah slid out of bed and pulled on a satin dressing gown. "Why did I give in to Marty? Because it's a good idea. That's all. A star needs to be married. And I need a man. And if Marty suggested it, well, I'll listen. Because he knows my secrets. All of them."

Lily could see real fear in her eyes. "That you like *girls*? That's not so horrible. The studio can cover that up. Stars don't have sex at all."

Deborah plucked a cigarette from her pack on the nightstand and sat down on the edge of the chaise longue. "No. There's something else." She was back in control of her emotions. "I was almost destroyed by scandal before. I won't take chances now. Glen Spangler and I have been very close friends, and he's strong and loyal and protective. He's everything I need and want."

Lily found herself again lying in someone else's bed feeling dirty and used. But she already knew she would not give up. She had come too far.

* * * *

Los Angeles audiences loved the magic turnip, and they loved Ted Hardy—and why not? As the leading human actor in the play, Ted had no reason to complain about being upstaged by a potato's poorer cousin. *My Friend Turnip* was a hit, and it had brought him from Broadway to Los Angeles and maybe all the way back to Hollywood. If one of the studios bought it, Ted was a cinch to play the role in the film version. He was Lloyd Schlenk, the wistful seeker, the innocent abroad in the land.

But even if there was no film sale, Hardy felt vindicated. He knew he had enemies here, and people who remembered him from his first go-round and wished him nothing but the worst. Any night some of them might be in the audience. He was a Methodist now, a married Methodist with a full gray mane and a clipped mustache. With a Methodist wife named Ruth who was the rock beneath his rock.

Ted took his bow and walked off the stage in a happy glow. It wasn't Othello, but he had a lot of lines. Ruth would be in the dressing room with a cold glass of Seven Up.

As he walked past the scene shop he caught a glimpse of three stagehands huddled next to a flat. The one called Van, or Vance, tipped up a pint bottle as the other two chatted. Van saw him and quickly lowered the bottle. Everyone in the company knew Ted was on the wagon, really on it, and they took pains never to drink around him, or to talk about drinking.

Van looked at him sheepishly. Ted gave him a smile and a wave, brushing off the incident. He didn't like to make people feel uncomfortable about drinking, he just didn't want to be confronted with it. He could resist temptation, but there was no sense in pushing it.

Ruth sat in the wicker chair in the corner of the dressing room, reading her magazine, her Kewpie-doll face scrunched with the effort in the dim light. Forty-five now, she still carried herself like the Charleston-dancing flapper she had once been, slightly plumper but still with the jet-black hair she had never dyed. No woman could look less like the soda-pop-drinking, scripture-memorizing, steel-backboned maiden she was inside.

She looked up with a delighted smile. "Maury came by in the second act. We're doing another two weeks at least."

Ted felt a welling of satisfaction and joy. He grasped both her hands in his. "Wonderful!"

"He's making the rounds now."

Ted picked up his glass of soda and handed the other one to Ruth. "To the turnip."

Ruth smiled. "And to you."

He could even do a toast without wanting alcohol. He felt a little bad that he'd interrupted the stagehands' party, even if it was by accident, and just for a moment. Van was a strapping young fellow who worked hard and improved himself constantly, as far as Ted could see. He deserved to have a drink if he wanted one. He could go about his life just as he pleased. Ted had Ruth, and he had his faith. That was a lot to give up for a slug of whiskey.

He set his glass on the dressing table, as Ruth did. She stood and they clasped hands and bowed their heads together, so close the feathers of her bobbed hair brushed his temple. He prayed in a low murmur. "Let me be exalted for you, or brought low by you. Let me be full, let me be empty. Let me have all things, let me have nothing."

Ruth did not speak in these personal moments they shared so often. To an observer it might appear Ted was abjectly beseeching his wife, rather than his God.

There would be something to that.

When he left Hollywood a decade before, Ted Hardy had been a broken down shitbag, a drunken faggot, a fatal disease. Standing here with Ruth, he could trace his progress, could see the valley of sin he had walked in for so long

Deborah had to divorce him, he understood that now. And she had to destroy him. His salvation had been to see that and to forgive it. It took a long time, but he forgave. A long time, crawling up from the gutter. He knew he'd left that behind when he met Ruth. She helped him see the light, helped him see who he was, and the Methodists had given him the backbone to stop drinking, absolutely and totally.

Between Ruth and her religion, he'd been able to understand that the source of all power, all good, and real love was not to be found in grasping and struggling for earthly rewards. And then along came this very funny play about belief, and magic powers, and the human spirit—though it was expressed satirically in the play—that took Ted all the way back to the top. As big as he'd ever been.

And Ruth had shown him the weakness of carnal love compared to spiritual, genuine, and caring love. And what Ted knew in his heart was that drinking and carnal desire were one and the same, and if he did not do the first, he could resist the second. It was really the second that had destroyed him before, and that beast must remain caged for all time.

And as long as he did not drink, it would.

* * * *

Lyman's lunchtime trip to Lucey's bar on Tuesday had not set him off on a bender. He was slyly proud of that. Oh, he'd had a couple of drinks since then, but not enough to even affect him. He knew when to quit now, and had the strength to do it. That was the difference.

Besides, he had been too busy to get into trouble. The Wilburs had moved this past week into a house in Pacific Palisades—took over the lease from a writer who returned to New York. After only a couple of weeks, those big paychecks were making a difference.

They'd ordered their furniture delivered from storage, and Lyman had even bought a big new English desk and chair. Thank God Tina felt strong enough to supervise most of the work. She was much revived from her previous weeks of illness.

And tonight, just as a special treat, because everything was going so well, Lyman had bought himself a flask of Lord Calvert.

Tina having gone to bed by eight, as usual, Lyman sat at the new desk enjoying the company of His Lordship. But the pleasure was limited by the presence of Archer Daniel, who had assumed the role in Lyman's mind, as he occasionally did, of a stuffy and unwanted conscience. *You're too old*, the alter-ego scoffed. *Too experienced to be having these feelings.*

"I'm no older than Edmond Glover," Lyman replied to himself. "And he's still a romantic lead."

No older! How old do you think he is?

"Oh, late forties. So just a couple of years older."

As Lyman raised his glass he could see his reflection in the darkened window. He turned away.

That sounds like the old real estate man talking—or the booze. You will only embarrass yourself! In his books, Archer was generally forgiving of the vices he encountered among his fellow characters. But he was born of Lyman's sobriety, and naturally he viewed this new side of his author with suspicion.

"You're only as old as you feel," Lyman countered. "And when I look at Tina I feel very old indeed."

Good thing you specified, Archer sniffed. *Because I would imagine that looking at* her *would make you feel pretty old, too!* And on and on it went.

Finally Lyman ended the discussion, took a jolt, picked up the phone and dialed the number.

Her voice sounded soft, but not sleepy.

"Hello, Miss Sheffield? This is Lyman Wilbur, from the other day. The writer who got fired?"

"Oh, hello. Yes. You."

"How are you this evening?" He was trembling so badly he had to grip the edge of the desk.

"Why are you calling, Mister..."

"Well, I know this must seem strange, but when we talked the other day, so briefly, I thought I detected a friendly ear, and I was hoping we might at some time be able to continue the conversation."

"I see. You were the one who asked me if I was married, right? And didn't you sort of go on about men who chase young girls? So what are you doing now?"

"Oh Lord, I know it must look like..." Lyman imagined April sitting on a sofa, a big Zenith radio across the room, hand on her bare knee. "Or rather, sound like."

She sighed. "Please don't tell me you're going to get me into pictures. I think the last fellow who tried that line was the kid who washes Harry Corvus's car."

"No, no. You see, I work with other writers, some a little younger, but no females, and none your age, and I thought—right now I'm working on a melodrama which features a young woman in an up-to-date setting, a secretary, in fact."

"Do tell." She was at least listening. Lyman forged onward.

"And I am trying very hard to make it more than just the typical gum-snapper role with the wisecracks and the sentiment. I just need to talk to somebody like you, and I thought... But this is an intrusion. Perhaps..."

After a moment she said, "I take it you did not get fired."

Lyman laughed nervously. "No, I was being a little over-dramatic. Melodramatic, I suppose you might say."

"Don't you have anyone you can talk to? Your wife? A niece, a daughter?"

Lyman panicked. He would not mention Tina. "As a matter of fact, our daughter...is no longer with us." He flung himself around in his chair, and almost fell over.

"She passed away? How long ago?"

"Oh, eight years ago, I guess it is. Seems like yesterday."

"I'm sorry, what was her name?"

Lyman's mind spun wildly, like a drunken sailor grabbing for a handhold. The only name that entered his mind was Greer Garson.

"Grndl," he fairly gargled.

"Excuse me?"

"Grendel. It's Welsh."

"Your daughter's name was Grendel? How poetic."

"She was eighteen." And they were off to the races. The odd thing was, Lyman had tried for three days to think of a pretext that would get his foot in the door with April, and had not thought of this one. It seems she died of diphtheria. He hoped they would not talk about his tragic mythical daughter too much, but at least the need to improvise this daughter's life would distract him from the ugliness and excitement of his real purpose, which was of course to seduce Miss Sheffield, to know her, to bury his face in her dark, wavy hair, her fulsome breasts.

Chapter Five

Virginia Beckerman flicked her cigarette ash into the black high-heeled pump and the ash rolled downhill into the toe. It was an expensive shoe, but she had only dropped in an ash, which couldn't harm anything. She reclined on the carpet of the large closet so she lay looking up at her clothes from almost directly beneath them. "What combination of colors and cuts will make my lover virile" she said, her voice muffled even to her own ears by the clothes hanging above her. "What hat will make him sensitive? What shoes will let me walk away from him with an ounce of self-respect?"

Virginia smiled. Her cigarette was warming her fingers. She rolled herself to her feet, walked a few steps to the bathroom and dropped the butt into the toilet. She slipped off her pearl satin negligee and began to dress, slowly, in a reverie of anticipation. They would not go to lunch, or anywhere but straight to the apartment, where she would embrace and tease Marty until he devoured her. In that warm, saggy bed that was used only for love.

Virginia shivered, whether out of disgust or desire hardly mattered. She concentrated on the image of Marty, tall and blond with dark eyelashes and ice-blue eyes. He could have been an actor himself, but he was too smart. He wanted to have real power. Control.

Again she trembled, which might have meant nothing more than that she had yet to put on any clothes except her nylon stockings. Virginia refused to let Max pop into her head. She had banished him from her thoughts, but here he came again. Dear Max. Dear husband. She loved him madly, but he was such a child. He brought this on himself, with his constant flirting and affairs right out of Balzac. What was a wife to do? God knows she was not keeping score, but what was a wife to do?

* * * *

Lyman sprawled on the office couch, enraged and exhausted. He looked up to see Fred Sheldrake standing in the doorway. Sheldrake held the nominal position of producer, but whatever a producer's job was, it did not seem to involve much interaction with the writers.

"I was on my way back from lunch and I heard shouting up here." Sheldrake's cigar waggled. "From the street, I heard it."

Lyman was not in the mood to show deference to his nominal boss. "We are having an argument," he grumbled. "About how butlers talk."

"It looks to me like you're sittin' on yer ass. Where's Max?"

"Mister Beckerman has broken off negotiations for one of his frequent trips to the can. Between his trips to the can and his telephonic seduction of starlets, I am spending a lot of time sitting on my ass, blowing smoke rings."

Sheldrake called, "Max!"

Through the bathroom door Max growled: "I am deep in thought."

"You are deep in shit!" The producer rubbed the top of his bald dome. His cigar ash fell on the rug and he kicked it to powder with the side of his toe.

Finally, Max came out of the bathroom. "It's not about the butler, it's about the babe."

Sheldrake stared at Max thoughtfully for a moment. "The butler...the babe." His face collapsed. "That's the first scene! Mother of Pearl, please tell me y'ain't still working on the first scene! Its April the goddam thirteenth, fer chrissake!"

"Of course not," said Max. "It's April eleventh. And don't worry. Not only are we progressing on the script, but conducting also a personal boot camp on screenwriting."

That at least got to the heart of the matter, Lyman agreed. Max insisted on instructing him, and Lyman was determined not to let himself be lectured to. "Writing is writing," he retorted. "Drama is drama. And I was writing in the English language when you were dipping Hildegard's pigtails."

Sheldrake cut in. "Let's move on. What is the particular problem with the butler and the babe?"

"Ach!" Max waved his hands. "Mister Wilbur has some confusion over this character. Young women of today are more sophisticated, not some kind of comic-opera Carmens."

"This woman," Lyman seethed, "is not young women today, she's a bleedin' psychotic! That's the bloody point!"

Sheldrake hesitated. "Are we talking about the Big Blonde?"

"Yes!" Max and Lyman shouted together, glaring at him.

Sheldrake peered at the ceiling, rolling the cigar around in his mouth, and looked at his watch. "Gentlemen! It's two thirty. What say we knock off early today and get a fresh start tomorrow."

Lyman stood up. His first thought was, *it won't be any better tomorrow*.

"And you are going to get along," said Sheldrake.

"Bah!" Max pointed at Lyman. "He thinks he knows everything about the story because he wrote it. Well, he only knows what he thinks he wrote, not what's really there."

"And you know everything about writing movies because you've done it for ten years," said Sheldrake. "So it is tough for two know-it-alls to get along." Sheldrake placed a hand on the shoulder of each of them. "But, if we don't start seeing pages, *you*—" he looked at Lyman "—are going to disappear. And *you*—" he turned to Max "—are going to be writing dialogue for Yutzo the Wonder Fern."

* * * *

Marty Nuco pulled his car into the deserted parking lot behind the nightclub and stopped next to the green Packard. Virginia jumped out of the car and slid in next to him, smiling and breathless. She wore an avocado-green suit. A jade necklace circled her throat.

"You din't have to get all dressed up," Marty Nuco said, but he didn't mean it. Virginia's clothes, the way they looked on her, gave him a warm feeling, like many of the things he saw in the world of wealth and enjoyment.

"I can't drive over here naked." She smoothed her skirt. Her hands were in butterscotch-yellow calfskin gloves. "Or maybe I could. Have you ever dreamed you were doing something in public, and you were naked?"

"Sure."

"Were you embarrassed?" She smiled, lips glistening.

"Of course. It's very bad manners."

He took her to the usual apartment off Crescent Heights. It belonged to a guy who worked for him, who got very cheap rent because he disappeared on cue. It was the perfect place to screw a married woman after lunch, and Marty had been thinking about Virginia all day.

The Gingerbread Mission style of the apartment building carried through to the interior, with brown terracotta tile floors, a curved archway between the kitchen and the living room, and the stained cherry wood doors. In the small bedroom, she undressed in front of him, very close. She raised her arms to unclasp the jade necklace, and her perfume and warmth surrounded him.

Before Virginia was out of her slip, Marty pulled her down and under him in one motion. He had at her hard, but after a half hour he let fly. He was no cabana boy, he had other possums to boil today. They dozed for a few minutes, but Marty's internal clock woke him at four thirty. Again, almost in one motion, he was up, dressed, and on the phone in the living room.

Virginia followed him a few minutes later, walking around the little apartment, tousle-haired and butt-ass naked, completely at ease. Marty had seen plenty of naked women, but he had never seen the kind of freedom that Virginia radiated, even out here in Hollywood. Only she seemed to have it.

He was on the phone with his office manager. "...that's thirty grand we get jewed out of..."

She was wearing only a black bowler hat. It belonged to the guy who lived here. In odd moments during his sexual encounters Marty had wondered about the hat, which always sat on the bedroom dresser. He had never seen the guy wearing it at the office.

Virginia bowed and held the hat in front of her face, then put it on and tapped the crown with a finger.

"Afternoon, Guv'ner," she said.

"What?" Marty said into the phone, "Wait, Mike." He looked at Virginia, impatient. "What?"

Virginia found the mirror by the front door, and tried out different looks with the hat, mischievously attempting to distract him, and doing a pretty good job. But he wasn't looking at the hat.

"Okay," Marty resumed his conversation. "The Hendelman contract."

"You know." Virginia turned to him. "I did not have lunch yet. And not much breakfast." Her face and nude body rippled with excitement. "I know! The Brown Derby!" She tapped the dome of the bowler again and gave him a dancer's exit stance. Then she opened the front door and went out.

"Hold it, Mike," Marty said, and laid the phone on the table. He trotted through the door and caught Virginia just as she was about to step past the protective foliage of the banana tree and head down the stairs. "Hold on, dahlin!" Marty hooked her around the waist and pulled her back in the door so fast that she giggled and almost lost the hat.

But he was smiling. Virginia picked up the phone and held it to her face. He grabbed it before she spoke and pushed her toward the bedroom. "Git dressed, now."

She laughed and went into the bedroom.

"Okay." He resumed the conversation with Mike. He wanted to follow her.

* * * *

Released early from work, Max decided that he indeed needed a break, and rather than switching to one of the half-dozen other projects he was involved with, he would indulge himself in some favorite personal pastimes. From the cabinet full of emergency gourmet items in his office,

Max pulled a tin of beluga caviar and slipped it into his pocket. He made the short drive to Lucey's, and went into the bar. He opened the caviar and ordered a bottle of Laurent-Perrier Salon, 1936. Crackers were provided, and Max sat at the end of the bar, wielding a butter knife and engaging the bartender in uncommonly witty repartee, at least as to Max's contributions to it.

The afternoon sun glowed behind the Florentine stained-glass windows, giving the nearly deserted bar the murky pallor of an abbot's library. As Max poured more champagne into his glass, Edmond Glover appeared at the bar and ordered a beer. Max glanced at him through the gloom, looking for makeup, which would mean that he'd gone AWOL from a sound stage. Off-screen, Glover was a thin, dour man with a threatening physical presence.

"Eddie, old chappy," Max chortled, his cares bubbling easily away.

Glover nodded at him. No makeup.

"Missed you at the *Rising Tide* preview," said Max. "The audience loved you."

"Last time I play a Frenchman." Glover flashed the little pained twitch of a smile that was his trademark. "Next time, they'll have to get Henreid."

After working with him on the picture, Max knew something about the mysterious hatreds and superstitions of Edmond Glover. These included an intense dislike of Paul Henreid, who had once been a rival of Glover's for certain roles. But why Glover still cared about Henreid now that Glover was a much bigger star mystified Max.

"Understood," Max replied. "Have some caviar. It was flown in from Stalingrad by communist pigeons."

"I don't eat that stuff," Glover sniffed.

"What do you mean? It's forty dollars an ounce!"

"It's *bait*. You celebrating something?"

Max shrugged. "Eh...just writing a new picture."

"With the Duchess?" Glover leered unpleasantly.

Max knew Glover was just needling him for sport. "I am no longer working with Mister Gladstone. I was not aware of that nickname."

"But you knew who I meant."

Rising Tide was done, and Max did not have to humor Glover anymore. Archer Daniel would be a perfect role for him, but no way in hell would Max go through that again. "Look, Edmond. Let's leave Gil out of it. I know we had a rough time on the film, you and I. But we don't have to be permanent enemies."

"I don't want to be your enemy, Max." Glover chuckled liquidly. "In fact, I feel sorry for you. I was there once. Fighting, scheming, pouring every ounce of energy into these magic lantern shows—and then some moron sabotages it. I'm afraid you'll find that what you're striving for isn't worth it."

Max studied the hangdog face, so unremarkable in life, so magnetic on the screen. "You may be right. This afternoon I have decided not to worry about much of anything."

Glover looked into his beer. "Good, Max. That's real good. I see your wife is returning to the acting profession."

"My wife? No."

"I believe she's meeting with an agent right now, though I don't approve of her choice. I saw her with Marty Nuco in the parking lot at Ciro's."

Max snorted. "Ciro's isn't open yet."

"That's why it was interesting they were there." Glover drained his beer and stood up. "Don't worry about it, kid. Just follow the yellow brick road." He walked out.

The champagne and caviar turned to swill in Max's mouth.

* * * *

Max drove down Sunset Boulevard, past Ciro's. Virginia's green Packard was in the parking lot—practically the only car there.

He knew what it meant. It had all been a waste. All the loving words, the tears, the slow building of trust, all the joy, the sudden surprises, the sweet moments, the pride. All of it was a lie. Virginia had never really been his after all. She had never belonged to anyone but herself. A crushing weight of sorrow pressed down on him. And that was the biggest lie of all, that you were ever attached to someone, or part of something bigger than just drawing another breath.

Max thought of what Glover had said. That was not just casual information. Glover knew. "*Verdammt!*" Max shouted in the car. If he knew, who else did? Who else *didn't*? Max lashed himself with anger and humiliation. And the idea that it could be Marty Nuco who soiled his nest made him nauseous. Nuco, who stank of the swamp, who wallowed in the *schmutz* of people's desires. A pimp! A dog of the street who had sniffed and licked a hundred diseased ratholes. Max knew he would never love Virginia again, and again the weight of sorrow crushed down on him so that he could hardly breathe.

But if Max's life was over, he had to make it count. Someone had to die today. He continued on home. From a cabinet behind the bar in the den, Max took out a wooden case and a squat tin box. A pair of antique dueling pistols snuggled inside the wooden case.

Max did not remember the exact lineage of the things. French, at least a century old. They had been an afterthought acquisition. A bauble. He and Virginia were on their honeymoon tour of Europe, in 1939. He had swept her off her feet, as he fully intended to do. The best of everything —again Max felt horror at his pride and his blindness. They came home with trunks of stuff. Two months later, Hitler invaded Poland. Poland was lost. Now Virginia was lost.

A low, horrible sound came out of Max's chest. He could not stop it. How ridiculous to compare the two. Who cared about *Poland*! But then who cared about Virginia, but him? And what had that come to?

Max picked up one of the pistols and hefted it in his hand, heavy as an ingot. With his other hand he reached for a bottle of cognac and slopped a big slug into a highball glass, then poured most of that down his gullet.

He pulled back the hammer of the pistol until it caught. He straightened his arm, closed an eye, and pulled the trigger. The hammer snapped forward with a satisfying clank. From the tin box, Max took out a lead ball the size of a cocktail onion. Somewhere, probably in his youth, Max had read or heard about the gaping hole one of these would carve through flesh. His hand already shook, so he would have to be very close, and aim for the middle of the chest.

* * * *

Marty drove her back to her car. Twilight. Time for a good wife to be home getting supper ready, and a good husband to stop at the tavern for a beer so the wife will have time to get supper ready. Marty laughed softly. She would probably make it. He didn't know if Virginia Beckerman burned canned beans, or whipped up gourmet chow with one hand. That was another life. Max's life. Marty Nuco would be home having dinner with Missus Nuco and all the striplings.

Marty could have many women, which was why he had few. Usually they wanted something from him. But not Virginia. She was totally indifferent to Hollywood, and in fact, longing to leave it. The fact that she was Mrs. Max Beckerman was not inconvenient for Marty. Like most people, Max had a secret he would do almost anything to keep hidden. And like a lot of such secrets, Marty knew it. So if there should be any trouble, Marty would have cards to play.

Marty turned into the driveway of Ciro's, and stopped in the slot next to Virginia's car, so she could slip out of the passenger side of his car and into the driver's side of her own. But Virginia was just taking out a cigarette. She offered him one of hers, and Marty took it, though he didn't really want it. He guessed he could spare a *Now Voyager* moment. He lit the cigarettes. Out of the corner of his eye he could see somebody in a white undershirt, maybe a dishwasher, sitting on a beer case by the back door of the restaurant, also smoking, looking at them.

"Sweetums..."

"I know." Virginia touched his lips with a finger of her soft, cool glove. "G'bye." She opened the door, and swung her feet out. Marty turned back toward the steering wheel.

He saw the pistol first. He saw the mouth of the barrel of the pistol first. The way the daylight angled into the opening for a fraction of an inch. It was right outside the car window, pointed at the middle of his face. A hand held the pistol, and farther back, at the other end of the arm, Marty saw Max.

"Get out." Max stepped away, and clearly expected Marty to open the car door. He did so.

"Max?" Virginia's voice came over Marty's shoulder. Still in the car, it sounded like.

"Did you thank I did not know?" Max's voice was low but strained with rage. "Did you thank I would let you do this?"

"Do what, Max?" Marty got out of the car. Now the gun pointed at his chest.

"Take my wife."

"Max!" Virginia spoke to him angrily in German, and Max spat out a reply in the same language, losing himself to anger briefly, his face red, his chin jerking toward her, his eyes leaving Marty for only a split second. In that moment, Marty collected himself.

"There is nothing going on here, Max." Marty looked at the pistol, the mouth of the damn thing like the entrance to the Rockfish Tunnel. He made himself believe his words. Everything depended on that. "I haven't touched your wife. She is thinking of going back to work, as you know. I am frankly discouraging her, but she is insistent. We went over to my office to draw up a contract. It has not been signed."

Max let out a short, harsh laugh. "I've got a private eye who says different."

Virginia said, "You *what?*"

Marty cut her off. "He's bluffing. Cut the bullshit, Max. There's nothing going on."

Something caught Marty's eye and he looked up. A young woman leaned out a window, in an apartment on the hill behind the parking lot. The apartment and the window and her face were all bathed in the golden light of the setting sun. Golden. This stranger stared down at them from her bleacher seat with round eyes and a slack jaw. Marty shared her disbelief. After all he had faced, to be shot by a jealous husband. It was a bad way to go.

"You've had your way too many times. I've looked the other way, and God damn me, I've even helped you." Max took one step back.

Marty realized he had a cigarette in his hand. He lifted the hand. It shook. He took a drag. His lips shook. His chest. He had one last plea. "Max..."

"No bullshit." Max's face twisted with a kind of hate Marty had seen before. He knew it was the last thing he would ever see. "You are going on a trip now," Max growled and pulled back the hammer.

Marty froze.

Virginia whispered, "Max, don't do it!"

The hammer slammed home. Marty flinched badly. That was it. A clang like the slam of hell's iron door, but no explosion, no fire, no lead tearing through his heart. Max lowered the pistol and croaked a raspy laugh. Marty exhaled a plume of cigarette smoke that had been caught in his lungs. He slumped down on one knee.

"No, it wasn't loaded," Max said mournfully. "The damn thing is too complicated. But it is better this way, anyhow. I won't be able to forget what you did to me for a very long time, and now you have something to remember as well."

Marty stood up, a fierce strength lifting him. He would kill this man with his bare hands, right now. He twisted the heavy, old pistol out of Max's hand as if it were a toy.

Virginia grabbed him. "No!" She pulled him back into the car with her. "Just go!" she shouted.

Marty threw the gun across the pavement. "You pathetic..." He couldn't think of a word that would fully contain his anger. Virginia pulled at him again, and he got in the car and backed out quickly. Jamming the gears, he roared out of the parking lot, almost hitting an ice truck that had just pulled in.

"What the croaking Jesus got into him?" he yelled at Virginia.

"I'm fucked if I know!"

Marty made himself calm down. He breathed. At a red light, he glanced at her. "I didn't know you spoke German."

She emitted a short, harsh laugh. "That was Yiddish."

Jesus Christ, thought Marty. Funny how you learn things at the oddest times. I've been fucking a damn Jewess and didn't even know it!

* * * *

With a free afternoon, Lyman took his own route home, working his way through a series of bars west on Santa Monica Boulevard and out the Roosevelt Highway. He was off on one of his benders, and he had already decided that it did not matter a tinker's damn if he showed up for work tomorrow. By midnight he sat at the typewriter in his study, bleary-eyed and disheveled, plinking away slowly, but with great resolve, on a list titled WHY I CANNOT CONTINUE IN THIS POSITION.

As Lyman typed, he recited. "Item the Third. I cannot work with...a man who...wears a hat in the...office. I feeeel that...he is about to...leave...mo-men-tair-illeee."

Tina appeared in the doorway. He could sense her worry. "Honey, aren't you coming to bed soon? It's very late to be..."

"Drunk? Yes. And I am almost done." Lyman did not look at her or stop typing. She remained in the doorway, and he went on, irritation rising. "If you must know, I am typing my resignation from the studio."

"That is what I was afraid of."

"I'm sorry, there's nothing else I can do. The man is a monster to work with. Let them film it any way they like. Let them make it a cartoon. I don't care." He continued typing.

Bettina watched him. "What will become of us?"

"What *becomes* of anybody? They die alone, rich or poor, loved or unloved..."

Tina shuddered as if she had been slapped.

"Damn it, go away!" Lyman cried. "If you stay in here one more minute I will lose my resolve! I know what it means to do this, but it is beyond endurance." He looked up, but Tina was as gone as a ghost, leaving him instantly sorry for the harsh words.

* * * *

The next morning Lyman came in to the office about a quarter to ten, unshaven, un-tied, shaking, feeling defeated and depressed. Max sat leaning back in the desk chair, looking out the windows, lost in thought.

Lyman took a folded sheet of paper out of his jacket pocket and stood before the desk expectantly. "What?" Max asked with a croak.

"I don't think I can work here anymore on this job," Lyman said quietly. "If you are interested here are the reasons." He held out the paper. Max, who had returned his gaze to the windows, gave a barely perceptible wince and reluctantly took the paper. He began reading.

"...waves an assortment of canes, batons and shill..."

"Shillelaghs. A bit of unpoetic license."

Max continued reading in a disbelieving mumble. He reached up and touched the top of his head. He was not wearing a hat. When he finished he tossed the letter on the desk and peered at Lyman. "Therefore you cannot continue in this position."

"That is right." Lyman braced himself for the gale, but Max did not react. He leaned back in his chair and gazed again out the window.

"In Gott Ve Trust." Max sighed. "All Others Pay Cash. *In hoc signo vinces*." Then he was silent. Lyman was nonplussed. Had the man come unhinged?

"You're right, of course," Max continued. "On our last picture, Edmond Glover called me a Prussian Nazi. Me! A Jew with a mother in Berlin whom I haven't heard from in three years! But he was right, too. What is Hitler but an asshole with too much power? Or too much powder."

Max twisted his fingers, contemplating something. "I've gotten pretty far up the ladder here in Hollywood. Was it talent that got me here, or vision? Or maybe just hard work." Max shrugged. "I think mostly it was snarling at the right people, and kissing the right asses. Oh, I did it with style, and for that you get extra points. But it leaves you not much at all to be proud of."

He gave Lyman a pained smile. "On the way, I met a beautiful young girl, an L.A. girl. Fresh-faced. Beautiful inside, too. Father was a set-painter right here at Colosseum. We fell in love. Me and the girl, not the father."

"The execs didn't know what to do with me until they hooked me up with Gil Gladstone. A decent, cultivated guy from New York whom they also did not know what to do with." Max laughed. "Together, we somehow clicked, and we wrote a dozen pictures together. We wrote words that Garbo spoke! And John Barrymore. We wrote for Lubitsch, and Hawks!" Max seemed briefly transported to happier days.

"But I got too big for Gilbert." Max frowned. "People said he was carrying me, and I couldn't stand that. So I moved on. That's where you came in. And now Gil hates my guts, because really I was carrying *him*, and after this picture everyone will know it, because I will be an even bigger success."

Max stood up and slammed both fists on the desk. "And now my wife is moving on from *me*. Because she got tired of carrying *me* in the marriage. I flirted with every pair of long eyelashes I saw. But I never really wanted anyone else. Why did I do it?"

He looked at Lyman, tears rimming his eyes. "Does any of this make any sense? You write novels about the sick soul of L.A. The poverty of the rich. The helplessness of the powerful. If you knew me better, you would know that I am one of those stories. You're too good a writer for this racket, Lyman. Go back to your novels. You'll be happier, and the work will last longer."

Lyman was fascinated by this completely uncharacteristic speech, and he had no response but the simple truth. "But I need the money."

Max nodded. "In God We Trust. *Ditat Deus*."

Quietly entering the room behind Max were Fred Sheldrake and two men—one tall and blond, one shorter and dark— who were unmistakably police detectives. Drawn by Lyman's stare, Max turned to look at them.

Sheldrake said, "Max, it seems..."

The tall, Swedish-looking detective cut in. "Are you Max Beckerman?"

"Of course."

"We would like you to come with us. We have reason to believe you may know something about the shooting of Martin Nuco."

Max grunted. "Yah, I shot him all right. But I think he'll recover. Unfortunately."

Sheldrake, who already looked scared and confused, turned even whiter. "Max! Don't say anything more!"

The Greek-looking detective planted himself in front of Max and leaned into him. "Were you at the apartment at 1101 Crescent Heights last night?"

"Crescent? What?"

"Come with us." The two detectives each took Max by an arm and headed him toward the door.

"Someone shot him? Where?"

"Where they were aiming. Twice." The Swede replied. "We know about your little scene in the parking lot. Maybe you caught up with him later and did the job for real? Or maybe not. Don't worry. We'll figure it out."

"Hold it!" Max shook loose. "Marty Nuco was really shot? When?"

"Oh, he's good!" said the Greek. "Shot, but not dead. Too bad for the shooter."

The whole group left the room, Sheldrake saying, "I'll call your lawyer...who is your lawyer?" Lyman heard them clump down the stairs. He had hardly moved since handing Max the paper, which still lay on the desk.

From the window Lyman watched them put Max in the back of a black Ford and drive away. He stood staring at the corner where the car had disappeared for a long minute, trying to understand the thousand and one implications of what had just happened. And the one thing that hadn't happened. He wandered around the edge of the room back to the desk, and picked up the memo.

His resignation had not been accepted.

Chapter Six

When Fred Sheldrake returned to his office, he had his secretary ring the studio legal department. No one was in. She got him the number for Max's lawyer, and Sheldrake called the head of publicity, and then the head of production, who said he would inform Mr. Corvus. The secretary brought in the Wednesday morning *Times*, and the first draft of the story was in there, without any of the damning details.

One of the most successful agents in the motion picture industry was shot last night at a west side apartment. Martin Nuco, 36, was found critically wounded about 10 p.m. after a neighbor heard several shots and called police.

By lunchtime, people were running all over the studio property carrying Extras and tut-tutting. By then, the papers had identified Max Beckerman as a suspect, and the story moved up to the lead: DIRECTOR HELD IN NUCO SHOOTING.

The arrest of Oscar-nominated director Max Beckerman for the shooting of Marty Nuco, agent to several well-known movie stars, was announced today by Police Commissioner Eugene W. Biscailus, who also revealed the involvement of Beckerman's wife, Virginia, in a love affair with the victim.

Gilbert Gladstone read it in his office, in the producer's wing. He walked down the hall toward Sheldrake's office, and caught him just coming out the door.

"Jesus, huh?" Sheldrake muttered.

"Max always goes for the dramatic." Gilbert didn't mind dancing on the German's grave, just for a moment.

Sheldrake gave him a hard, impatient look. "There's no way."

"Oh, hell, I know. Max is much more likely to be shot than shoot."

Gilbert Gladstone circled back to his office, motioning his secretary to follow him in. He was considered a producer now, not a writer, which meant he had a higher status, but a worse job. That was thanks to Max, who'd been terrible to work with, and worse to leave. He wasn't so sure Max wouldn't shoot a man, but what shocked him was the idea of Max as a cuckold.

He sat behind his desk, and glanced again at the picture of Virginia on the front page. A glamour shot from her days as a pre-starlet. His secretary waited, steno pad on her knee.

Gilbert said, "I knew it would end badly for Max."

The secretary wrote it in shorthand.

He shook his head. "No, not that."

She scratched it out.

* * * *

According to the Commissioner's statement, Max Beckerman confronted Nuco at least twice, once to threaten the powerful talent agent, and a second time in an attempt to kill him. Nuco at last word was clinging to life.

In the first incident, about six p.m. Tuesday, Beckerman pulled a pistol on Nuco in the parking lot behind Ciro's Restaurant. Also present at that time was Virginia Beckerman, the wife of the Colosseum Pictures director.

Edmond Glover, wearing a white dinner jacket, read the newspaper in his dressing room, while a makeup woman dabbed at his hairline with a cotton pad. To himself he muttered, "Christ on a crutch, Max, can't you take a rib?" Then he whacked the paper, as if the makeup lady wasn't a foot away.

"Wha-ut?" Her eyes did not move from her task.

"I tell this horse's patoot that I saw his wife talking to a man, and he goes out and blasts the poor slob with a gun."

"Well, whaddaya wanna do that for?" she said. "You don't go and wave a red hanky in front of a bull."

Virginia Beckerman, who has admitted to the tryst with Nuco, told police that the gun was not loaded. Another witness, 17-year-old Phyrne Medwin, who lives behind the nightclub, said that Beckerman actually fired at Nuco at this time.

Sometime around 10 p.m., Max Beckerman purportedly surprised Nuco in the latter's "love nest" apartment on Crescent Heights Blvd, shot him twice, and left him for dead. Beckerman and his wife had been arguing at the couple's home, Mrs. Beckerman said, when the director stormed out, and did not return. He was arrested at Colosseum Pictures Studios this morning.

* * * *

In a room at the Ambassador Hotel, Ted Hardy rose at noon and called room service to order breakfast and the morning paper. His upswing was continuing. *My Friend Turnip* was selling seats, and Ted's agent was in negotiations with Galactic Studios for a film. Ted Hardy had bought half the play when Chase Elmont was still writing it, and then acquired the rest, along with the copyright, later on.

When the paper came and Ted read the front page, he became so excited that he forgot to eat. Marty Nuco mortally shot by a jealous husband, caught with his pants down, literally or figuratively. It was Nuco who had engineered Ted's disgrace, back in '34; Nuco who had set him up, had got him drunk, had paid that boy to come and bat his eyelashes, and the photographer to break in when Ted had the boy's cock in his mouth. Nuco was just a young punk then, and he'd held the photos in front of Ted and sneered his demands. And Ted was so ashamed, he got on the first train east with a case of scotch, and woke up in Baltimore two weeks later in a pool of his own puke. That had been the first lap of a three-year bender.

Now Nuco was cut down in one swing of an archangel's sword, maybe dead, but surely shamed. Ted Hardy dropped to his knees and began his prayer of obeisance and thanks, but emotion overtook him, and he could do nothing but shake and sob before the power of the Lord.

* * * *

Beckerman, along with screenwriter Gilbert Gladstone, was nominated for an Academy Award for best screenplay in 1941. Beckerman has directed several successful pictures for Colosseum in the last two years. He is a German emigré, a former journalist and actor. Marty Nuco is a talent agent and manager of some of the movie industry's biggest stars. He is a known associate of several members of the Los Angeles-area crime syndicate.

Lily Torrence read it over Deborah's shoulder. They had been sitting in the clubhouse at Santa Anita race track when one of their escorts, a rugged young actor named Peter something, came bounding back to the table with the Extra of the *Examiner*.

Deborah had a horse—El Chico Capitan—running in the fifth race. Lily had been able to come because the rehearsal for her new picture had been cancelled today. The women had not been betting, drinking, or paying much attention to the races, just chatting and sipping ginger ale. Now Deborah sat hunched over the folded tabloid, clucking worriedly.

Lily knew that the most important thing for her to do right now was comfort Deborah, if she wanted comforting. There was no way for Lily to know how she would take it. Deborah was certainly friendly with Nuco, but she had said that he could ruin her. So perhaps Deborah's secret was about to die with Lily's own. And now the complication of Deborah getting married, well, that might die also. Lily would comfort Deborah, but she would give nothing away.

* * * *

Virginia Beckerman, 29, is an artist and former actress who was under contract at Medallion Studio from 1938 to 1940.

That was about all the press knew about Virginia. So the reporters and photographers came and camped on the street in front of her house. She could see them from her bedroom window. A few clumps of curious people from the neighborhood, or from somewhere, also appeared, drifting along the sidewalk like nosy little wisps of cloud after a storm. Virginia smoked a cigarette and looked at them. Then she went back to bed.

As long as they were quiet. Just quiet.

Chapter Seven

Lyman Wilbur sat at the typewriter early Thursday morning, thinking about Scene Six, the first appearance of Chloe. He turned his head, and part of his brain registered that the sky outside the office windows was just beginning to brighten. But only a part of his brain—the rest of it conjured Chloe as she walked through the conservatory toward Archer Daniel.

Lyman's pipe jutted jauntily from his mouth, unlit, unfilled. He plunked the keys of the machine in short bursts. By moving his jaw, he caused the flat diamond of the pipe stem to rock gently back and forth, making a clicking sound against his teeth. A part of his brain registered the motion and the sound.

Peering through the bottom of his bifocals, Lyman read what he had written, sighed, pulled the paper out of the typewriter and dropped in into the wastebasket next to him. He ran a fresh sheet into the machine, sat back, and stared at it.

After the detectives led Max away yesterday morning, Lyman set about piecing the story together. Last night he had meditated at length on what it all meant for him. Despite his total lack of involvement in the shooting, these were events in his life. If Max went to jail there would be no movie, no need for a scriptwriter, no need for him, no thousand a week.

The job that he had almost quit now seemed precious to him.

The resignation—attempted—had been an unseemly burst of rage, caused by—what else?—alcohol. It was the oldest story in Lyman's book. Now the thought of losing this job gave him an actual pain in the gut. The poverty, the loneliness, the despair for Tina's health, all that had ended so suddenly, so gloriously because of this job. He could not think of going back to his old life.

But even if Max did not go to jail, would the studio still want to make a movie about a murdered lover directed by Max Beckerman? Lyman's conclusion was that his days here were probably numbered, but two more weeks, even one week, could make a difference for him. So he resolved to squeeze every last dollar out of this place by coming to work every day and every hour he could until someone—probably someone with a big cigar—told him to stop.

In fact, he had come in early this morning to guard against the office being taken apart and put away somewhere like an office set. Now Lyman sat, as still and round as a Buddha, and frankly as content as a Buddha, at the typewriter, free to write the screenplay as he saw fit, even though it might never see the light of day. The idea that Max had shot someone was still unbelievable, and impossible to get a grip on. The shock of it, and the scandal of it, gave him a little tingle, but he found himself unmoved about Max himself.

Light of day had come, but stillness shrouded the building. No one around to hear the clearing of his throat, the squeak of the swivel chair, the clicking of the pipe stem between his teeth.

Lyman stood and stretched, half singing, half humming a song that had bubbled up from the soup of his memory about a doughboy who found a rose in Ireland. Or maybe it was a Jew boy. If Max was here, they would probably have a twenty minute argument about it.

He stepped around the desk, and headed for the can. There would be no arguments today.

He pulled the door open, and nearly jumped through the ceiling.

Deborah Boynton was sitting on the toilet. "Do you *mind!*" she said frostily.

"Oh, of course." Lyman closed the door. He returned the way he had come and eased himself back into the swivel chair behind the desk. Not wanting to even look in the direction of the bathroom, he turned again to the typewriter, pulled the blank sheet out of the carriage, and put in a fresh blank sheet. He began typing.

New news of the day. Flash: what the hell is going on?

Lyman heard water swish, and it faded away, but still Deborah did not come out. Maybe she never would. Maybe she lived there, some false wall opened up to her mansion attached behind the office. A secret passage. The Phantom of the Studio.

The door opened and Deborah stood there, dressed simply in slacks and a crisp cotton blouse, no makeup, hair pulled back. Lyman expected embarrassment, perhaps a self-deprecating chuckle, but in her first glance she conceded absolutely nothing.

Lyman rose. He couldn't forget what he had seen. A half a giggle died in his throat.

Deborah smiled. "Well, I suppose I should explain."

"Oh! Well." Lyman blushed.

"I came in to see you."

"Really?"

"This is embarrassing." But she seemed utterly unembarrassed.

"Please, sit down." Lyman indicated the couch. Deborah sat in the armchair. Lyman remained standing behind the desk.

"I didn't mean to startle you."

"I just had no idea. You were either very quiet, or I was very distracted." Lyman could not understand why *he* felt foolish. After all *she* had been caught with her pants down.

She looked at the bathroom door. "Must be soundproof," she mused. "I think we are all somewhat distracted by this tragedy. About Max. In shock, actually. That's what I came to talk to you about."

Lyman lowered himself into the desk chair. "About Max?"

"Yes." She rose, walked over to the windows, and stared out for a long minute. She turned to him. "I think he's being set up."

"Set up? You mean framed? By who? And how?"

"Marty has a lot of enemies in this town. Enough to form a line around the block. Maybe Max just had the bad luck to be seen threatening him, and someone took advantage of that."

"Perhaps."

"Or maybe it's just coincidence." She chuckled unmerrily. "That comic opera in the parking lot of Ciro's—that's Max. Sneaking into an apartment and really shooting a man? No."

"Well, I'm sure that the police will work it out." Lyman felt she was just stalling.

"I'm not so sure. That's why I came to see you. Will you help me find out who really shot Marty?"

Up to now, Lyman had been extremely solicitous towards her, but he could not stifle a derisive snort at this. "Good Lord, no. This is a real crime, not a movie caper. The police would not look kindly upon a couple of well-meaning bumblers romping in their sandbox."

"You won't help me?"

"Do what?" Lyman asked. "Find whom?"

"I don't know exactly. That's why I was hoping..." She wilted a little.

"I'm afraid not."

"Would Archer Daniel turn down a rich lady in trouble?"

"Perhaps." Lyman could not but be amused by her appeal to his alter-ego. "He would only take the case if he thought he could help, and if there was a clear-cut job to do."

"Yes. In one of your books you said that Archer only does *reasonably legal kinds* of detective work, isn't that it?"

"Well, well." Lyman smiled. "You have read me. Yes, something like that. It always starts with routine stuff, like finding a person who is missing. It starts routine, and then goes very haywire. There's a lesson there for us."

"Yes, I suppose you are right."

Lyman felt like he was getting his bearings. She had had an impulse to action, but she really just wanted to be talked out of it. A very common reaction to bad news. "I think we should let it work itself out," he told her. "Keep an eye on things, of course. And if we have any concerns, we should take them to the studio legal people, wherever they are. Max will have his own lawyer, and he'll listen to him. The rich and powerful don't get railroaded."

With that, he gently ushered her out, though in different circumstances he would have done anything to keep her there. Walking back to his desk, he trembled a little. Deborah Boynton in the bathroom was quite a shock first thing in the morning—any morning!

This vulnerable, tender side of her was something he had not seen before—except in every one of her movies. He sat down in the desk chair, dreaming of scenes from those movies, especially the old melodramas: *The World Moves On, Trans-Oceanic, Ladies Who Lunch.* And there were others, half-remembered, half slept-through in the little second-run houses of the Depression, where you could stay all afternoon for a dime, nursing a cheap bottle, out of the sun, away from the world. That had been a refuge, and she had been there, along with all the others, of course. All the stars in heaven.

But how the hell did she get in the bathroom? Had she walked in while he sat there typing? Sure, he couldn't see the door without turning, but he wasn't asleep, either. Or she was there when he walked in and she stayed there for—he looked at his watch—forty-five minutes? And how to read her request for him to become involved in Max's case? Could that be sincere?

Staring into space, Lyman reached into the lower desk drawer for the bottle of Five Crown. Normally he wouldn't, in the morning, but normally a blonde bombshell wasn't sitting in his can. He giggled a little at the memory of being cheek to jowl with her.

His fingers, expecting the smooth, round neck of the bottle, stumbled on something heavy and hard. His hand grasped the thing, and only when it appeared before his eyes did he realize he held a revolver.

Lyman laid it on the blotter before him. Stylized letters spelled "Colt" on the oval shield at the top of the grip. He thought perhaps—no, *definitely*—he should not be handling the pistol, because it had never been in this desk drawer before. This was his drawer, and all it had contained in the month he had been working here were a few books and papers, sometimes a sandwich or a Milky Way, and lately, the bottle.

The gun had not been there yesterday...or had it? Had he opened this drawer yesterday? Had Deborah placed it here? Is that what she was doing, and he surprised her? Planning to frame Max herself? But why would she have the gun that shot Nuco unless she shot him?

Or, Lyman thought, was she trying to frame *him*? It seemed ludicrous. First of all, only Max would know this was Lyman's drawer, if he had even paid attention. Lyman had no reason to think Max was trying to cast suspicion on him. He had too much respect for Max's plotting skills to credit that idea.

But a real weapon lay there before him, not a plot device. And now with his fingerprints on it. Lyman did not know if this was definitely the weapon that shot Nuco. But what other pistol would suddenly appear in his desk drawer? He looked in the drawer. Yes, the bottle still lay there, on a telephone book. And no other ordnance. He pulled the whiskey out for a quick swig.

Lyman leaned over and sniffed the barrel. He recognized the biting smell of burnt gunpowder. Without picking it up, he looked into the cylinder from the front and saw the round heads of two unspent bullets. An Archer Daniel line came to him: *like two larcenous aldermen resting in their chambers*. It was not a large-caliber gun, maybe a .32. And it did not look like it had been cleaned or oiled for a long time. A street gat, or a longtime resident of someone's sock drawer. Certainly not something a fastidious snob like Max would own.

Lyman heard voices in the hall. The wrong kind of voices. He hooked his pinky finger through the trigger guard and lowered the revolver into his briefcase. He snapped the briefcase shut.

* * * *

The office door swung open. The detective from yesterday walked in. The Swede. It was a couple of hours earlier in the day, but otherwise a repeat performance. The congruity of it threw Lyman off. Why had he come back?

The Swede saw Lyman sitting at the desk and stopped abruptly. A man who was following bumped into him, then backed up. "Oh, hel-lo!" The Swede glanced at his watch. "Didn't realize you started so early. We wanted to get in and out before we bothered anybody."

"You won't bother me." Lyman forced a smile, and leaned back in the swivel chair. "I have a meeting in a few minutes anyway." He had been wondering why the gun appeared in his desk, and who it was meant to ensnare. Now he was much more certain that it was meant to ensnare *someone*, but not him. He could feel the briefcase nestling against his leg. "Do you mean to search the place?"

"No, we're not searching. Just looking around, trying to get a feel." The Swede folded his arms across his chest, a pose which made it obvious that the sleeves of his rust-brown suit coat were too short for his long arms. He commenced a leisurely tour of the room, while another plainclothesman, a fat, slit-eyed specimen this time, remained in the doorway.

"Has Mister Beckerman been charged?" Lyman put the question out for whoever wanted it.

"It's all in the papers," said the Swede.

"The papers sometimes get it wrong."

"No kidding," the detective sneered. "What was your name, sir?"

"I don't believe we've actually met."

"Soderman. Detective." He flopped a blue and gold shield in Lyman's direction.

"I'm Wilbur. Lyman."

Soderman pulled out a small notebook and wrote in it. Lyman knew he was being recorded as Wilbur Lyman, but he let it pass.

Soderman continued. "How long have you known Mr. Beckerman?"

Lyman fought to keep focused. They weren't here for him. "What's the date today?"

"April thirteenth. I'm only looking for approximate."

Lyman thought a moment. "I've known him approximately since Saint Patrick's Day. Of this year. By the way, has the gun been found? That shot Nuco?"

"No, but it's not a crucial piece of evidence." The Swede sniffed. "We're pretty sure he was shot." The beefy underling coughed a laugh at this.

The Swede inspected the artwork above the mantel. "Now, on Tuesday, were you here at work?"

"Yes."

"And Mr. Beckerman was here?" He fingered the whips and canes hanging on the hatstand.

"Yes."

"All day?"

"We quit early," Lyman said. "I left about two thirty."

"You didn't see him after that?

"No, I never see him outside the office," Lyman proclaimed, perhaps a little too eagerly. "I don't know very much about Mr. Beckerman. And I don't consider him a friend. Or an enemy." Lyman felt like he would snap if he did not get out of the room. "I just work here. Look, I've got to go." He rose, patted his jacket pocket for his pipe, and made his way around the desk. The Swede waved him away with disinterest.

The underling stepped aside and Lyman walked out the door. He no sooner reached the hallway than he remembered that he had not picked up the briefcase. *Idiot!* He cursed softly but kept walking down the stairs.

After pausing a moment and mentally thrashing about in indecision, Lyman turned around and walked back up the steps and into the room. Again he surprised the Swede, who gave him that saggy eyed, querulous frown of his. Feeling distinctly like Bob Hope in one of his cowardly-heel roles, Lyman picked up the briefcase, pointed at it, mouthed a silent explanation at no one in particular, and left.

* * * *

Lyman went to his car and drove away, glancing too frequently in the rearview mirror, shivering every mile or two with fear and excitement. He had a lot to think about. Max, Deborah, the pistol, and the absurd risk he had just taken. The only intelligent thing to do would have been to show the gun and explain what happened. Simple instinct had led him to drop the pistol in his briefcase. He did not clearly understand why he had then taken it away. But he knew he now had a lot to lose.

Deborah had lied to him about her reason for being there this morning. But it was hard to conceive that she had placed the gun there. Why would she even have it unless *she* shot Nuco? Lyman had to shake his head on that one. Yet, clearly the Swede had come to the same spot to collect it, with a couple of witnesses. Lyman did not feel anyone had any intent to frame him. He had just gotten in the way. Twice. It occurred to him that if they had to plant evidence to make a case against Max, he might very well be innocent.

Lyman went over it again. Whether Deborah had planted the gun or not, she must know whether or not Max did it. And if Max didn't do it, Deborah must know who did. Then, the cops showing up. Was that Act Two of the same play, or something out of the blue? Had he just prevented an injustice, or caused one? He could get no traction on any aspect of this, sliding all over the road. He needed more information.

He took his eyes off the rearview and looked around him. He had reached Olympic Boulevard. The sun slanted through the grimy windshield, across the dusty dashboard. He checked his watch. Eight thirty. On a chance, he headed downtown to the county court building. After some searching, he found Assistant D.A. Jim Daggett, an old acquaintance.

Daggett occupied a cubicle made of dark wainscoting below frosted glass panes that did not reach the high ceiling. Neatly stacked papers and folders covered every horizontal surface in the tiny office. Daggett cleared the upright wooden chair that stood next to the desk, and the two men sat down. Lyman took a deep breath. The sounds of telephone bells and typewriters mixed in the space above the partitions.

Daggett was a slight man with a slight mustache and a natty hunter green double-breasted suit. He and Lyman went back twenty years, to when Lyman worked as a land agent and Daggett as a junior attorney for the company law firm. They worked together on land purchases, leases, and evictions. Daggett was also an early fan who encouraged Lyman's writing when almost no one else cared. They had not been too close lately, but Lyman knew him as a solid guy, someone who could be trusted.

Lyman got right to it. "Did Max Beckerman shoot Marty Nuco?"

"Well, good morning to you, too."

"I share an office with Beckerman, and an interesting series of events took place there this morning." Lyman narrated the story, but he left Deborah out of it. "It sure looks like someone is trying to plant evidence to incriminate Max. And it sure looks like Detective Soderman is part of this...conspiracy, would you call it?"

"Nasty word, probably a misconception. It is possible he was telling the truth and just wanted to look around. So now, you have a gun."

"I have a pistol." Lyman opened his briefcase, hooked the trigger guard and took out the pistol. He set it on the stack of folders on the corner of the desk. "Is this the gun that shot Nuco?"

"Since I am not on this case, I have no idea." Daggett pulled on his lower lip. "You're quite sure this was never in the drawer before, or in the office?"

"I'm sure I've never seen it." Again Lyman decided to leave Deborah's name out of it. "I did touch it inadvertently in two places, here and here."

Daggett looked at the gun as if it was cast iron dog waste on his desk. "Even if the police were tipped about the gun, it doesn't mean they're in on something dirty. Anybody could call in an anonymous tip."

"That's true, but it sure looks like someone planted it last night, and then called them." Lyman snapped his briefcase shut, "Anyway, my conscience is clean now."

Daggett sighed. "All right. I'm not sure how to explain this without getting you into some trouble, but I guess I can. You will have to make a statement as to where and when."

"Now?"

Daggett picked up his desk phone. "No. I'll let you know. You sure there weren't any other murders by studio personnel last night?"

"Only a few screenplays." This bit of repartee was completely mirthless. Lyman stood up.

"You did what you thought you had to do," Daggett said. "And you came clean. Now, if you're smart, you will stay as far away from this case as you can. If your neighbor's house is burning, call the fire department, don't go over there with a garden hose."

"Believe me." Lyman smiled, relieved. "That is my strong desire. I stumbled on this, but that's the last you will see of me."

He had not told Daggett anything about Deborah. That could have been because Lyman wanted to save her from needless involvement. Could have been, but even he didn't believe it.

* * * *

Lyman returned to the office around eleven. He ascertained that the police had not ripped the place apart, and in fact had left no evidence of a search. Almost, he thought, as if they had looked in the drawer, failed to find the revolver, shrugged, and left.

Lyman walked to the office door and looked down the hall. The writer's wing was quiet but not deserted. He found Jeff Ehlers lolling at his desk in the office two doors down—a far smaller office than Max's suite.

"You see the cops here this morning?"

Ehlers thought he was joking. "What, again?"

The tall, stiff-legged Oklahoman was perhaps the only one of the studio writers with whom Lyman could have a simple and sincere conversation.

Lyman closed the door. "What do we know about Deborah Boynton?"

"She's down-home, cautious, conservative." Ehlers unhooked his steel-rim glasses from his ears. "Doesn't put on airs. Not a publicity hound. But she is ambitious."

"Ambitious? How ambitious?" Lyman wanted dirt, but did not want to be seen as digging too hard.

"Well." Ehlers chuckled. "I don't know. Assertive. And she's smart to be that way. She knows she's in competition for everything. Roles, lines, screen time, billing, lighting, angles. She's very savvy."

Lyman pursued. "But what about her personal life, outside the business?"

Ehlers smiled. "There's a school of thought that she doesn't have one. So what is your interest? Thinking of getting involved in the personal life of Miss B?"

"No, no," Lyman fibbed. "She approached me about a project, an adaptation. Some historical romance she's fond of. That could come in handy, under the circumstances."

Ehlers leaned back in his chair, stretched out his legs, and nearly spanned the room. "The only thing I recall about her is that scandal about her back in the thirties. Her husband was Ted Hardy, a fairly big deal in New York, but he never made it out here." His voice contained an unmistakable tinge of sympathy for someone who had been relegated to the small-time.

Lyman knew the name, if not the story. "Ted Hardy. Song and dance, light patter."

"A mean drunk, and they said he beat her. But he was Catholic, and wouldn't give her a divorce. Then when she sued him, he fought for custody of their son, and put it out that she was a rotten mother. I know it was a story I kept up with. It was pretty juicy stuff."

"So what happened?"

"Typical Hollywood dustup." Ehlers shrugged. "They got divorced after all. Hurt her career for a while. Never heard what happened to the kid. Hardy moved back to New York. Never heard anything about him either. So how did you meet Deborah? She is not that easy to find around town."

"I met her through Max. She was supposed to be in *Double Down*, which I assume is now double dead.

Ehlers nodded. "Too bad for you."

"Worse for Max."

"Worse yet for Marty Nuco."

* * * *

"They finally have fresh strawberries," Tina said. She and Lyman sat at the dining room table of the new abode in Pacific Palisades. "Didn't cost us any points."

Lyman sipped coffee. "I didn't think vegetables were rationed."

"They aren't." Tina chuckled. "By the government. But they were going fast, and the store would only allow one box. It will make up for the dinner a little bit."

The dinner was actually one of Lyman's favorite cheap meals. Welsh rarebit: cheese on toast with Worcestershire sauce. "I don't mind the rationing. I'm proud that you get us by without cheating. It seems the least we can do."

Lyman had enlisted in the Great War in 1917, and ended up a First Lieutenant and platoon leader. He wished he could enlist again. Not because he loved the military, or fighting. But he had followed the rise of Hitler, who looked, to Lyman, like the Kaiser in short pants, and who had bombed Lyman's beloved London. So giving up a few foods seemed the least they could do.

Tina was anxious to hear about his day of adventure, and Lyman tried to convey it, even as he was still trying to understand it. As they began the strawberries, Tina said, "It seems to me—or rather, my question is—if a scandal was bad for Deborah Boynton ten years ago, why is she getting involved in this?"

"Or is she already involved and trying to cover it up?"

"Deborah Boynton a killer?" Tina scoffed.

"First off," Lyman cautioned. "Nuco's not dead. Who will he finger? Max? Deborah? There was a story in the paper today that Nuco's in with gangsters."

Tina smiled. Lyman knew she enjoyed it whenever she thought he was talking like a pulp story hoodlum. He would deny it and pretend to get offended, of course.

"Maybe he won't squawk." Tina made a comically sinister face.

"Do you mean talk?" He laughed. "Or squeal? I don't believe it is considered squealing if you identify the person who shot you."

"That's another thing. If Deborah wanted to kill him, would she shoot him with a gun?"

"What should she shoot him with?"

She spooned a bit of whipped cream. "I mean, maybe she would have poisoned him, or, I don't know."

"But somebody did *something*?" said Lyman.

Tina frowned. "Well, at least you are done with it."

For a moment they ate in silence, their teeth snapping the tiny seeds of the strawberries. Lyman tried to think of a way to tell her.

Tina sighed. "You're not thinking of helping her, are you?"

"Not without getting more information."

"Information from Deborah?"

He shook his head. "Assuming she is telling the truth, Deborah doesn't know anything. I want to talk to a woman who knows something."

Chapter Eight

Joseph Dujanovic had washed for dinner, and now he waited with the rest of the stable hands. They lounged on the porch of the trainer's house, waiting for the dinner bell from the main house, combing dust out of their hair, walking around in their socks, draining bottles of beer, tossing peanuts into their mouths and shells into the yard. They knew Deborah Boynton's was a once-in-a-lifetime job. Dujanovic could see that. Imagine a mug from west Chicago having anything to do with horses.

Lily Torrence's red Plymouth approached on the county road. All the men knew about Lily. She would ride the gray gelding a couple of times a week, and she could handle him.

The red car slowed as it approached the driveway, and some of the men, recognizing the car, turned to look at her. Dujanovic turned, too. They all liked to look at Lily. Sometimes she waved. As she turned in the driveway Dujanovic caught a flash of her finely-molded face in the sun before it was obscured in a shadow. She drove up to the main house. No wave today.

Dujanovic went into the kitchen of the trainer's house to make a telephone call. Three short sentences. "Hey, it's dinner time." Pause. "Yeah." Pause. "Okay."

* * * *

When she walked into the big house, Lily was greeted by Moira with the news that Deborah had gone into town to have dinner with the Sid Bermudas. "But we'll be having supper at the big table, as usual."

Lily's knees and ankles twinged with every step. "Oh, I'm not really hungry," she said. "I think I'll just have a little something and go to bed."

"Are you all right?" Moira looked at her more closely.

"Yes, just tired. Exhausted." Lily could feel the tightness of her smile and the puffiness of her eyes. "They drove us like mules today."

"I know, I know." Moira smiled. "You're like me. I was always the last one standing."

Moira was old enough to be Lily's mother, but still strong and energetic. Lily craved her approval almost as much as she did Deborah's.

Moira gently patted Lily's back. "How about, I'll bring you a plate. I'll bring it to your room."

"Oh, gosh, Moira."

"Go on."

"Thank you so much."

Lily went to her room, took off her coat and lay on top of the bed. She kicked her shoes off—blessed relief. The Sid Bermudas? The childlike clown with his hand puppets was a real person with a family? It just showed the difference between Deborah's life and hers. At least, the difference now.

Lily wondered what Deborah's past had been like, her youth. She often talked about being poor, about struggling to make it. When she was just starting out, what had she done? What had she sold? Who had she spread for? Who had she crawled over? The images made Lily shudder.

"You have to sleep your way up," Marty Nuco had told her. Lily had scoffed, not wanting to believe it. Then she began to look around her. Every day, at the studio, Lily found herself surrounded by very talented people. Unbelievable dancers, actors and singers that no one had ever heard of. Some of them were younger than her and they already had Broadway experience, or they had been developed by a studio, and even had feature roles. But for some reason their careers had stalled. If talent couldn't do it, what could? Luck? Or cheating.

Lily knew it wasn't easy to cheat, either. In show biz everyone says, "ya gotta sell it." Lily had always assumed that meant on stage. Then she had learned different.

Moira came in with a tray. Dinner, coffee, and a bottle of aspirin. Lily smiled, really touched, and thanked her again as she closed the door. Her hunger came up instantly. There was some sliced chicken, peas and potatoes, and a biscuit. The door opened again, and Lily looked up, ready to say something to Moira. A dark man in a blue work shirt stepped in, smiling, acting very casual. It was that Dujanovic. The convict. Lily didn't want him there. "Yes?"

He closed the door. Lily really didn't want that.

"Hi there. If I could just have a minute?"

Fear, impatience, and hunger fought in her. "What?"

He immediately assumed an insolent attitude that Lily had not seen in their previous small encounters. She knew right away what it meant.

"You see, we've been keeping an eye on you."

"You went to all that trouble?"

"No trouble." Dujanovic sneered. "It's an exercise cure for me. I'll be staying on for a while. I think they like me."

"I discussed it all with Koch," said Lily.

"There's been a little shakeup since then. Koch wants to talk to you. He wants to settle things."

"A shakeup? That's what you call it when they shoot Nuco?" Lily knew she had to push back or be flattened. "Did Koch do it?"

"That's not my biz," said Dujanovic. "Not yours either. You're going to see him."

"Tonight?"

"Right now."

Lily shook her head. "No."

He didn't make a move to threaten her. He didn't have to. "We've got you good, baby." He made a motion like flicking ashes away. "One word."

"Yeah?" said Lily. "That easy, huh?" She was trying to sound hard-boiled, but didn't. What did they want from her? Probably just to kill her in the most convenient way. They must know about Maria. And about Marty. But was it possible they didn't know anything, and she would actually get away with everything?

"You go on your own," he said. "Or I'll twist your neck a little and then you'll go with me."

Lily sighed. "Jesus Christ. I'll go. *Hijo de la gran puta*. Where?"

"You don't have to thank me." Dujanovic put his hand on the doorknob. "The Swamp for you. Now." He was gone.

The plate of food on her lap made her stomach churn. She put it aside. She wiped her mouth with a napkin, put on fresh lipstick, and looked at her face in the dresser mirror.

Beneath the blonde dye job and the plucked eyebrows, and without the makeup that made her nose look smaller and cheeks stand out, she saw the Mexican girl from Montebello, Lily Torres, who became Lily Torrence. Who had given up so much of herself, who had gone too far, much too far to stop now.

Lily put on her coat and took the tray back to the kitchen. Moira stood wrapping leftovers for the icebox.

"I've got some things I have to take care of. That I forgot. I have to go home. And I'll spend the night at my Tia's.

Moira shook her head. "But you're so tired."

"Funny thing—that went away."

"Oh God, the energy you kids have."

They both smiled. Lily left.

* * * *

About eight fifteen, Lyman rolled to a stop a couple of houses down from the Beckerman residence. When he phoned ahead to set up the meeting, Virginia Beckerman had warned him about the reporters in front of her house. They were certainly making themselves comfortable.

A brakeman's lantern had been hung from a low branch of a sprawling magnolia tree that canopied the sidewalk and a third of the width of the street. The newspapermen and photogs were gathered around a folding card table that had been set up on the sidewalk. They seemed thoroughly engaged in portraying a hard-boiled image right out of The Front Page *for the genteel neighborhood. I could hear the flick of cards, and smell the gentle perfume of cheap rye in the breathless twilight air.*

They paid me no attention, but as I turned up the walk, a figure emerged from the shadows, stuck a Speed Graphic press camera in my face and made it explode.

"Who're you?" he demanded.

"Nobody." I said. "She been getting any visitors?"

"You're not a cop. Another lawyer?"

"Life insurance salesman. I'd like to give you a quote on some low-cost term."

"Pug," he growled listlessly.

Lyman strode up to the door with a show of confidence that betrayed his doubt about what he was doing. In his business career he had learned to forge ahead in uncomfortable situations. At times that had worked out well.

All Lyman knew about Virginia Beckerman came from the newspapers. So he did not know much. But two powerful men had fought over her. This afternoon, a columnist in the *Herald* had called her "The Woman in Green" because at the confrontation behind Ciro's she wore a green dress and drove a green car. Lyman had never heard Max talk about her.

A dark and wary woman answered the bell. The woman was not Mrs. Beckerman, based on the newspaper photo Lyman had seen. Whoever she was, her demeanor did not invite unnecessary conversation.

The woman led him through double doors into a formal parlor, then excused herself and disappeared into the house. Someone, probably Max, had done a great job of transforming the parlor into a reproduction of the reading room of a London club. Landscapes and harbor scenes lined the walls, the gilt and brass frames of the paintings complementing the dark wood paneling and finely upholstered furniture of the room. Lyman stood there awhile, fighting the impulse to walk out after all.

Virginia Beckerman opened both sides of the double doors and swirled into the room. Lyman was very glad that he had not fled, for he immediately felt a strong but undefined attraction to her.

A petite, slim woman, her large dark-blue eyes darted glances from beneath a valance of black eyelashes. Chestnut hair caressed the shoulders of a red and gold silk Mandarin dressing gown. Her smile and manner welcomed Lyman as an old friend, even though he was probably little more than a rumor to her.

"A drink, Mister Wilbur?" she asked, instead of shaking hands.

When he shook his head, she proffered a cigarette box, and Lyman plucked out a Chesterfield. They sat down in wing chairs, knee to knee. A heavy brass lighter stood on the table next to them, and he tried it, but it clicked sparks without igniting.

"Oh, my," said Virginia automatically.

"Let's see..." Lyman fumbled in his jacket pocket, his shirt pocket, and finally located a box of matches in his trouser pocket. "Ah!" He half stood, slipped them out, and sat again. This fumbling, which could have made them both impatient and uncomfortable, instead brought a small, shared smile as he lit first her cigarette, then his own. The matchbox made a friendly rattle when he dropped it on the table.

She leaned back. "I love to smoke." She was wearing a heavy gold and amethyst manacle that slid down her wrist when she raised her hand to her face. Lyman nodded and puffed. He avoided cigarettes, but Chesterfields were okay. The taste always reminded him of gingerbread.

"We haven't met." She seemed about to say more, but a dark cloud passed behind her eyes and stopped her.

"I haven't been around for long. And most of the time I think Max considers me more of a burden than a help. So I'm not surprised he doesn't spend a lot of his off-hours talking about me. Or even off-minutes." Lyman quickly realized what had halted her words. Every topic led to something bad. The shooting. The adultery. Her faithlessness. Max's. It was useless to try to find happiness around this couple, or even conventional morality.

Lyman felt great empathy for her, but he needed to get her talking. "I am just here to offer my help."

"Max has a lot of friends, at the studio, the club. But no one has called. I guess that's not too surprising. They're not *my* friends."

The loneliness in her voice pained him. "No one?"

"Oh, I'm exaggerating a little. A few. Some of the Germans, the old friends. Willy Wyler. And Deborah Boynton."

"Miss Boynton came to see me. She seemed distraught. She couldn't believe Max would do it."

"She's lovely." Virginia smiled warily. "I hardly know her."

"I mean she really thinks someone else did it and tried to frame Max." Lyman watched her closely.

"Really? She didn't say that to me."

"Yes. And I have reason to believe she may be right."

"*Really.*" For the first time her mask of caution dropped away.

"Yes." Lyman paused. Being a busybody really was not his forte. He called on his business experience: you know the number you have to get to, so get there, or leave. "But I need to know more. I'm not sure how to say this. It would be helpful if I could ask you a couple of questions."

She smiled coolly. "I have told everything..."

"I would ask you at this point to trust me just a little." He smiled and flipped his hands open in a friendly plea.

Virginia stood up, walked to the fireplace, and tossed her cigarette into the blackened grate. She stood there for a moment, a clenched form covered in fiery silk. Lyman thought she was about to launch into a dramatic monologue, but she merely turned and nodded. "All right."

"Did Max shoot Nuco?"

"I don't know. Before yesterday, or rather, the day before yesterday, I would have said no. But he was so crazy, so angry, he might have done anything. And he did not come home that night at all."

Lyman tapped fingers on the point of his chin. "Did he have reason to shoot him?"

"You mean was I having...an affair with Marty? No." She faced him, anger flaring in her eyes. "Now, I need to ask you, why are you asking? Did Corvus send you?"

"Corvus?"

"Corvus. Harry Corvus."

Lyman understood that she meant the head of the studio, but beyond that he was at a loss. "No. I don't know." He straightened in his seat. "I don't have any connection..."

"You work at the studio?"

"Yes."

"And they didn't send you over to pump me?"

Lyman felt his face burning. "Who, the studio?"

"Or are you here to deliver a message?" Virginia jutted her chin at him. "How am I supposed to play it? The grieving wife? The wronged woman? The vamp?" She made a quick burlesque of a gesture for each role. "If you can tell me whether they love Max or hate him this week, that will help."

The relaxed, charming woman had melted before Lyman's eyes. "Mrs. Beckerman." He kept his voice calm. "I work at the studio. That's all. I've never met Corvus, or any of the other poobahs. No one could be more completely an outsider than I am."

She sat down, panting from emotion and exertion. "*I* could."

Lyman felt someone enter the room behind him, and he knew the other woman was watching them. "Look, I frankly don't care that much about Max. If he did it he should pay the price. But if he goes to jail because someone set him up and the police were too lazy or corrupt...and I knew it, then it's my duty to do something. For the good of society, not Max." Lyman had not put the thoughts together like that until now.

She gazed over his head at a painting. "For the good of society? Really?" She said it without sarcasm. More like baffled.

"Yes, in a way. I think Deborah Boynton may be right. Whoever was trying to set Max up is the one who shot Nuco."

A glimmer of hope, or some new suspicion, showed in her eyes. Lyman leaned closer, but did not take her hand, though he wanted to. "I just have two more questions, you can answer them, or not." He plunged ahead without waiting for an answer. "Did you shoot Nuco?"

"No."

"Do you know who did?"

"No."

Lyman heard a door bump shut, and looked at it. The woman, if she had been there, was gone. He continued. "Do you love Max?"

"That's three."

"Okay."

Her voice turned husky, as if the tears that could not be seen in her eyes had found some inner passage to her throat. "Yes. But that's all over. Max has always wanted a devoted wife. A wife, do you understand? Marty wanted *me*. He was handsome. And flattering. But he didn't treat me any better. I lied to him and he lied to me. Love was never in the picture."

"So you had an affair with him."

Virginia stood up, glared at Lyman as if he was an overpriced piece of furniture, and walked toward the double doors. One of them opened before she got there, and Mrs. Beckerman stepped through it, leaving Lyman to show himself out.

* * * *

Maria sat at the tiny table in the kitchen. She had made coffee. It sat on the table in front of her, steam rising. Now she didn't want it. Or booze either. She just wanted to get out of the empty apartment. Her jacket hung on the back of the chair and she slipped it on, putting the apartment key in the pocket.

On the roof, she could feel the damp coming in from the coast, but the stars shone in the black sky. She reached up to them. Not knowing the constellations, she made up her own: The Brush, The Ship, The Jumping Dog. The roof had a clear view to the south, where other lights shone. Clothes hanging on a line and the box of the stairwell kept her from looking north.

Life was beginning for her now. Lily said it, and Maria believed it—at least she tried to. She had a real job, like a real person, thanks to Hosey.

She'd met him at that little bar on the corner, and he'd been so good to her. He didn't say anything about a new life, because he knew what kind of woman she was. The kind who showed up at a cheap bar and went home with the first good-looking guy with fifty bucks to his name. But he'd steered her to this job. He knew a guy.

It was money, and honest work. So why wasn't she more grateful? Yes, the work was hard, and she couldn't tell anyone. Big war secret. But she could tell the stars. She looked up at them. "I make parachutes, at the Nu-Life Laundry. Downtown."

There. The stars understood. The stars saw into her soul, saw the desperation, the pain of her past, of her whole life. They saw that you can't make a happy future out of a sad and lonely history. "What? You didn't know I could sew? Oh, yes, I can sew. But this machine is a beauty. Double needles, but I'm getting the hang of it. They give me diamond-shaped pieces that I sew together to make a big triangle. The more experienced girls sew the triangles together."

She realized that a breeze had come up behind her, shifting the clothes hanging on the clothesline. A mist was starting to lighten the sky and hide the stars. "Everything has to be just so, because it's a parachute that could save a guy's life. There can be no mistakes."

The door from the stairwell opened, and Lily appeared.

"I thought I might find you here. Shouting at the stars again?"

"Silently, I shout."

Lily walked over to where she stood by the waist-high roof wall.

Maria said, "I was just thinking I'll never go home again."

Lily gave her a firm hug. "I don't believe that. I know how you feel. But you will get there. Don't worry."

The kind words did not lighten Maria's mood. "It's a long way. A long way. And I'm not as strong as you."

"Count your blessings."

Maria saw the worry in Lily's brittle expression and hunched shoulders. "What's wrong?"

"I was just wondering myself...can you see the stars in jail? Or in hell?"

* * * *

As Lyman drove away from his meeting with Virginia Beckerman, he felt frustrated and confused. She had cleared up nothing, and had in fact muddied things considerably.

Despite the assurance he tried to present to her, Lyman had no clear idea of how to proceed. He had stupidly crossed over into detective fiction, expecting the dame in the kimono to blurt out some clue that would set him on the track to the inevitable but surprising solution.

Nothing of the sort had happened, and he was way out of his depth. Not a cop, but an aging, pudgy conjurer, a writer of dime novels; not a detective, but a guy milking an angle. After all, his primary motive was not really the pursuit of truth and justice, but getting his ass of a boss out of jail so he could keep his cushy job.

The force of that truth hit him hard. Part of his recovery, his trip up from the sewer, had been the belief that he would never again sacrifice his integrity. That was the main personal trait that he put into Archer Daniel. But he had developed that belief when he had nothing. The thought of going back to nothing gripped his spine like a steel claw.

He left Virginia in her house, the press sideshow out front, and drove down the hill to where the city blocks were square. To get home, Lyman had to take either Sunset or Santa Monica. Normally he would take the straighter, better-lit Santa Monica Boulevard. But just now he was not thinking about his driving. Sunset came first, and Lyman automatically turned west.

Traffic thinned out after he passed the old Warner Bros. studio. The houses were fewer and set back from the road. Lyman saw a flashing red spotlight in his mirror, and a siren growled at him briefly. He slowed down and hugged the shoulder, assuming the police car would pass him and go on its mission, but instead it also slowed down, and flashed its high beams.

Lyman cursed softly. He could not find a place to pull off the road here, because of the thick growth of manzanita on the shoulder. He kept driving, slowly, another three-quarters of a mile, until he came to a little side road where he turned in, pulled up fifty feet or so, and stopped.

The police car stopped behind him. The engine was cut and the spotlight went off, but the headlights stayed on. A large cop in a dark blue uniform with sergeant's stripes climbed out and bounded up to Lyman's car. "What the hell's the matter with you!" he howled, his belly swelling around his Sam Browne belt. "Don't you know when you are being pulled over?"

"I just wanted to get off the road safely. What is this all about?"

"C'mon, get out of the car," the cop barked at Lyman.

Lyman slid out and stood beside the car. Surely this was a coincidence. But something tickled his memory. He told himself to keep cool and things would be fine. The road where they stood, or it could be a driveway, was dark and quiet. A quarter moon shone directly overhead.

The other cop walked up waving his electric torch around. He was a scrawny specimen who looked like a 4-F reject from the army. The only things holding up his oversized patrolman's cap appeared to be his winglike ears. "He was weaving pretty bad, Sarge," the 4-F wheedled. "You better smell his breath."

The sergeant stuck his meaty nose in Lyman's face and sniffed noisily. "Yeah, stinkin'," he crowed. In that second Lyman realized he had not had a drink since his tiny swig in the office that morning.

The patrolman leaned in the driver's door of the Chrysler, pointing his torch around. Lyman smelled the dust the cars had kicked up on the little dirt road, and a familiar whiff of burnt oil that he knew came from his engine. Behind that there was the menthol smell of eucalyptus, and in his throat, a metallic taste of animal fear. He heard the glove compartment slam.

The patrolman stood up and waved a pint bottle. "Looks like he was right in the middle of a highball, Sarge. Black and White. That's the imported stuff with those cute little Scottie dogs, ain't it? Don't you know you are s'posed to drink in a tavern, sonny boy?"

"I was just taking it home, officer. I haven't had a drink." He had bought the scotch on his way home the other night, on his bender.

"Don't tell me about it!" brayed the fat one, his tarnished shield waggling on his shirt pocket.

"Right now," said the skinny one, "we got you on speeding, illegal lane changes, failure to yield. There's a couple of ways we could go on this." He held up the bottle and unscrewed the cap. The bottle was about half full. He handed it to Lyman.

"I don't want it," Lyman said.

"Then we're headed downtown."

"Look, there's been a mis—"

The sergeant grabbed Lyman's tie and twisted it hard around his fist, pushing knuckles into Lyman's throat. "You heard him."

Lyman raised the bottle. The fat sergeant released the necktie, and Lyman took a large sip. The other man reared back and aimed a vicious punch at his stomach. Lyman flinched and swallowed hard, but the cop pulled the punch, only grazing Lyman's shirt. The cop laughed. The whiskey went down like kerosene.

When the sergeant laughed, Lyman knew where he had met him. This morning at the office. He was the other plainclothesman with the Swede. Lyman had thought of him as a hapless chair-filler. Now the man had tracked him down—in uniform, in a patrol car—to threaten him. Had they been following him all day? What did they want from him?

"That's enough." The sergeant knocked the bottle away. It bounced on the running board of Lyman's car and landed on the road without breaking. He kicked it into the bushes, and it still did not break. "I think he was beginning to enjoy it too much," he said to the other one with a harsh chuckle.

"He's ready for his drunk test."

The sergeant spun Lyman around. "Yeah, I want you to walk the line."

"What line?"

"Draw a line, Ed."

The patrolman scraped a careless toe a few feet down the approximate middle of the road.

"Look," Lyman pleaded. "If you think that was my gun? You need to call Daggett."

"What the hell you talkin' about, Pops?" the patrolman taunted him. "Are you about to spill something?"

"You need to get in contact with Daggett, the county attorney's..."

"Never heard of him." The fat man laughed malevolently. "Walk!"

"I can't see the line."

"Walk!"

Lyman began to walk down the road.

"Heel and toe! Heel and toe!" The sergeant kicked Lyman in the ankle, making him stumble. Anger shot through him like an electrical jolt. But an old instinct, remembered from his days at the front, kept Lyman's fist locked at his side. It wasn't fear. It was survival.

The cops did not even watch him. "All right, now come back." The sergeant began kicking his ankles on every step.

Lyman tripped and went down hard on his knees. He yelped a little and both cops found this very funny. Humiliated and heedless, he grabbed the fat one's leg and tried to ram his head into the overstuffed crotch. All he succeeded in doing was to spin himself face up in the dust. This made both of them guffaw.

"All right, that's enough," said the fat one. He grabbed Lyman's arm and pulled him up. "In you go." He opened the door of the police car and Lyman eased himself unsteadily into the seat. One leg of his pants had ripped at the knee, with sand ground into the raw scrape of the skin. Both his ankles throbbed. The car door slammed with a finality that almost made him cry.

* * * *

Lily drove down Avalon, way down, out in the marshes between an oil field and an army base. The bar they called The Swamp looked like it used to be a highway cafe, with a row of tourist cabins behind. No sign or light identified the place.

Lily parked her car at the edge of the dirt lot. A couple of small lights on a telephone pole provided a dim and ghostly illumination. In the bar someone was banging boogie-woogie songs on the piano. The windows of the cabins glowed—some of them—behind thin curtains. If she sat there for a little while, Lily knew she would see men and women slipping or staggering between the bar and the cabins. When Lily went back to Nuco, she'd ended up in the cabins and the bar. In the bar, it was seduction and promise. In the cabins, all business. It was the standing joke—they made love in the bar, and worked in the cabins. Lily shook her head and sighed. Everything had been a joke, because without the jokes, it would not have been possible to go on.

She walked up to the side door of the bar and went inside.

It was darker inside than it was outside. Young men, some in uniform, some not, shuffled around shouting, laughing, baiting each other, pawing the bar girls, who laughed or scowled according to their mood of the moment.

One pair of eyes spotted her as soon as she walked in. They belonged to Kris, the bartender, a big, young, blond-headed kid with a beard. The Swamp was his domain, and though he usually stayed behind the bar pulling beers, his main job, Lily knew, was to watch. The girls, the suckers, the other bartenders.

She leaned over the bar and he gave her a little nod. "I'm supposed to meet Koch. He's expecting me."

"He's not here."

"What should I do?"

"Wait."

A ridiculous answer. She was not dressed like a party girl: her long coat, buttoned to the throat, covered everything above the ankles. She had on no makeup, and her hair was held back by a rubber band. She looked like she had come to deliver lunch, or scrub the toilets. It did not matter.

"Hello, springtime!" A young man veered into Lily. He wore civvies, but everything about him, from the haircut to the sunburned nose to the dangling Lucky Strike, said *recruit*. He looked just like the kids at the Hollywood Canteen, but he was drunk, and looking at a slut, not the girl next door. He waited a moment for her to say something. You couldn't be standoffish at the Swamp. You either jumped in or got out. She headed for the door.

"Hey." Lily heard a husky voice beside her, and it took a second to recognize it as a female voice, directed at her. She glanced in that direction. A rinsed blonde with pink cheeks and big, liquid blue eyes was staring at her. "Hey!" Louder. "What yew doing here?"

Lily couldn't get through the bodies, and the girl grabbed her arm.

"I don't know," she muttered.

"Don' remember me? I rem'ber you!"

"Sure, I remember."

"You goin' to work? Just remember, if they ask for Dottie, you send 'em over. I got my reg'lars."

Lily pushed toward the door. Dottie called after her. "Don't cross me, sweetie, and we'll get along."

Lily glanced back. Kris's eyes glared out above the blond beard. But nobody tried to stop her. She made it to her car and sat there. Her skin crawling, but not from the cool night air. Koch wanted to play games with her. So small-time.

He realized he could not just grab her, because now Deborah and a movie studio protected her. But the other side of the sword was that he could destroy her with words in the right ear. She wondered how long they had been following her, and how they found her. It might have been that night when she went to the apartment with Yaqui's gun. If they knew what happened there, would they kill her?

Or would they reward her?

Shadows moved from the back door of the bar across the driveway. Murmurs floated out from the shadows. Lily could not stand it. She drove away.

* * * *

Lyman Wilbur sat in the Westwood police station in a chair in a windowless room. They'd brought him here, Fatso and Eddie—now very businesslike, even bored—and they left, closing the door. On the table in the middle of the room sat a notepad, and a pencil that had been clawed or chewed to a dull point.

Nothing had been taken from him, so Lyman still had his pipe, tobacco, and even his matches. He smoked a pipe unenthusiastically. The liquor he had been forced to drink boiled in his stomach, and his mouth tasted dry and sour. Lyman's anger at the abuse of the two cops was filed away as his weariness grew heavier. Both his ankles throbbed, and the torn knee of his trousers lay against his scraped skin and stuck to it, no matter what position he put the leg in.

Around two a.m. a detective—or anyway, a guy in a rumpled suit—directed Lyman out to a car, and drove to the downtown police station. There Lyman sat in the processing room on a wooden bench the rest of the night. Nobody told him to stay put, or tried to detain him, but on the other hand, nobody said he could go. The big room reminded Lyman of a train station, busy but not really crowded, rather quiet except for the echoing bang of unseen doors. Lyman dozed and woke repeatedly as different faces and bodies appeared and disappeared, mumbling and murmuring, joking and complaining.

By five o'clock, the place seemed to clear out, and Lyman pulled his feet up and lay on the bench, using his jacket for a pillow. Soon he was frying hamburgers in a large iron skillet, and looking up at the Hudson River Palisades, glorious in the bright sunshine. But the smell of the meat made him very hungry, and the hamburgers took a long time to cook.

Someone called his name, and grabbed his arm. "Mister Lyman? Mister Lyman."

Lyman swam upstream to wakefulness. It was the Swede shaking him. Detective Soderman.

"Will you come with me, please?"

Lyman stood up with difficulty. His right leg had fallen asleep, and his ankles had stiffened up. He tottered after the Swede into an orderly room, and they sat on opposite sides of a dark desk. A clock high on the wall said eight-thirty. That seemed impossible, but Lyman's watch agreed.

"First of all, thank you for coming in this morning." The Swede sat back, sleek and content after a good night's sleep and a hearty breakfast. "I understand you have something more on the Nuco case?"

It was all too much. "What are you talking about? I was beaten up, arrested and dragged in here by a couple of thugs in uniforms." Lyman twisted in the hard chair, trying to ease the pain in his legs. "At ten o'clock last night."

Soderman's eyes tightened. He had a sheet of paper on the desk that he reviewed with a sober expression. "I don't show anything about that. I was told you wanted to make a statement."

"A statement!" Lyman jackknifed upright.

The Swede appeared genuinely surprised. "About a weapon, identified as a thirty-two Colt revolver?"

The first light of dawn peeked into Lyman's clouded brain. "Am I free to go right now?"

"Of course."

"And I have not been arrested or charged..."

"No! Charged with what?"

"...on your orders?"

The detective stared at him so uncomprehendingly that Lyman almost doubted his own memory. Almost. The anger that rose in him like a gas flame put an end to that doubt. But the anger subsided very quickly. Lyman slumped back in the chair. He just did not have the energy. "May I have the name of the booking officer?"

Soderman glanced at his sheet of paper again. "You were never booked. Now look, do you have a statement or not?"

"Where is my car?"

The Swede turned pink. "I don't know where your car is! Did you leave it in the city lot across the street?"

Lyman let out a phlegmy laugh. "No, I don't have a statement."

Detective Soderman shook his head. "Then what the hell are you doing here?"

"What, indeed." It had all been a message for him. Stay away from this case. Who exactly the message was from was unclear. And unimportant. Lyman looked across the desk at Soderman. It was entirely possible that he did not know anything. In a big-city police department, all kinds of scams and cross-purposes were possible.

"When you came to my office Thursday morning..." Lyman studied the detective carefully. "...to look for the gun."

Soderman smiled venomously. "Don't presume too much."

"There was another man with you. The fat one. Who was that?"

"You mean Sergeant Shira. What about him?"

The detective was being cagey. Whether that meant he was smarter than Lyman, or just in over his head, mattered little to Lyman at that point. "Sergeant Shira. Sounds like a good title for a war movie."

The Swede shook his head, annoyed. He took Lyman back to the waiting room, pointed him to the door, and stomped away. Lyman fought off a surge of bone weariness, and trudged out.

* * * *

Lily drove back to the apartment, hurried into the stairwell without being seen, and made it up to the fourth floor of the sleeping building.

The door to the apartment hung wide open. The side of the door frame had been splintered. No light came from inside.

She stood listening to the quiet, but nothing could penetrate the ringing in her ears, the roar of her own breath. She stepped through the door.

On her left, the kitchen seemed empty. Lily reached for the light switch by the door, but hesitated. She flipped it with her finger, and flinched when light filled the room. The brightness in the kitchen made the rest of the apartment more fearsome.

Knowing she had to plunge ahead or leave, she rushed into the little living room, spinning around to see everything at once. The awkward movement caused her to slip on the bare floor and she fell against the wall next to the open window. No one there.

A new horror gripped Lily, and she rolled away from the window. Convinced now that no one was inside the apartment, she glanced into the bathroom and the bedroom. The bed looked slept in. There was no sign of a physical fight anywhere.

Lily returned to the living room, her heart pounding. The window was open, and a breeze ruffled the curtains. She forced herself to approach the window and peer out. Four floors seem farther, much farther, when you're thinking in terms of jumping, or falling, or being pushed. She gripped the window frame and looked down.

The dull orange glow of the city against the low clouds produced enough light that Lily could see there was nobody on the roof of the drugstore. And logically, a fall like that would probably have attracted someone's attention. A scream, maybe. Lily sat down hard on the floor, then lay down, sobbing. They had followed her tonight. All the way from Deborah's. She thought she had outsmarted them, but the game was over before she walked into The Swamp. Lily did not know what they would do to Maria. But anything that happened to her now was Lily's responsibility.

* * * *

When Lyman limped out the door of the downtown police station, he found himself on First Street. He could see a parking lot across the street. He wondered if someone would have brought his car here. But why would they? To make it convenient for him? He stood on the corner to hail a cab for the trip home. He'd have the cab go down Sunset, and see if he could find the little side road where he'd parked. If the car was there, he'd drive it home. If it wasn't, the hell with it.

A movement or a noise made him turn and look at a group of people spilling out of a doorway across the street. It took Lyman a moment to realize that the building was the L.A. County Jail, and that he knew the short man who seemed to be leading the charge. Max Beckerman, dressed in a sharp navy blue suit, but for once without a hat, hurtled down the sidewalk. The short, sturdy apparition, trailed by what appeared to be a gaggle of reporters, made a point, jabbing the air with an angry finger. The noise of the downtown street prevented Lyman from hearing what exactly Max was blustering about.

Striding along next to Max was Virginia, wearing a black and white suit that, added to her natural beauty and carriage, made her the visual center of the group, the street, the universe. A large black car waited at the curb for them. Virginia and Max climbed in, and the car pulled quickly away while a couple of reporters continued to scratch at their notebooks, the rest of them straggling away.

Lyman's anger grew slowly, like a long comber headed for the beach. Why would they let Max out? Because Lyman had found the gun? Because he'd been buffeted around by the police? Were the two events connected, or did they amount to another incontinent emission of a perverse legal system?

It didn't look like Max had changed much, or learned any humility. Still a blowhard, and still in possession of *her*. What kind of sick hold did they have on each other? Lyman had never seen Virginia before last night, and she was already like Mona Lisa to him—far more fascinating than she ought to be. And yet, there they went, he accused of murder, and she perhaps guilty of it, and they looked like they were going to the goddamn yacht races. Driven off in a limousine, complaining all the way.

Lyman looked down at the heel of his hand, which itched intolerably. He had scraped it when he fell on the dirt road, and it still oozed blood.

"And here stand I, the hero of the piece, beaten, forgotten and left on the corner with a few shekels in my trousers." The force of Lyman's anger broke over him. He pounded the scraped hand into his other palm. "Damn, damn, damn!" It hurt.

People walking by stared at him. His bloodshot eyes burned. His breath wheezed. What the hell had he been doing, playing detective? Lyman was angry at the police, at Max, Virginia, Deborah. But his disgust with himself overshot all the petty villains. What the hell had he been doing?

Chapter Nine

The car pulled away from the cawing reporters, headed west out of downtown. Max stared at the back of Irv Jensen's head. The thick neck, the shiny gray hair, the flaps of his ears. Jensen was not a criminal lawyer. He did contracts and business disputes. Max and his bohemian friends back in Berlin in the twenties would have ridiculed him as a bourgeois tycoon. Now Max wouldn't take out a revolving loan on a Frigidaire unless Jensen reviewed the papers.

How far Max had come from those idealistic days. Self-righteous days. He had learned to flash anger like lightning, had come to enjoy the interval of surprise he could see in startled opponents, the flinch between the flash and the thunder of his sarcasm, his indignation.

The car headed west, the junior lawyer, Strouse, driving unhurriedly through heavy traffic. It would be a while until they reached a part of town Max recognized. Virginia sat behind the driver, to Max's left, staring out at the mundane sights of downtown. When the car drove into a shaft of morning sun, the strong light through the window made her hair and perfect skin glow.

Virginia and the two lawyers seemed occupied with their thoughts. Max, however had spent two days chasing his thoughts around a very small room. "Mike Romanoff brought me dinner from the restaurant Wednesday night, and they let him."

Jensen turned his head a few points to the left. "What was the dinner?"

"Beef Stroganoff, what else?" Max wondered if he had mangled the pronunciation of *stroganoff*. "And a strawberry tart for dessert. No wine."

"That's not a bad dinner."

"Don't get the idea I enjoyed it. I had about three bites. They had not questioned me then. Not really. Thursday morning they put on the boxing gloves." Talking about this made Max's neck and shoulders tighten up. It would never be a party anecdote.

Jensen turned himself a little more, so Max at least could see an angle on his face. "So they started to question you closely. And the more you told them, the more obvious it became that you did not shoot Nuco in the apartment."

"Nor anywhere else." Max loosened his collar. They had brought him a clean shirt, but he had not showered or shaved. "I could not describe the apartment. I have never been there."

Jensen spoke to Virginia. "Whose apartment is it?"

"A man that works for Marty." She still stared out the window. "He said. I don't know."

"The two of you went to this apartment after the incident in the parking lot at Ciro's?"

Virginia's face flushed. "The *incident*? My husband pulling a pistol? Yes. We went there and talked about what to do." She looked at Max for the first time since, then turned her gaze back out the window. "You were insane."

"Yes," said Max. "Of course."

Virginia opened her purse and spoke to its contents. "I stayed there an hour, and called a cab." She took out a cigarette. "Marty was on the phone when I left. Story of my life."

Max sighed. "But the next morning, when they came to get me, I did not know where you went, or what you did, since I never went home that night. I really thought you had shot him."

"Why would I shoot him?"

"I did not know. I knew that I didn't."

Virginia addressed Jensen. "And you let him confess?"

"I wasn't even there. Strouse had to talk him into recanting."

"I don't understand what you were thinking of." She glanced at Max, and looked away. "Where were you that night, honestly?"

"Honestly, I drove around. Ended up at Redondo Beach. I sat in the car. I fell asleep."

Jensen untwisted himself. Max appreciated the lawyers walking him out of jail, though he thought it unnecessary. He saw it as lawyers marking their territories. Though Max had been released without charges, the investigation was still underway, with no other suspect.

The kid driving, Strouse, had been the one who visited Max at the jail, both Wednesday and Thursday. Apparently he was sort of the office celebrity specialist, and now Max would be one of the Hollywood scum he took charge of. And Max had resigned himself that there would now be a divorce from Virginia, sooner or later. That would be more business for the law firm, more money out of his pocket. This would end up costing Max almost as much as it cost Nuco. All Nuco had to do was lay there and die. Max would be paying for this for the next ten years.

They approached the Beckerman house. The reporters were ready. Three photographers blocked the driveway, so that Strouse had to come to a complete stop. Then the reporters converged on either side of the car.

"Chrrrist," muttered Max. "They got out here fast."

"They've been out here the whole time," said Virginia. "I'm getting so I recognize them."

Of course they had. They yelled through the rolled-up windows. "Max, why were you released, Virginia, are you a suspect, if Nuco dies, or lives, someone else? Do you regret, how long did you know, make any threats? Smile, honey, and cross your legs."

Strouse nosed the car forward and the photographers grudgingly parted, looking for the angle at which the light of their flashbulbs would penetrate the window glass rather than bounce off it. The car broke through the wave and pulled up the short drive to the house, where the driveway and side door were hidden from the street by a sour-orange hedge.

"Why don't they go away now?" asked Virginia.

"They're bound to increase." Jensen twisted around again to face the unhappy couple. "This story is going to turn into an air raid. And until there's another suspect, you two are London."

Strouse let the car idle in neutral. He peered at Max in the rear view. "Who is another suspect?"

"I don't know," said Max. Virginia also shook her head.

"The police didn't give you any info, any questions they asked that you could get an idea where they are looking?"

"No."

"Is there anyone *you* suspect? Either of you?" Strouse's question met with silence. "I know I have asked each of you before, but any fresh ideas?"

"Everyone, and no one," said Max. "Marty got where he is through extortion, blackmail, bribery and threats. But who knows, he may have crossed the line at some point." Even Max did not laugh at this black joke.

"Any chance he had another lover?"

"You're asking *me*?" Virginia flared.

The Beckermans got out of the car, and the lawyers left. Virginia walked into the living room and stood staring out the French doors at the garden.

Max followed her. He looked longingly at the decanter of cognac on the bar. But before anything else happened he needed to ask the question. "Why?"

"I can't talk about it."

He walked over to her. "Okay. Something simple. Why him?"

She shook her head. "I'm too angry to cry, and too tired to be angry. I've got nothing left."

"You are angry? Let me catch up. Why him? Do you hate me so much that it was not enough to be unfaithful. You had to spread your legs for that despicable—"

She jabbed a long finger toward his face. "*Don't* you talk to me in that vulgar way! You care about *his* reputation! *Your* pride! Ha! That is so funny."

"I don't give a Gott-damn about his reputation, or my pride. Except...damn it!" The sunny, verdant garden mocked his misery. He wanted to drive a fist through the window.

She walked away from him and sat on the couch with her purse next to her, as if it was a bench in a train station. She took out a cigarette, lit it, and took a deep drag. "Except?"

"Except I have to care. You know how much I despise him."

"I had no idea."

Max realized he had become so expert at hypocrisy that his wife did not know how much he feared Marty Nuco, and how much he hated him. "Well, for the record, *I despise him!*" The room rang with his shout. He lowered his voice to a whisper. "He humiliated me once before. A long time ago. And he's held that over me ever since. And I've been under his thumb ever since."

And then he told her why.

* * * *

Bettina had not had a good night either. As bad as Lyman felt, she had been his first concern. He knew she would have worried about him all night. Thank God she was reasonably healthy now.

"I'm sure you were worried," said Lyman. "I wanted to call you, but every time I asked to use the phone, they left the room. Like a Franz Kafka story, or a vaudeville routine."

The chain of events seemed even more incredible as he narrated it to her. To wit: On behalf of Max, whom he loathed, and Deborah, whom he mistrusted, Lyman had concealed evidence and called on Virginia, a woman he'd never met before she was implicated in a murder. He had been strong-armed by cops, who never explained their purpose, and in fact denied their interest in him. And then the only drink Lyman had had all night had been against his will. All because twenty-six hours earlier he reached for a whiskey bottle and found a revolver.

"I had no business getting involved," he summarized. "I can't believe I was so naive."

"But I don't think you were naive." Tina dabbed at his scrapes with a warm washcloth. "You went over there because you suspected the police were up to something, and their actions certainly seem to show that you were right. You saw a situation that was wrong, that you could do something about, and you tried to do it. That's what Archer Daniels does, even though nobody pays him to, and people keep telling him to stay out of it. And so you did something. Was it brilliant?" She smiled. "Oh, well."

Lyman's heart swelled. "You're sweet. Of course you would say that, and I appreciate it, even though I'm not sure I deserve it."

"Well," she said. "It's not like you don't have an interest. If Max is in jail, what becomes of your job? The movies are a great opportunity for you. I am proud of you."

"Well, it was idiotic. Let's leave it at that."

Lyman spent the day in bed or in his bathrobe, sleeping, eating, reading *Jane Eyre*. He picked the book at random and opened it at random, and he found the gothic romance oddly comforting, with its night coaches, whipping winds, and brutish and deceitful minor characters.

That afternoon, the paper said that Max had been released, and a gun had been found that might be the one that fired two bullets into Marty Nuco. The reporting of these facts in the same story implied a connection, without stating it directly. The paper again mentioned that Nuco had underworld connections, and added that his "hard-nosed style" had earned the agent a number of enemies in the movie business. The implications of these statements were not related to any suspect.

Lyman wondered to what extent his blunderings had contributed to these developments. He wondered because the phone did not ring that day. Not Daggett, not Deborah, not Max. He had not gone in to the studio, and no one called to ask why.

* * * *

Pacific Palisades was misty Saturday, with a spanking breeze from the sea. But it warmed up early, and Lyman arose to find Bettina determinedly working in the garden, shaping up a bed of neglected succulents and pink geraniums along the back fence. She seemed to have more energy now, and she loved this place as she had loved no other. She was starting to fix the house up, confident that they would convince the landlord to sell it to them and that this would be the home where they would live out their lives.

Lyman had no quarrel with that idea, and he went out to be with her. He did a little raking, but mostly he just lolled on the grass, still recovering from his long night in stir. Occasionally he would wrestle a weed out of the ground. If he came across a snail he would toss it into the trash can as well.

By the time the sun rose overhead, Lyman's energy had increased, and he was using an old table knife to dig a stubborn runner of Bermuda grass out of a crack in the patio. A familiar voice in an unfamiliar place made him look up.

"Hello!" A manila straw hat had appeared in the cutout curve in the top of the redwood gate. After some fumbling with the latch, which was inoperable, Max pushed on the gate and it swung open. "Hello," he said again.

Although Lyman had been expecting some word from Max or Deborah, he was surprised. Max had never been to his house, did not even know where it was, Lyman would have thought. He managed to say, "Well!"

"I got your address from the office. I could have called, but, when I found out the extent of your help, I thought the least I could do was express my thanks in person."

"My help?"

"My lawyer was told that you found a gun in the office and turned it in. It's hard to believe finding the murder weapon in my office would exonerate me, except that you told them it was absolutely not there the day before."

"It is hard to believe," said Lyman. "In fact, I am not sure that I do."

Max chuckled uncertainly. He stood in a most uncharacteristic pose, that of the supplicant, nervously rotating his hat in his hands. Lyman introduced Tina, who suggested lemonade. When she went inside, Max said, "I also appreciate your calling on Virginia. I hope...she's under a lot of strain. I don't know how well she held up with you."

Lyman could tell that Max did not know any details of Lyman's visit with his wife on Thursday evening. Max also would have no way of knowing what happened to him the rest of the night. Lyman did not at that moment feel like enlightening him. "Well, I knew the gun had not been there before, and suddenly a large sector of the population seemed intent on discovering it." Lyman cut the irony. "But you've been released, everything seems on the up and up, and hopefully they will move on to finding the real suspect. So. All's well that ends well."

"What did Deborah have to do with all this?"

"She came to me, and was most emphatic that you could not have been the one. In fact, I had no inkling, and to be perfectly frank, I didn't care much about your fate one way or another, except that it probably meant I would be out of a job."

Max let out a cackle that sounded a little more like his old self. "I understand completely."

"I think you should know, if there is anyone I suspect of setting you up, it's Deborah. I haven't a molecule of an idea of why she would, but I practically caught her at it. Red-handed, as they say on the radio."

Max squinted at the sky. "You see, that's the other reason I came. I have heard from her. I don't know what's going on either, but she wants us to come out there to see her."

"See her?" This sudden turn drove home to Lyman that he really did not want, anymore, to get at the truth. He just wanted to be left alone. "No. I don't think I have any further business with her. No, I don't think so."

"She asked me to give you this." From his jacket pocket Max produced an envelope. Lyman unsealed it.

Mr. Wilbur,

I feel that I owe you an explanation of certain things, and I need your advice on a very important matter. I hope you will come out this afternoon to my place. Lyman, I regret the inconvenience to you, but I hope you will see that I have no choice. I have also asked Max to come, and I trust you both will keep this confidential.

Deborah

Lyman read it twice, looking for an easy out. "How did you get this?"

Max shrugged. "Her chauffeur brought it to my house this morning."

Lyman whapped it on his palm. "Is this what a royal summons looks like?"

"You have every right to refuse."

"Do we have time for lunch?"

"Certainly."

"Let's have lunch first."

* * * *

"Rain will be good for the grass," Deborah said to Lily, standing with her on the cement plaza between the house and the garage.

Deborah pointed past the garage to the pastures and the hills beyond. "I lease all that open area. All the way up to the ridge." Her arm swept across the landscape to the north and east, though she barely glanced in that direction.

Sunlight flooded the driveway, but a cool breeze was blowing, and a heavy bank of dark clouds loomed toward the early afternoon sun. Deborah had received a call. Max Beckerman and some writer were on their way over. She had told Lily they would be going out to the horse barn, so Lily had put on dungarees. But then they had come out to wait for the visitors in the driveway. And Lily felt uncertain about her clothes, and about everything else. She was going to have to admit to everything she'd done, to the man who had gone to jail because of her.

Lily had foolishly thought she could handle Nuco and Koch herself. When she failed, she had to ask for Deborah's help, and now she had it. Deborah made it clear, though, that the trouble and danger she had taken on was not entered into primarily for Lily's sake, but to protect her own reputation and career. Any affection she felt for Lily had been replaced by businesslike coolness, and worrying about the present crisis. She kept saying that, *the present crisis*, sounding like that Lowell Thomas guy on the radio.

Lily's only hope was that Deborah would somehow understand that it was to save her that Lily had committed her crimes. In the last three days she had seen how Deborah—warm, giving, common Deborah—might almost match her ruthlessness. But Deborah had not confided in her, so Lily could only see the results of her plan, not the thinking behind it.

Now Deborah stood in the bright sunshine next to her, squinting, shading her eyes, face turned downward in the glare. She turned and stared out the driveway to the road, and Lily heard the rough burp of a car engine. A small bug-eyed roadster bumped along the gravel drive and onto the plaza where they stood. Max Beckerman smiled at them from behind the wheel. The larger man in the passenger seat looked rather shoehorned in. He did not smile.

The car pulled up next to the women and shut off with a shudder. Max hopped out and almost hopped into Deborah's arms. She gave him a long and fervent hug. The kind of hug people give at funerals. The other man took longer to unfold himself from his seat, and by the time he did, Deborah had moved in front of him, and gave him an even warmer squeeze. The old man's arms remained stiffly at his sides in surprise or shyness.

Deborah introduced Lily to the two men. "Max is an old friend. He knows Marty as well. Mister Wilbur is also a screenwriter. But perhaps we can get acquainted as we walk. I'd love to show you the stables." She smiled and steered the group north, indicating to Lily that she should walk next to Max.

Despite Deborah's forced chirpiness, little was said. They walked past the house with its tile roof and the window bars looking like something right out of *Zorro*. Lily gave Max a long glance, and his eyes passed over her without a spark of recognition. He had been pretty drunk that night she'd brought him back to the apartment. She hoped he'd forgotten, but she had better assume he hadn't.

They followed the driveway, which became a narrow dirt road between the pasture and the riding ring. Deborah walked with her hands clasped behind her back. She would forge a step or two ahead, then slow down for them. The old man tottered feebly, and Lily wondered if he would make it.

"What happened to your leg?" Max asked him.

"Nothing." The man hitched himself up. "Tripped getting off my seaplane."

Lily glanced at him curiously, but Max chuckled, so it must have been a joke. As if the little exchange reminded Deborah to be sociable, she turned to the others. "The horses have already been put in for the night. Rain coming." The clouds behind them had finally caught the sun, and the edge of their shadow ran across the fields, and up the slope of the hills. Lily wished she could race ahead like that, as quickly and silently.

They entered the barn. It smelled like the corral behind her *padrino's* house in Fresno. The fine dust, the fog of manure and hay. Deborah switched on the lights and slowed her pace. Each horse had a generous stall, and their mangers were full. Lily wondered where the stable hands were. Then she remembered. On Saturday afternoon, most of them took off. That's why Deborah had brought them to the barn. But it would not make Lily's confession any easier.

As they went past the stalls Deborah made a few comments about the horses. The men were polite, but they didn't really care. They just wanted to know why they were there. Some of the horses eyed the visitors to see if treats would be offered. When they came to the tack room, Deborah opened the door and the others followed her in without a word. The long, low shed was crowded with saddles, blankets, and all the tools and medicines necessary for the horses. At the end of the room there was a clear space where a few mismatched kitchen chairs huddled around a tin stove. A half-empty bottle of root beer sat on the stove, along with coffee can filled with sand and some cigarette butts.

"Please…" Deborah flicked a hand at the chairs, and they all sat down. Lily sat last, and reluctantly at that.

"So!" Deborah smiled stiffly. "How do you like my office?" The two men clucked softly at the joke. Deborah blew out her cheeks with a long breath. "Thank you for coming out. Max, you have been the victim of a terrible mistake—thank God the truth came to light, and you were released."

Lily stared out the one small window of the room and wished Deborah would just stop speaking. She felt as if someone was sitting on her, pinning her to the chair. A couple of fat flies buzzed around, regularly returning to tap the window. A spider's lace curtain stretched along the sides of the glass.

"I hope you have been completely exonerated," Deborah continued. "We both have known Marty a long time, and yet." She shook her head. "And yet, it's not exactly a shock, what happened. But you had enough heartache to deal with without this totally unnecessary suspicion, which, unfortunately, I have contributed to." Her gaze shifted to the old man. "Thank God you found the gun, Lyman, and averted what could have been a terrible miscarriage of justice."

Lily did not know what she meant by that. Did this Lyman have the gun now? Why was he here?

Lyman said, "So this is about the gun?" He had a hard glint in his eye. He didn't seem so old now.

"Yes." Deborah turned to Lily. She had that cold look in her eye that meant, *don't mess this up*. "Lily is going to tell you something now. She is a young girl who has been living here. I met her at the Hollywood Canteen. She was like so many young women, working hard to get into movies and not having much luck."

"You are a dancer, too, Miss...?" Max addressed Lily.

"Torrence." Lily and Deborah said it together.

"Used to be Torres," Lily added. She looked at the ceiling. Her lips were trembling, and so dry she did not think she could get the whole story out. She turned to Deborah. "I can't tell them, I could hardly even tell you!"

Deborah touched her hand. "Tell them about Tuesday."

"I shot him."

They all stared at her. Deborah seemed to be expecting more. "Lily..."

"If he...if he lives, I will shoot him again."

* * * *

One of the horses whinnied, and several others joined in, as if the joke was just too rich.

Lyman had only come out here this afternoon out of curiosity, the vanity of knowing something the rest of the world did not, especially something the police did not. He had written four novels and three dozen stories which intimated an inside knowledge of the scandals and gossip of the powerful and the corrupt. But it was all fabrication. In reality he had had very little access to the lives of such people. So how could he pass up a backstage pass to the best Hollywood scandal of the year? Besides, his throbbing ankle reminded him, he had earned it.

The girl sat slumped in her chair, her eyes riveted to the stove across from her, her voice as flat as old paint on a beaverboard wall. "You see, Nuco...as important as he is and everything...he's really just a pimp. Controls girls, lots of them. I was one of them."

A long moment of silence followed. "But you need to tell them *why!*" Deborah prompted her. "There are reasons. Powerful reasons."

"He didn't take anything from me!" Lily hissed.

Deborah considered this. "I suppose it falls to me to explain."

The girl glared at her, then stood up abruptly, knocking her chair back against the wall. She opened the door. "I *gave* it to him." She spat the words at Deborah. "I gave him everything."

"Gave what?" Deborah asked. "Why?"

"Because I wanted to be...*you!*" She stalked out of the room and slammed the door, which failed to latch and bounced open again. She was gone.

"Lily's story is as old as Hollywood." Deborah shook her head. "Max, you and I know that Marty Nuco was capable of just about anything. Was. Is. Ever shall be."

A significant look passed between them, which did not invite Lyman into its meaning.

The sound of a horse moving came from the barn, then, outside, a little cry, a grunt, and a thump of hooves. Through the tiny window of the tack room, Lyman glimpsed the girl, bareback on a gray horse, heading across a field toward the open hills.

"She's from the country. She's a mustang herself." Anxiety tightened Deborah's eyes. "She told me it started with an audition for an acting school. She wanted to sing and dance and play dress-up. Like we all do. Innocent young girls. Truly innocent. In the beginning. But in that world they grow up fast."

"Yes." Max growled mournfully.

"But she got away from him. She was on her own when I met her. Marty called her that night, the night he was shot, and convinced her somehow to go to this apartment." Deborah stood up and turned away from the two men. "She says he threatened to expose her past to me, and if necessary, to the studio and the newspapers. Because now she had something to lose. He also threatened her with a gun, but he was careless, and she got it away from him. There was a struggle. The gun went off."

Lyman spoke to her back. "When did you find out what she had done? That night?"

"No, I did not see her until the next night." Deborah turned and gripped the back of the chair. "Wednesday, when she got home late from rehearsal. She was distraught, but wouldn't talk about it. Later that night she told me she had gone to Max's office and put the pistol in the drawer."

"*She* put it there!" Lyman could not contain himself. "To frame Max? But how did she know where the office was?"

"It wouldn't be hard," Max muttered. "Once you're on the lot there aren't many locked doors."

"My God! I was horrified." Deborah picked up the chair and banged it back down. "I didn't sleep all night. I went in at makeup call, as if I was on a picture. No one questioned it."

"Of course not." Max squirmed in his seat.

Deborah shot a tense glance at Lyman. "When we...met, that morning, I was looking for the gun. I don't think she put it there out of any malice toward Max, but simply to throw off the police. I guess she heard about the incident in the parking lot at Ciro's." Deborah waved a hand at Max. "She thought they would suspect you." Her voice broke. "I'm sorry I dragged you out here. I can't control her."

Lyman could hardly contain his disbelief. "You are telling me this Nuco threatened her with gun, and then let her take it away from him?"

"I know." Deborah shrugged.

"I saw the gun," Lyman said. "It's a thirty-two caliber pocket gun. Not the sort of thing a gangster would have around."

"I was hoping she would answer those kinds of questions, that I don't know anything about."

Lyman had many questions that did not require Lily Paloma, or whatever her name was. "What is your relationship with her?"

"What do you mean?" Deborah looked out the window as if she'd caught a glance of the girl.

Lyman cleared his throat. The dust of the barn irritated his sinuses. "You said Nuco threatened to expose her past to you. But you don't strike me as someone who would hold an unfortunate past against a girl."

"She's ambitious. She thinks she's going to have a movie career. And she thought she was protecting me." Deborah returned to her chair and sat. "She thinks I give Marty too much control of my career. I tried to tell her that my relationship to him was not the same as hers, but she sees things differently."

Lyman was hardly satisfied with this circular tour of Deborah's wants, needs and excuses. "What is your connection to Mister Nuco?"

"He's my agent." Deborah's voice rose a half tone. "That's all. That means he sometimes gives me advice about personal matters that could affect my career. Sometimes I take that advice."

"How long have you known him?" Lyman asked.

"I've known of him for years. And I was one of his first clients. Nineteen thirty-six. Or thirty-five." Deborah sighed wearily. "The problem began when I accepted Glen Spangler's proposal."

Lyman had glanced at Max several times for his reaction, and had found him mostly staring at the patterns of the saddle blankets hung next to the window. Now he turned his eyes back to Deborah. "Proposal of marriage?"

"A proposal that's been on the table for a long time, I might add." Deborah mustered a brief smile. "Lily misinterpreted. She overheard some phone conversations I had with Marty about Glen, and she thought that I was somehow being forced into the marriage. She sees Marty as pure evil, and everything he does as evil. But she was wrong about this. Anyway, that may be what motivated her to act."

Deborah held her hand out over the dead stove as if warming it. "And to make a long story short, that is how I ended up in your office Thursday morning. The problem, of course, was that you came in almost right after me. Before I could find the damn gun. When I heard you coming, I didn't have time to do anything but hide in the bathroom. Which was stupid, and idiotic. At least one good thing happened. While I was in there, I decided that I wasn't much of a secret agent, to say the least. That's when I asked you to help."

"But you did not tell me the whole truth," Lyman challenged her. "Or really the least part of it."

"No, I didn't."

Deborah had run out of words, though her hands continued to flutter. She sat down. Max pulled out a pack and gave a cigarette to Deborah. So far his involvement in the conversation had been limited to a couple of grunts and some waggling of eyebrows—certainly not the same old Max.

There seemed to be nothing to do but have a smoke. Lyman pulled out his pipe and began filling it from the Bond Street pouch, wondering about Max and Deborah, and the look he had seen pass between them. He finished loading and struck a match. "With all due respect." He paused and puffed, thinking. "What you should have done, as soon as you could, was to call the police. If Max is really your friend, how could you let him take the risk of being charged for murder, when you could have cleared it up so easily?"

Deborah stared at him but said nothing. She had that distant, hollowed-out look Lyman had seen in the trenches in France.

Lyman tossed his box of matches on the table. "Maybe it would be fair to say that although you wouldn't hold Lily's other life against her, you feared that someone would hold her past against you."

"I was just trying to help her!" Deborah protested. "But people could make it look bad, I know."

Lyman nodded the stem of his pipe at her. "So there is enough to make some juicy gossip, which is the same as the truth."

"She is guilty of trying to safeguard her reputation." Max reached across to Deborah and patted her knee. "Of course, she should have called the police. This girl committed a crime by hiding the gun there, but it was a very minor crime compared to shooting someone."

"Yes," said Lyman. He turned to Deborah. "What were you going to do when you got the gun back? It was a dangerous game."

Deborah sat with her elbows on her knees, staring down at the smoke from her cigarette.

"And if you were trying to cover up Lily's crime, now you have made a great difficulty for us by telling us what you know. I presume the reason that we are here in this shed and not in a more open place is that you want us to keep the secret as well."

"No," she said. "What I was hoping was that you would help me convince Lily to turn herself in. As you can clearly see, I don't have the power myself to make her do anything. So now what should I do?

"You should do nothing," Lyman said.

"But here is a young woman—a good girl, I believe, with talent and heart—who was a victim of Marty and his gang." Deborah held out her hands, pleading. "If there ever was a case of self-defense this is it."

"Investigators, lawyers, judges." Lyman counted with the pipe. "They should make those decisions."

Deborah sighed. "There's something else. Lily helped another girl too, and now that girl has disappeared."

"Helped her what?" Lyman asked.

"Get away. Out of the whorehouse. Whatever it is. She was a prisoner. A slave."

"*Mein Gott!*" Max sputtered his disbelief. "When does she sleep?"

"Lily was trying to get her to Phoenix or Denver or someplace and help her make a new start." Deborah's hands were fluttering again. "Now she has heard from them. The gang. They have this Polack girl, and they will release her and let her and Lily alone for five thousand dollars. I'm willing to pay that."

A startling bang came from the barn. Probably a hoof against a stall, Lyman assumed. The stench of the place seemed to be growing. "If that's all they want, they must not know she shot Nuco."

"I don't know." Deborah shrugged. "I don't think so."

They all sat still, thinking.

"Well," said Max. "I am willing to go along with whatever you want to do."

Lyman was so sure that Max was going to tell her to go to hell that he started to nod in agreement. It took him a moment to find his voice. "Are you saying that after already spending time in jail, you are still willing to hide the identity of the guilty person? Even to the extent of obstructing the investigation, which could be a crime itself?"

"Of course not." Max stood up and turned to the rack of saddles, running his hand over them. "I was just agreeing that I will talk to the girl. And that it is important that she get good legal representation, and that this whole matter be handled as quietly as possible. There are people who can help."

Deborah nodded. "I think I can talk Lily into giving herself up if she knows the girl is safe."

"How will you know the girl is safe?" Lyman asked.

"I was hoping you would do one more thing for me. I was hoping I could count on you to deliver the money and get her."

The pain throbbed in Lyman's ankle like it was being pounded with a ball peen hammer. He had a feeling of being on a trolley that would not stop at his station.

* * * *

As Max listened to Deborah's tale, and Lyman's protests, his depression returned, blacker than ever. Sitting in jail, Max had stared at the walls, and remembered, and planned, and contemplated, but mostly he had regretted. This was his first incarceration since Berlin in 1925, when he was a reporter for a socialist rabble rag, charged with abetting a riot. But really they picked him because they suspected him of plotting to overthrow the government. And they were right.

Then he had been in real danger and did not care, and he had emerged from his cell as prideful and headstrong as ever. The Los Angeles jail was like a supermarket compared to the prison outside Berlin, but Max had been terrified, not of his jailers, but of what the incident meant for the rest of his life. He certainly had reason to question whether his marriage and his career would ever be the same again.

The charge this time was shooting Marty Nuco, but his real guilt was that he was so much like Nuco. Not a pimp, extortionist, and thug, but like him in a basic way. He was a man of wealth and power who exploited the weakness of others.

Max knew plenty about illicit and meaningless affairs. Since rising above the clouds of Hollywood, he'd been able to bed, feel-up or fitzle starlets and serious actresses, waitresses, and secretaries. Before that, as a penniless wise-ass *yiddishe* squirt from the streets, not so much.

There were hookers and vamps, the ambitious and the *meshugeneh*. He had never been in love with any of them. And though some had beguiled and even enchanted him, he knew none had ever loved him. And Max knew some were gifts, the fleshly equivalent of a bottle of champagne sent to his table. Max was careful. He never flirted when drunk, never went to a strange girl's house, or a hotel he didn't know. And sometimes, if he caught a whiff of bad herring in a situation, he just pecked them on the cheek, paid for their dinner, and took off.

When the meeting with Deb was over, she kissed him again, and he was filled with the shame and bewilderment of his pointless unrequited lust for her. He led Lyman back through a gathering wind to the Bugatti. As Lyman coiled awkwardly downward to get into the low-slung car, he banged his foot on the door sill.

"Christ!" he yelped. "Did we have to come in this coffin?"

"Sorry." Max reached across ineffectually to help him. "It's a better car for short people. What *did* happen to your ankle?"

Lyman plopped heavily into the seat, and arranged his legs in front of him. He stared at Max for a moment. "I was rousted by cops on the way home the other night. And pushed around a little."

"Rousted? Were they following you?"

"Yes."

"As a suspect?"

Lyman pushed his owlish horn-rims—therefore his great horned owl rims—up on his nose. "It was revenge for finding the gun, and for hiding it from them. It was also a warning. Stay away."

Max had not known this. He wondered if Deborah did. "Do you think the police are handling this correctly now?"

"You mean, since they realized you didn't do it?" The color rose in Lyman's pasty face. "Hell, no. Maybe they're too stupid to figure it out. Maybe they're too corrupt to follow the trail. Maybe Deborah or the studio bought them off. Maybe they wanted Nuco dead, or the mob did." He looked out the windshield. "I don't have high hopes for justice in this case."

"Do you think the girl really shot him?"

"That's not our most pressing concern." Lyman looked out the window again. A hard burst of raindrops pattered on the fabric roof of the car, then died away. "Don't you think we should get going?"

Max started the car and pulled out onto the gravel road that served as a driveway. "What is our most pressing concern?"

"Despite Deborah's protestations of innocence, she has now involved us in a conspiracy to manage or massage the truth. Okay. I know why I'm in this conspiracy. A combination of ethics and circumstances. And I know why Deborah's in it. She's trying to hide her indiscretions with this girl. But what I can't figure out is, why the hell are you involved?"

Max wondered how much he should tell this man, who had proved very useful, but remained as snooty and irascible as ever. "Deborah is my friend, I—"

"Bull hockey!" Lyman cut him off. "You should be running from this like Seabiscuit."

They had reached the main road. The rain fell straight down in sheets. "Deborah tried to help me."

"And from what I could see, she was about the only one."

"I was accused of shooting my wife's lover. I don't blame anyone for thinking I could do just that. This girl, if she's telling the truth, was fighting for her own life. Yah, there's a seamy side of it, but that part can be finessed. No one ever heard of her, and no one really cares." He was telling a story now, warming to it. "If Deborah is in peril because she was trying to help a poor young woman, the audience will root for her."

Lyman smiled at him. "You said *audience*."

Max stifled a laugh. "Public, I meant. I meant, in the court of public opinion, which has a lot to do with the court of law. If Nuco can be shown to be half the things we think he is, that this girl said he is, she will get off with a lenient sentence."

* * * *

"So someone kidnapped this poor girl," Tina said, after Lyman told her what he had learned at Deborah's. "And they want to ransom her for five thousand dollars? And all there is to go by is this girl's word and a man's voice on the telephone?" She snorted. "What's to prevent Lily and this girl from faking the kidnapping to get five thousand?"

"Why not?" Lyman chuckled. "I can't decide if five grand is cheap for a human life, or expensive for a prostitute." They were side by side on the couch. Every time Lyman returned to this safe haven lately, he appreciated it more.

"Since they told you this secret about the gun, you're required to tell the police or be liable for, I don't know what. Withholding information on a murder?"

"But if I go to the police alone, Deborah and Max are incriminated, and they are powerful people. You might say they are my benefactors. I've got to convince them to turn her in." Lyman bumped his fist on the cushion next to him. "Turn her in and tell everything. I see that now more clearly. I should have put my foot down. But they are intimidating."

"I can only imagine."

Lyman sighed, "Welcome to high society."

Tina stood and walked toward the kitchen, where a teakettle called. "Society. That reminds me. Khaggar Newman phoned to ask if you were going to the Nightshade dinner."

Thank God she was walking away from him so she couldn't see his reaction. "Nightshade, eh?" His heart raced.

"He thought you might have missed the invite."

"Because we moved," Lyman finished the sentence. Tina turned the corner into the kitchen.

Lyman had received the invite, and he had planned to go, but in the chaos of the last five days it had dropped from his mind. The dinner was an informal annual affair for the West Coast writers and alums of *Nightshade*, the pulp mystery magazine in which Lyman got his start.

It could be a pretty dismal affair. Most of the writers were dirt poor, and considered themselves unrecognized geniuses. That made for a lot of tedious umbrage-taking. Lyman had, however, been looking forward to going, for three reasons. First, he felt it his duty to go and buck up the boys with his tale of success, and stand them and their dates, if any, to a few rounds. He'd hit the bonanza, and custom and conscience demanded he be generous to those still struggling—at least for one night. And if it looked like he was showing off, well, maybe he was. They didn't have to drink with him.

Secondly, Lyman had heard that Deal Table would be there. Table was the hero of them all, about the only one who had broken out of the pulp ghetto artistically, but still managed to exploit it commercially. His books sold, and people paid him to adapt them into movies, radio shows and even comic strips. In other words, he had done something like what Lyman wanted to do. Though they'd not had a warm relationship in the past, Lyman wanted to at least observe what success looked like, now that it seemed possible for himself.

Those were as nothing compared with his third reason for going to the dinner. He had invited April Sheffield. Tina had never gone with him to the dinner, and the only one who would be there with whom the Wilburs socialized was Khagger Newman. And anyway he could pass himself off as the girl's mentor, a witty, wise, generous uncle-figure.

That had been his actual role in the budding relationship, which had so far been limited to a few lunches together in the studio commissary and a couple of his drunken phone calls. On these occasions, Lyman would draw her out, listening carefully, learning her likes and dislikes, and tidbits about her personal life. He gathered April had had a fling or two, but was presently unattached, which was presently to her liking.

Lyman knew that the instant she perceived him as pursuing her, as a man, their relationship would end. So he approached her falsely. Every word, every attitude, every solicitude had been a lie. It had been torture. Glorious torture.

April only gave him any time at all because she wanted to be a writer. Not a mystery writer, she didn't think, but also not a baker of brainless serials for the *Saturday Evening Post*. She read literature, and loved to talk about it. She used the language of aesthetics, of criticism, and she loved poetry, especially her own, and that written to her by young men.

The fact that she knew poetry-writers meant to Lyman that April was already morally compromised by romantic notions and the bohemian spirit. Twenty years before, art and poetry had helped Lyman win another lover—the beautiful, sophisticated divorcee, Mrs. Bettina Green. Tina had fancied herself a free spirit, an Isidora Duncan, a Nazimova. Lyman knew the tune.

Tina returned, bringing two cups of tea and setting them on the table before him. Old, ill, sixty-five now, but sometimes she seemed eighty. Her illness had etched itself on her skin, criss-crossed it with a spider web of lines, and pouched her face with the constant pain of breathing, and the struggle between hunger and nausea which made it impossible to enjoy most meals.

And Lyman was in his prime, more or less: mature, careworn, craggy, perhaps, but not old.

"Do you want to go to the dinner?" he asked.

"No, I don't think so, dear. Working outside today wore me out."

"Gee. Well..."

"Why don't you go?"

"I was thinking of it. It can be an awful bore." She seemed to have no suspicions of his nefarious plan. Lyman knew that if he went he would drink, and make a fool of himself, and probably never see April again, and endanger the marriage that meant everything to him. But he had been drunk when he proposed the outing to April. Lyman licked his lips. Maybe if he got drunk again, seducing her would seem like a good idea again.

Chapter Ten

Lyman heard himself talking and thought maybe he should pay attention to the words. The writers had adjourned to the saloon. Deal Table, an armchair Bolshevik, stood at the bar rhapsodizing about the Russian divisions, and Stan Brown, who wrote clever but phony courtroom thrillers, sat in a booth hammering New England Naturalism as if it was a bad automatic toaster.

Lyman would have none of it. Too many ideas! Not enough action! Empty pettifoggery! Effete didacticism! Or something like that. Lyman could handle ideas, but he preferred action when possible. No one was listening anyway.

The people at his table were dully watching Newman and a young writer Lyman did not know play euchre. So he began to tell the whole ridiculous story, starting with his war with Max Beckerman. The Nuco shooting wasn't exactly the big story of the day anymore. Everyone else had already weighed in on the subject and grown tired of it. So they ignored him, or made perfunctory comments.

Lyman just kept on. Then he felt April's eyes on the side of his head, and noticed the young writer peering at him over the top of his glass. Pretty soon others began to lean in—did he say Debbie *Boynton*? The growing silence fueled Lyman's enjoyment. All they knew about Marty Nuco was what they'd read in the papers. And what's this about the cops?

"...slams me in the gut—I've still got the bruises—and I swallow the whiskey. The whiskey." Lyman looked up. Ten or fifteen people stared down at him, straining to hear. "Won't someone come and give the fiddler a dram?" he sang tunelessly. Then he realized he had told these people things he had not yet told Tina. Or the police. And he remembered that he had every reason to believe that Max and Deborah were lying to him.

"Bastards," he said.

A fat writer interrupted. "Were they L.A. cops or sheriff's? Because I heard..." Someone else said something about how all the real cops had gone in the service, and now it was all cronies and bums.

Lyman felt his stomach knot up, from fear, disgust, or maybe the liquor. Yes, he could still feel the places he'd been kicked, and fallen.

Things were moving too fast. Lyman pushed himself up from his seat. The table tipped, hands grabbed drinks and lifted cigarettes overhead as he jostled a couple of people. He walked down the dark barroom with the pink and fudge floor tile towards the men's room. He should go into the men's room. Things were moving too fast.

He went past the men's room into the little hotel lobby, past the front desk, where a plum-faced clerk sat doing the night books. Into the street. A steel pipe railing along the sidewalk kept drunks from wandering into traffic. He gripped the cold, damp pipe and held himself up straight. Better now, or worse? The light drizzle might cool his brain, if he could just...

"How are you doing?" April walked up beside him. She had her raincoat on, and held his.

"Oh, okay, I guess. Got a little stuffy in there." The drizzle suddenly increased.

"Come here," she said, and they stepped back into the covered entranceway of the hotel.

"To tell you the truth," Lyman said, "They scared the hell out of me."

"The cops?"

"Yeah." Lyman shivered, but he felt better now.

"Is that story really true?"

He felt like an idiot schoolboy. "Yeah."

"Is Max Beckerman really innocent?"

"Well, yes, I think so. Somebody, y'know, put the gun in our office after he was arrested."

"Really?" Her eyes studied him closely.

"Yeah," said Lyman.

A man in a military uniform—an Army officer—came out of the lobby, and stood near them in the entranceway. He looked out at the rain, pulled out a pack of cigarettes and lit one.

She handed Lyman the raincoat and he put it on.

"Have you got a cigarette?"

She shook her head.

The captain—Lyman could now see his collar—turned to them and shook a loose cigarette half out of the pack and held it up to Lyman. Lyman took it and thanked him. The man flicked open his Zippo and Lyman could smell the lighter fluid of the fat orange flame under his nose. He thanked the officer again.

"Nothing," the man said, moving off into the rain.

"Look, I'm sorry. I haven't been much good. I should not have started drinking."

April had a sly, hard look. "Oh, I don't know. You can sure handle it. And it sounds like you've been under a lot of strain." She took his arm. A gust of wind blew down the street and she pulled herself a little closer.

"Yeah, I-I'm-I," he stammered.

She held up two fingers of her other hand in a pale, smooth V, and Lyman slipped the cigarette into them. "Actually, I'm intrigued." She puffed the cigarette smoke into her mouth and out again. "What's your next move?"

"My next move?" The dark wave of her hair brushed against his cheek.

"Are you going to turn her in?"

"No. I don't know." He needed to think about this, but could not. "I want to be done with it."

"Do the police know about her? The girl?" She slipped the cigarette into his fingers, and her hand seemed to linger on his.

"Not from me."

She cocked her head minutely. "You mean, none of you told the police."

"None of who? Oh. I told you what happened when I tried to help Max before."

She nodded. "Yeah, you're right. Better to lay low. But what about them?"

"Who?"

"Those people you just told this story to."

Lyman snorted. "Nobody was listening. They're all drunk."

"I think they were all holding their liquor very well. Did you speak out of school?" Her dark eyes were blazing intensely.

"There's more I haven't told you. It would be dangerous and foolish."

"And the people in there, you think they won't repeat this story?"

"Confound!" he growled, his hubris fully revealed. "Look, we're talking about a whore who disappeared into the underworld. No one cares about her. But they care about the crummy agent who got shot, and that damned little sauerkraut Max. And now I've spilled the beans and it's going to turn out bad for everybody. Especially me." Man of action! A regular Continental Op!

"There's only one thing you can do," she said. She was grasping both of his arms now, almost pressing into him.

"What's that?"

"You've got to get that girl back, fast. And get the other one to turn herself in."

It was so easy. When he moved his arms to encircle her, her hands slid around onto his back. He kissed her. Hard. The cigarette was heating his fingers. He dropped it and it died on the wet concrete without so much as a hiss.

* * * *

Ted Hardy lived by routine, by schedule. That was how he stayed on course. But Saturday night was different. Subtly so, to all appearances, but different. Saturday night was a ritual.

After the show, Ruth and Ted returned to their hotel for a fine supper brought by room service from the hotel's excellent restaurant. Whole crabs with butter, roast potatoes, crisp early peas, Parker House rolls, coffee and Angel Food cake with dark chocolate icing. The meal was slow and relaxed. Ruth opened the windows and closed the sheer white curtains, which waved slowly in the breeze, a most pleasing effect. The conversation was carefree, if sporadic. They were content with stretches of silence.

Finally Ruth stood, went into the bathroom, and Ted could hear her preparing for bed. He poured himself a final splash of coffee, and lit his last cigarette of the evening. It was past two in the morning, and the noise filtering up from the street had almost completely died away.

Ruth returned to the room in her robe and nightgown. Seeing him sitting there, she said, "We should go to sleep."

Ted felt a warm glow of expectation. "Yes, of course."

"Matinee tomorrow."

"I know, I know." Ted did not get up. "You say the same thing every Saturday night."

Ruth pulled back the bedspread and the blanket. "And every Saturday night, you say..."

"I'll sleep late on Monday."

"Oh, Ted, Ted. Must it always be the same?" Casting him a peevish glance, she walked over to the room service trolley. There was a frosty pitcher of ice water, and she poured some into a glass and sipped it. "That stagehand was very fresh with me tonight. During the show, he came into the dressing room."

"What stagehand?"

"Ben."

"You mean Van?"

"No, his name is Ben. He's the big, good-looking one with the blue eyes."

"Not good looking to you, though?"

"Of course not," she said coldly. "Just objectively speaking. He stank of cheap whiskey. It was repulsive. I was on the point of calling the stage manager, but he left."

Ted stood and walked to her. She turned away, looking at the trolley, and lifted a silver lid. She picked up a bit of leftover crabmeat and swirled it through some congealed butter. Then she popped it in her mouth, and searched the tray for another morsel, ignoring his closeness. It was exactly what Ted expected.

"So he was everything I am not."

"If you mean drunk and horrible, yes."

"And that just might be his charm."

"Don't be absurd. Our Lord commands us to submit to his will, to tend to the spirit and not the flesh."

Ted bowed his head closer to her shoulder. "His will be done."

"We really should get some sleep." She finally smiled. "I didn't mean to upset you."

"I'll get rid of him."

"I think that's best."

* * * *

He had come home late. Tina didn't like it, but at least he had come home. Now that he'd started drinking again, there was always the chance he wouldn't. She hoped that being with the writers would distract him from Max Beckerman, Deborah Boynton and all that. Since Lyman had gone to work for the studio, their lives had changed a lot, and not all for the good.

But going out hadn't had a good effect. He was cranky as all get-out this morning. Mumbling to himself, slamming the kitchen drawer shut. Roaming around the house. Probably hung over.

Finally, just standing in the kitchen, he said, "I am going to do what Deborah asked. Table convinced me. Whether this Lily shot Nuco on purpose or in self-defense is not the point. He's a bad man and he got shot for that. The point is to save a girl who is an innocent pawn in all this. Who has faith that the law will do that? I don't."

Tina felt a jolt of suspicion. "You told Deal Table about this?"

"Yes, privately. He can be trusted." Lyman rolled his eyes impatiently.

"Was that wise, to tell somebody?"

"Of course not." Lyman's sharpness increased. "But I realized that whatever I'm going to do, I should do it as soon as possible."

Whatever he was hiding was beside the point. "It's dangerous, honey, and foolish. I thought we had agreed on that. If you don't want to inform on them, all right. But don't get any more involved! If they want some girl rescued, why don't they do it? Or hire a detective, or send their chauffeurs! Anybody but you!"

He crossed his arms and leaned toward her slightly, his glasses glinting in the kitchen light. "You said that the theme of my books was that a man has to do the right thing, no matter what. Well, this is the thing I have to do."

She sighed. "It's because those cops humiliated you."

"They only embarrassed themselves!" He clenched his hands. "They didn't hurt me. I am the only one who can do this, and good will come of it. If not for me, for an innocent girl. If you weren't so..." He trailed off.

His defensiveness was a dead giveaway that he was hiding something. Usually he hid his reasons, rather than the actions themselves. So what was he hiding here? Probably his infatuation with Deborah Boynton. But Tina understood how it could happen. She was a beautiful movie star used to dominating people and getting her way. Lyman, for all his pride, was a sucker for a pretty face with a tale of woe. Tina usually didn't let his little flirtations bother her. But she'd never gone up against a movie star before. And neither had he.

She couldn't say any of that. She went to the sink and began rinsing out some dirty cups that stood on the drainboard. Maybe she was overreacting. She hadn't slept well, and her cough was worse today.

Lyman went into the living room and made a phone call. By the tone of voice she could tell he was talking to Deborah Boynton, who was getting all the sweet reason he'd just denied Tina.

His voice rose. "From them?" After listening again, he said, "What would you like me to do?"

He listened for a long time, then hung up and came back into the kitchen, where Tina now sat. By his very expression he showed his shame at doing the woman's bidding. But that was not what mattered. "Please don't!" she said.

"It's nothing. It's a business transaction." Lyman squeezed Tina's hand, and she did not squeeze back, or look at him. He turned and left. She regretted that she did not tell him she felt poorly. That would get him to stay, but it was against her principles to play the wilting violet, even when it was for his own good.

* * * *

Deborah again met Lyman in the driveway. When he stopped the car she slid into the seat next to him. "They called me. They have Lily now." She was wearing a dark blue suit and a white hat with a veil, as if she had just come from church.

"How did that happen?"

"Not sure. I didn't see her after she rode off on the horse. Someone called last night. They want twenty-five thousand."

Lyman stared through the windshield. After a rainy night, the clouds were still low and the wind was blustery. "Did they get her when she was riding?"

"No. The horse was back in the stall."

"Are you going to pay?" he asked.

"Of course."

"When will you get the cash?"

"I already have it."

Lyman whistled softly.

"I don't keep it at home." She held up a fat envelope. "I got it out of the bank."

"On Sunday morning? That's even more impressive."

"At seven o'clock Sunday morning. I've already been downtown and back." She handed him the envelope. Inside were five packets of bills.

Lyman took one packet out. Fifty hundreds in a tight pink paper band. He put it back in the envelope and licked the gum on the flap and pressed it closed. Was that the right thing to do? Should she even have shown it to him? For a man who plotted crimes for a living, Lyman was remarkably confused. It all depended on who was using whom for what—factors he sketched out with no concern when he was writing one of his melodramas, when he was consigning this or that character to a bloody end, just for the sake of the blood.

"You're to go to a place down south. Signal Hill. It's a bar. No name. No address." Deborah gave him a slip of paper. "Here are the directions. It's on Avalon. The bar is closed. Park by the front door. They will bring the girls out and get the money. Then you leave."

Lyman squinted at the paper. "This is putting an awful lot of trust in them. In fact, I feel like the only thing protecting me—and these girls—is their intention to extort more money from you in the future."

Deborah slowly bent forward, her eyes squeezed shut behind the ridiculous veil. "I know."

"If I do this, we give her to the cops for shooting Nuco. No more persuading. No permission. No bargaining."

She sat up straight. "Yes. Period."

* * * *

When Deborah gave him the directions, it was clear she had no more idea of the location of Avalon Boulevard than the Road to Zanzibar. But Lyman knew Avalon, and most of the other long roads that cross the L.A. basin from town to country to city, from neighborhood to orange grove to oil field to air base. Imperial Highway, Western, Lakewood-Rosemont, Olympic.

He knew them from his days in real estate, when there really were farms and small towns, and *Los Angeles* was a place north of Florence Avenue and south of Griffith Park. Now Avalon Boulevard below Rosecrans was clusters of cheap auto courts, hamburger stands and "ranchos" which harvested mostly weeds, mosquitoes and junk. It was some of the cheapest land still available because it had not been properly developed. Lyman knew that somewhere down here the government had expropriated a large tract for a temporary barracks and an airfield.

This morning all was washed clean by the recent rain and wind, and the sun blasted through the scattering clouds on the wet, vibrant green grass which grew up around every fence post, abandoned tiller, and rusty fender. Lyman felt nauseous and out of breath, assaulted by the colors and the brightness through which he drove, the sound of his tires upon the road, the drafts of cool air leaking into the car. He had to consciously remind himself to make the simplest actions of operating the vehicle, and to blink.

He had gone out the night before to get drunk and be foolish, and now his body retained a physical memory of a kiss and an embrace he had longed for.

But a kiss is just a kiss. He had walked away then, into the rain, knowing that they had changed for each other now, that he had become a man to April, not a character, not an uncle or a professor. And she was a woman to him. That was enough for one night. So Lyman had not been foolish with April, but he had been foolish. He had put Max and Deborah, and himself, in danger with his loose lips.

Up ahead Lyman saw the pea-green roadhouse on the right, with the tomato-red door. That had been the description. The building itself was little more than a quickly constructed barracks with the windows boarded up from the inside. An array of oil-drum trash cans in blue, yellow, and rust stood along the side wall. Two cars were parked near the door, but otherwise the narrow parking lot of crushed seashell and gravel was vacant. A row of old motor court cabins behind the place also seemed deserted. Not an unusual scene for ten forty-five on a Sunday morning in a place where people stayed up late and drank.

Lyman parked in front of the building as far north of the other two cars as he could get without blocking the driveway that went around to the back. He sat and waited, fighting to control his fear, staring at the front door of the bar.

A sound caught his ear and he looked around. A car had pulled off the road and was rolling up behind him. As he looked in the mirror, it skidded to a stop directly behind him, blocking any escape. A big body in a blue jacket came quickly out of the car and walked toward him. A meaty knuckle tapped on Lyman's window and he rolled it down. It was the fat cop who had pushed him around on Sunset.

"Give," said the creased pink face. Dark orange hair bristled over the scalp, zigzagged above the slit eyes, and shot out of the nostrils. The white lips were pulled back in a grimace, showing yellow teeth. "Give," said the teeth, with no change in tone.

Lyman hesitated. "The girls."

"At the apartment."

"What apartment?"

The creases of his face shifted slightly. "You don't know?"

Lyman shook his head.

"Huh." The cop cleared his throat. "You should find out. It's up in Silver Lake. Soon as you give, the guy in the bar makes the call, and they walk away."

Lyman handed over the envelope. "They're okay?"

The face and the blue jacket had gone, along with the money. The car pulled away and disappeared into thin air. It was over. Lyman's heart leaped with the joy of survival. He didn't have the girls, but he had not been beaten up or arrested, or killed. And the girls would be released.

* * * *

They brought Maria back to the apartment late that last night, and the two of them sat there all night long. Two men stayed in the room, skinny bastards with sharp eyes. Every hour or so a third man would let himself in the front door, and there would be a muttered conversation in the kitchen.

The men didn't seem to care if anyone saw them or heard them. Lily and Maria stayed on the couch, weary and terrified. The two with sharp eyes were like twins. One or the other of them kept saying "don't worry, we won't hurt you, but we have to get the money."

In the middle of the night, one of the twins and the other man took Lily down to a car. They shoved her down behind the seat, and drove for a long time. When they stopped they were at a phone booth outside a closed liquor store somewhere. Lily didn't recognize the street. They told her to call Deborah. Then they took her back, and she spent the rest of the time on the couch with Maria.

"It's okay," she whispered to Maria. "She's sending the money. Then we're getting out of town and never coming back."

"I'm sorry," Maria muttered. "I feel like it's my fault."

"No, it's not your fault." Lily realized her dreams were gone, and had never been more than a fantasy. "I was stupid to think I could stay in California and they wouldn't find me. We'll have to go. You can go home. I'll help you."

"Yeah, but what about you?"

Lily had been thinking about it. She had to get out of Hollywood. And she was afraid of New York. "Maybe Chicago. Maybe I can get a fresh start there."

Maria fell asleep, and Lily thought she was fighting it, but she woke with a start. She was still on the couch, but it was daytime and Maria was gone. A man, two men, held Lily so tight she couldn't move. Sylvan Koch leaned over her, looking at her arm, and he had a shot, a needle, what do you call it? He stood up and stared at her with his black rat face. Then a wave knocked Lily down and she was at the beach, floating on the sand, or the water. Anyway she was floating.

* * * *

Lyman drove fast for a while. Then he slowed down, and made a conscious effort to slow his thoughts down as well, to try to understand exactly what had happened.

Lily's story made no sense, of course: she had terrible things done to her, and then Nuco physically threatened her and got what he deserved? Then she found the perfect fall guy and hid the gun in his office? Just because it was there, more or less? To call it a tale for morons would be charitable.

And how could Max, who could go apoplectic if his tea was over-brewed, sit there and agree to patiently reason with the girl who had already sent him to jail and ruined his reputation, and might cause him even more trouble?

Then what about Deborah? Could Lyman or anyone else believe that Deborah had just picked up this poor girl out of nowhere for a sort of personal finishing school, the opportunity of a lifetime? And that this scholarship included covering up an attempted murder and involvement in a white slavery ring? This from a woman who was so concerned about her public image that she would not play a villainess in a movie.

Nuco, Deborah assured him, was capable of anything. But she could have told Lyman whatever she wanted, and he'd have had no choice but to accept it because he had no firsthand knowledge of any of this. For that matter, he had no way of knowing whether the story of Lily shooting Nuco was true.

And then these two "cops" that kept showing up. Or at least the fat, ugly one—Lyman didn't get a look at the other one this morning, but he knew they were not in a patrol car. Were they really cops? Or part of this supposed gang? Or both?

And finally Lyman had to question himself. Getting stupidly and needlessly involved not once but twice! For what reason—to do the right thing, or because a pretty woman cried wolf? At one point, he had thought himself the only one who had all the puzzle pieces. Now he felt like the ultimate dupe in the affair.

Driving aimlessly, Lyman ended up in Santa Monica. He stopped at the bus station and called to tell Deborah what had transpired. No one had called her, and she didn't know anything about an apartment in Silver Lake. She didn't even ask what happened to the money. She just said all right, and hung up. The job was completed.

By the time Lyman arrived home, the rain was pounding down, the streets were liquid with a thick coating of water that could not run off as fast as it fell. He wanted to go in, lock the door, and never come out. The walkway to the front door was blocked by a deep muddy pool of rainwater, and he soaked his shoes and socks getting through it. Once inside, he took off the wet footwear and headed for the bathroom, where he wiped off the shoes with an undershirt from the laundry hamper and hung the socks on the edge of the tub.

He found her on the floor in the bedroom, kneeling at the side of the bed. For a second he thought she was praying, like a child prays, and he wondered why, and even thought maybe he should join her. But of course she was not praying.

He leapt to her side. "Tina?"

Her face was ash gray, her hands cold. She looked at him in mute terror, trying to speak. "My God, my God!" he whispered.

* * * *

She heard sirens very far away. They had nothing to do with her because she was in a canoe, a rowboat, cold against her skin. She wanted to get out of the rowboat because someone needed her help. Yes, Maria needed her help. They were pulling her up now, telling her to wake up, but she was wide awake.

Was she dead—was that what happened? You still saw everything and heard everything, but you couldn't speak, you couldn't make them realize you were still alive, still here? She was moving now, they were holding her up. It was the bedroom, but it seemed a very long distance to the door. They stopped in the living room. Maria was bent over on the floor in front of the couch. Her hair had been pulled back from her head somehow, and clumped off to the side. Lily tried to reach out to touch, but her arms wouldn't move. Maria lay there, hunched over. The darkness stained the floor there. And her hair clumped off to the side. She just wanted to smooth Maria's hair, then it would look better, it would cover the white skin, and the dark red line on the skin, and it wouldn't bother anyone. But she couldn't move her arms. The policemen stood on either side of her like statues, and nobody moved.

Someone said, "She's dead, sister."

Chapter Eleven

"**I**t's really a miracle. It was developed for high-altitude flyers. Aids inhaling, and lets her exhale on her own."

The doctor was reassuring, but Lyman couldn't look at his wife. She lay in the bed with a hose and mask strapped over her mouth and nose, and a rubber tube from a suspended bottle taped to her arm.

"It takes the pressure off her heart." The doctor turned the dials on the breathing apparatus. "It was a pretty serious heart attack. She'll recover." He was a large, tan, balding young man with an easy smile and a southern accent, maybe Texan. Lyman wanted to believe him.

Tina lay quietly. She had been unconscious or delirious since Lyman found her and called the ambulance. Now they had her hooked up to machines. They knew more about the equipment than they did about her.

"The emphysema complicates things," said the Texan. "That's where the oxygen comes in. I mean, it really helps her."

How long had she lain there alone before he found her? Two minutes? Two hours? He wondered whether Tina would ever leave this hospital, would ever leave her bed. He walked out of the room into the corridor, the floor of which stretched shiny and empty and cold to the window at the end of the hall.

Tina had gone first to the busy emergency ward. After examining her, they brought her up to this floor. The treatment would consist mainly of rest, by her, and prayer, by Lyman.

At the desk next to the elevator hung a panel of colored lights, fifteen or eighteen columns of three, like miniature traffic lights with green on top, blue on the bottom, red in the middle. All the little stoplights were on blue, except two which glowed green. Lyman wondered what made the red lights go on. There was no one at the desk, and the only activity on the floor seemed to be the procedure in Tina's room that he had just left.

Lyman walked toward the dark end of the hall. In the room on the other side of the elevators a light was on, and he could see, from the knees down, a patient in the bed. A radio in the room played very low, syrupy orchestral music. A burly but genial-looking nurse sat in a corner chair with her white-stockinged legs crossed, reading a paperback book. There's the audience, thought Lyman. Twenty-five cents a copy for those paperbacks, but times a million copies. Twenty per cent of that, even fifteen percent. He continued aimlessly on. All the rooms were empty, lit only by the little bit of evening light seeping in around rolled-down shades.

He went into one of the rooms. The mattress had been removed from the bed. If Tina died, Lyman's life would consist of writing and whiskey. But writing was hard work, and how much comfort and affection would that give him? That left whiskey. So he would not be long in following her. Whacked on the back of the head with a trash can lid on 9th Street. To take his last buck and a quarter. That's how he wanted to go out. And too drunk to even feel it.

He lay down on the tight steel springs. And he wept, keening silently to himself.

* * * *

Dinner was two hamburgers with onions and ketchup, and metallic coffee in a paper cup, brought to the cell. Lily felt both tired and alert. Jangly, like the one cup of coffee had been three.

Hours passed, yet it seemed like time had stopped, and nothing would ever start it again. Her head pounded, her stomach was queasy. To pass the deadness of the wait she traced the corners of the room with her eyes. Up the corner, across the ceiling, down the next corner. Over and over, varying the pattern, going backward, skipping between lines.

Finally they came and got her and took her to a bigger room with a table. She sat in one of the wooden chairs. The door opened abruptly, and a man in a rather sharp gray suit tripped in.

"You Miss Torres?" He sat one haunch on the table, looking down at her. "Como esta? Me yammer Detectivo Robbins." It was the worst Spanish accent Lily had ever heard.

"Fine." That was a lie. She felt awful and probably looked worse. "What do you want?"

"So what happened in that apartment?" He had precisely parted hair, and gold-framed glasses. "Witnesses heard screaming. Heard a struggle."

"Nothing happened." She had to be careful what she said. "I mean, there was no struggle. These men came in. They gave me a shot. I woke up here."

"And they killed Maria."

"I know." Lily's eyes filled with hot tears.

"They killed her, but not you." His sad smile made Lily feel that he wanted to understand. "Why is that?"

"I don't know. I think the shot was supposed to kill me."

Robbins tugged the sleeve of his jacket down over his white shirt-cuff. "Yes, the heroin. Brought by these bad men."

"I swear."

"But you have dope in your bathroom. And a hypodermic kit in your dresser drawer."

"They must have put that there. I'm not a hophead." So they had drugged her and left her alive to take the fall.

"And your fingerprints are on the ashtray. The one she was beaten with."

The door opened again, and a large man in a blue suit stepped around the door and closed it.

"Hello, Shira." Robbins was surprised, but looked like he knew this man.

"She said anything yet?" said the new cop.

"She's a suspect in something else?" Robbins sounded annoyed.

"I hate to pull that on you, but, yeah."

This new guy knew something, or suspected something, about her. It had to be about Marty. The two men looked at down at Lily, one standing, the other hunching toward her.

She sighed. "You're just never going to leave me alone, are you?"

"Never," said Robbins. "I'm camping here until you're ready to talk."

Lily pushed and twisted herself, trying to find a comfortable position in the hard chair. These two could be in Koch's pocket, helping to frame her. Or they could be honest, true-blue good guys who would give anything to nail the rat. Since she didn't know, she couldn't take the chance of telling the truth. She needed a frame-up of her own. "So let's talk."

"You said something before," Robbins purred. "About the bad men who did all these—"

"*He* sent them."

"Who sent them?"

"Hold on." The man in blue held up his hands.

"Who's this?" said Lily.

"That's Sergeant Shira. He's from...he's helping me with this. Who sent the men?"

"Nuco."

Robbins shot a glance at Shira. To Lily he said, "Nuco who?"

"Marty Nuco."

"He's a vegetable, sweetie. He's not sending Jack and Jill up any hill."

"His men." Lily made sure not to seem like she was watching for Shira's reaction. "His thugs."

"Whose thugs?" said Robbins. "Nuco? You got the wrong guy here, babe."

"Go on," said Shira.

"He was a pimp."

Robbins glanced at Shira. "Is this your other, uh—"

Shira nodded.

"Great," Robbins whined, "but I just need who bashed Maria in the head."

For Lily it was very simple. If she wanted to die, she could give them Koch's name. If she wanted to live long enough to get out of town, she had to blame everything on Nuco, who couldn't hurt her anymore.

Robbins turned back to Lily. "So Marty Nuco was a pimp. Okay. But he had help, right? Who?"

Lily's mind grabbed at something, hoping it would hold. "There was this guy. Johnny. Maria and I worked out of his apartment."

"The one where we found you?"

"No, over on Crescent Heights. The one where Nuco was shot."

"Describe the inside of the apartment," said Shira.

"Tile floors. All the furniture was brown. One bedroom, double bed, a black hat always on the dresser. We kept a gun for safety, and that night Nuco came, he beat me, and Maria shot him."

"Maria shot Nuco?" said Robbins.

A sob welled up in Lily. She nodded.

"And when the men found you last night, did she admit that she shot him?"

Lily nodded.

Shira ran his tongue inside his lower lip. "I need for you to say it. Did you see Maria shoot Nuco?"

"He walked out of the bedroom and I heard a shot and he fell back into the bedroom."

Shira stared at her for a long moment, fingering his sunburned cheeks. "That could change our view of the crime. But Maria can't answer anymore. Neither can Nuco. That makes your story worthless. Maybe you shot Nuco."

Lily said. "I might've, if I'd had the gun in my hand."

"What kind of gun was it?"

Lily shook her head. "It was like a black bulldog."

Shira looked at Robbins. "But you still need who bashed Maria. I'm thinking as a junkie whore, this one seems a likely suspect."

* * * *

"Sir? Sir?"

A pleasantly horsey face surrounded by a black and white halo was much too close to his eyes. The overhead light was bright. Lyman pulled himself up. Had he been crying out loud in his sleep?

"She's better now," said the nurse. "She's resting."

"Good, good. What time is it?"

She studied her watch. "It's... eight twenty-one or twenty-two."

Lyman scarcely believed her, but his grogginess and disorientation told him the truth. He had been asleep for three hours. His self-loathing almost boiled over.

"We didn't know where you had got to. Hiding in here, really, sir." The nurse clucked disapprovingly at him. "She's stable now."

"I just needed to lie down."

"Well, if you would just let us know—"

"Is she conscious?"

"It looks like she's coming around."

Lyman went to Tina's room. If anything, she looked worse. But the breathing machine clicked and wheezed, and she seemed to be asleep. Sleep was what she would need for a while. Lyman sat down and watched, walked the room to the door and back, sat down again, leaned over her, leaned against the window jamb. For the next four hours.

At one in the morning, Tina opened her eyes. Lyman was dozing in a chair next to the bed, but he felt her move. She looked at him, over the black neoprene of the breathing mask. The black bladder which hung from the mask looked like an absurd cartoon nose. She made a sound that he could not understand. Lyman stood and unhooked the mask. "It hurts," she whispered.

He grasped her hand and squeezed it softly. "What hurts? This thing?"

Tina shook her head minutely. "I hurt."

"My love." That she could feel something, even pain, and speak, even two syllables, made him joyous.

She coughed a little, and winced. Lyman could hear her chest rattle. "Water."

"Just a little." He picked up the cup from the bedside stand and tipped it into her mouth.

Tina swallowed the trickle, and licked her lips with painful effort. Her eyes closed, and she seemed to be sleeping again. Lyman watched and waited. Her eyelids flickered. "Missin."

"What?" Lyman leaned closer.

"Missin."

"Is something missing?"

Tina shook her head. She was fully awake now. "MISH-en."

"Mission? The mission?"

Her face said *yes* with a slight smile and nod. She closed her eyes.

"What about the mission?"

Tina had returned to sleep again, or something like sleep. He squeezed her hand, but her eyes did not open.

Lyman thought of Spanish missions, like Capistrano or San Luis Rey. He thought of war, and of his army service, when they called every dangerous day a "mission." He wondered if the words came from some dream he could not see. Or did it apply to what Lyman had done this morning—actually yesterday—his mission to ransom the blonde and the other girl. He wondered if they had been returned. They should have, by now.

Lyman thought he should report to someone that Tina was conscious. He went out into the hall and down to the nurses' desk a few feet away. A pale, chubby young woman sat there, filling in a crossword puzzle.

"She's awake. She spoke."

"Did she?" The nurse stood up and followed Lyman back into the room. She passed a hand over Tina's forehead, took her pulse. "We should put this back on," the nurse said, fixing the mask back in place.

"I know. She was trying to talk."

"That's good."

"She said it hurts," Lyman whispered. "Does a heart attack hurt?"

"Lord, I would think so. I'm not the RN. I'm to call down if help is needed."

"Why is this place deserted?"

"Shortage of staff. A bunch of them formed a hospital unit and went to Hawaii for the Navy. They closed this floor until Knuckle showed up."

"Excuse me?" Lyman followed her out into the hall.

"That guy in the other room. And then your wife. Now a couple more. But don't worry. The RN can be here in ten seconds, and I've been checking in every few minutes. You've been asleep." The girl smiled approvingly. "He has a private nurse." She flicked her chin toward the other occupied room Lyman had seen. "So your wife's getting a lot of attention."

"You mean he hired his own nurse in the hospital?"

"He didn't, obviously. Someone else. He can't do anything." She pointed a finger at her head.

Why did she keep telling him about some other poor sap? "Should I hire a nurse?"

"There's really no need. The RN and the resident are right there. We're fully staffed during the day." She shielded her mouth conspiratorially. "I think that nurse in there is really a cop. At least the one I've seen looks like a lady cop. And she can't do anything for him."

"Why not?"

"Cuz, y'know." She pointed a finger at her head again, and this time held her thumb up and tapped it down. "Lot of damage. He's done for, poor guy. But I guess they don't know who did it."

Then Lyman understood who Knuckle was. "I think it's pronounced *New-co*."

* * * *

Around ten a.m. Lyman walked back into the room from having a pipe, and Tina was awake. She smiled as he leaned over her. "How are you?" he crooned, with as much jollity as he could manage.

She shook her head. "Weak as water. I don't think..."

He waited expectantly, ready to reassure.

"Why?"

"Why what? The doctor said it's not uncommon..."

Tina shook her head. "Why...everything? Why the struggle? What's it for? A lifetime. Young and fresh and hopeful." Tears appeared on her flaccid cheeks. "Learning everything. To speak French. Square root. Now s'all over. Useless. It all dies with me."

Lyman wanted to comfort her, but he could not. He stared at the floor, overwhelmed by her honesty and despair. Finally he roused himself. There are certain things you have to do, no matter how you feel or what you really think. "Please, dear. You're going to get better. It's not all you what." done. I tell He smiled. "As soon as you can, we'll go to a French restaurant. That one on Wilshire. You can order for us. Anything you want."

"I don't think so."

"Just try. Just want to. It's not in your hands."

Tina nodded, maybe more out of weariness than assent.

"I'm sorry that I was not there when you needed me." It was an admission of guilt and failure that he truly felt. "You asked me not to go."

"Who called the ambulance?"

"I did."

"Well, then." Her smile was brief but sincere.

"But I—"

"You couldn't have stopped the heart attack. You can't always be a hero." She closed her eyes again.

Lyman got by on coffee and tobacco for a while, but by late morning he was exhausted, and followed the nurse's advice to go home and rest. He picked the morning newspaper up off the porch. His hunger slightly exceeded his weariness, so he fried two eggs and made toast, but no more coffee. Lyman covered the shimmering surface of the fried eggs with salt and pepper and sat down to eat.

On the lower left side of the front page was a small article. "Brutal killing in Silver Lake Apartment." Lyman knew what it was before he saw Lily's name.

Maria Bielecki, a known prostitute, had been bludgeoned in the head with a heavy ashtray and then smothered. Allegedly, she had been sharing the apartment for several weeks with Lily Torrence, a chorus girl. Torrence told police that unidentified men entered the apartment early Sunday morning and drugged her. When she awoke, Miss Bielecki was already dead. Neighbors did not report seeing strange men in the building.

He pushed away the plate of uneaten food. Each word of the story increased Lyman's dread and shame. They had taken Deborah's money and then killed one of the girls. That they had not killed Lily was confusing. Was there some message in that? Or another aspect to the story Lyman did not know? He wondered if Max or Deborah had tried to find him at home yesterday while he'd been at the hospital. Or maybe someone else? Lyman experienced profound revulsion at being caught up in a real murder mystery. The terror and disgust affected him physically, roiling his gut and swirling his brain. The death of this girl he had never seen cast a heavy, dark, inescapable weight over his life.

His investigation of the case had begun, what, last Thursday? In the five days since, he had been easily convinced of Max's innocence and Lily's guilt, and of the official police indifference to the truth. The newspaper did not mention that the girls had been kidnapped. Now what should he believe?

Again, Lyman had that feeling that the more he learned about all of it, the less he knew.

* * * *

Marty lay there like a wounded soldier, quiet, eyes half-open. Because of the oxygen, Virginia could not smoke. She found a stick of gum in her purse, and chewed it as primly as she could. She wasn't supposed to be there. They let her in because they thought she was his wife, or maybe his sister. The nurse in the corner ignored her and read her magazine.

Sure she did.

Virginia had to be discreet, but she had come for a reason. She leaned closer, and took his cool, dry hand. "I'm going away with Max. We're going to try to save it. Don't know if we will." He did not seem to hear her, but how could you tell? "I mean, neither of us have done very well at being married."

She thought back to their first meeting. They were at the Hillshire Country Club. Max was off playing tennis while Virginia passed the time in a dull bridge game. Marty walked into the room and two women at her table got the vapors. And these were women who would consider the average leading man barely worth a second glance. He had on white flannel pants and a van Gogh-yellow jacket, and he glowed with a casual confidence.

Marty might not know who she was married to, but by the rock on her hand, he had to know she was married. It didn't matter. Suddenly, every time Virginia went to a party or a show, Marty was there. When she went shopping, she would see him nearby, looking at handkerchiefs or some other improbable excuse. Without a direct word, he made it clear he was pursuing her, and she quickly found herself looking forward to it, wondering when he would show up, what offhand remark he would make, waiting for him to casually touch her hand or chin or sleeve. When they became lovers, he was the first man she'd known who fulfilled her romantic dreams—direct, yet sensitive; passionate, yet in control.

Now here he lay, pale and inert, a machine breathing for him, a tube collecting his urine. Even if he lived, he would never be the same.

Virginia leaned closer. "No, you were not my first *liaison*." She slipped into the French pronunciation. "You probably guessed. But the others did not matter. You knew that." She rolled the ball of gum around her mouth. The nurse continued to strain to not listen to her whispers. "I have a feeling you can hear me, even though you can't show it. I know I don't even have to say this, but you were...are..." Sadness and loss choked her. She finished the thought in her head: *My one true love. The one I will carry to my grave.*

* * * *

It was two o'clock in the afternoon, and Ted Hardy was not at his appointment with the tailor, as he had said to escape Ruth, but walking into Marty Nuco's hospital room. He carried an armload of flowers, blooms he could immediately see Nuco would never smell. What had been a tall, powerful man was now a rotting log with tufts of hair poking out in places like moss. What you could see of his face looked slack and sickly.

"I heard you were done for," said Ted. "Now I believe it." He put the flowers on a chair. "So maybe these will be for your funeral."

The nurse, amazed at his rudeness, stood and left the room. Ted was also amazed at the fearlessness of his words. The last time they met, this man held Ted's life in his hands. Everything that had happened to Ted since, both evil and good, had flowed out of that moment. Now Nuco lay motionless, the breathing machine clicking and whooshing.

Ted had long ago forgiven Nuco for exploiting what were, after all, his sins and his alone. "You were God's sword on me. Stern yet merciful. I'm not bitter. Oh, for a long time I hated you, and yes, I felt like I'd been given a portion of grief I did not deserve. But no, it wasn't a matter of fairness."

Ted realized he was doing *My Friend Turnip*, talking to and for something—in this case a consciousness—that might not exist. "But it's worked out well for me. Just at the exact moment when things went bad for you, I made a comeback. I doubt you will. Like I said, I'm not bitter. You humiliated and bullied me. But I deserved it." Ted took a moment to swallow the fear that still appeared in his throat when he revisited that day. "But I grew. Stronger. Straighter. Like an elm. I used to be a joke. Now I tell jokes and the world laughs at the jokes, not at me."

Ted Hardy wondered if he really meant his forgiveness. He looked in his heart through the lens of belief that God had given him, and found it to be true and pure.

"So I forgive you, I thank you, and I bid you adieu."

* * * *

When Marty awoke, he saw Janet. Just like in his dream. He tried to say her name, but nothing came out. He tried to ask *what happened to me?* and his mouth did not seem to want to move. But he must have made some sound because she jumped up and ran out of the room.

When he opened his eyes again, a man was shining a light in his face. He wanted to see his kids, not this man. He had seen him before.

"Do you know where you are?" said the man.

Marty nodded. At least he tried to nod, and he must have succeeded because the doctor smiled. Yes, the man was a doctor, and Marty was in the hospital. But why?

He had a memory of driving. Had he been in an automobile accident? But he also remembered talking to people from his past, some of whom he barely remembered. He was pretty sure that hadn't really happened.

Now Janet was in front of him again, grinning and crying. "But the important thing is that you're going to get better. You're going to get better now."

Marty Nuco was very glad to hear that.

* * * *

Calvary Cemetery covered a large, rolling slope east of downtown. Lily had been here before, five years ago, for the mother who had abandoned her. She would not be visiting that grave today. The mausoleum where Maria would be placed was a wall of the dead four high by many long, looking out on a stretch of worn grass and gravel shaded by a coral tree.

This was part of her deal. What she had negotiated. They allowed her to plead voluntary manslaughter after she signed a statement that Maria shot Nuco. Lily would forever be legally known as Maria's killer. But she would have a chance at life, somewhere. She had insisted, however, that she be allowed to attend this service.

The jail matron stood next to her. An officer leaned on the unmarked government car and stared at her. There was another funeral going on not far away. By the number and age and condition of the jalopies parked along the narrow road, Lily guessed a Mexican was being buried. Her mother's funeral had drawn two extended families, half of Montebello, it seemed like, everyone expressing their fear and sadness and regret not for the woman being buried, but for their own lives.

Maria's service was attended by no one. The priest, a young man with blazing red hair, stood to the side in his black tunic, next to the funeral director. Two men in dark blue suits stood by the hearse from McDougald's Funeral Parlor, and two other men in green uniforms stood near them. The four workers chatted in soft, unhurried mutters, waiting to do the work of sliding the casket into the crypt and sealing it.

All paid for by Deborah. A man had shown up at the jail and said he was Lily's lawyer. He was going to defend her. He handed Lily a letter from Deborah. *Dear Lily*, it said, and how it was a terrible tragedy, what had happened, and Deborah was still willing to help her out. There was not a word of condemnation or judgment, and not a word of real feeling. When she finished reading, the lawyer took the letter. He said, "I have to give this back to her."

On the other side of the crypt, an old couple and a single man stood staring at the casket. Lily did not know who the old people were, but the man was the same one who had been at the stable with Deborah and Max. Lyman. He stood a little apart. Everyone stood a little apart until the priest approached the casket and opened his book. Then the sparse little group gathered around.

Lily placed her hand on the box, about where Maria's hand would be. She didn't know if Maria had been Catholic, but she was Catholic now. Posted and paid for by Deborah.

The priest unfolded a silk ceremonial stole and draped it around his collar so that the ends hung flat against his chest. He raised his right hand and painted a cross in the air before him. "*In nomine Patris, et Filii, et Spiritūs Sancti. Amen.*"

After a short preliminary prayer, the priest took a silver scepter from a bowl held by the funeral director, and used it to sprinkle holy water on the coffin. "I am the resurrection and the life," he intoned, then continued on in Latin, calling for the mercy and help of prophets and saints. Lily knew the end of the prayer— about a shining light on those in darkness, the shadow of death, and a guide for our feet to the way of peace. He closed his leather-bound book, took up the scepter, and again sprinkled the casket with water, peering at each of the people in the group in turn, very deliberately. Then, in plain and stern English, he said, "Grant this mercy, oh Lord, we beseech Thee, to Thy servant departed, that she may not receive in punishment the requited of her deeds who in desire did keep Thy will."

He nodded and the attendants stepped up to the casket. They cranked the pallet higher until it was level with the second row of crypts. At a signal from the funeral director, they gently lifted the casket, walked two steps forward, and slid it into place in the wall. All this was done with a respectful smoothness and lack of hurry, and Maria, free at last of earthly movement, settled into the place where she would remain forever.

* * * *

Lyman parked his car at the office and chapel near the gate. Inside the office, a soft man in a dull charcoal suit sat at a high desk eating a sandwich. A freshly opened can of potted meat sat in the middle of the desk next to a can opener, a knife, and a jar of yellow mustard.

"Hello," said Lyman.

"Howdja do." The soft man spoke around his mouthful of food.

"I'm looking for a funeral. It's, uh, the girl who was murdered."

"Which one?" The man picked up his butter knife and twirled it.

"Murdered." Lyman said it a little slower.

"Yes, sir." The man twinkled with secret knowledge. "Bullicki or Modrano?"

"Uh, the first one. Who's Modrano?"

The man wiped his lips with a finger. "Patricia *Modano*. Shot by her husband." He took out a half-sheet of white paper and drew a simple map. The lunch meat was growing more pungent by the moment. "Down the lane to your right, then right again. Just look for the people. Modano is on the right, yours is on the left, at the mausoleum."

Lyman headed back to his car and drove not more than a quarter mile until he came to the back end of a long row of cars parked along the narrow lane. He got out and walked toward the solid stone block of the mausoleum.

The funeral gathering for Maria Bielecki was small indeed. The service was just beginning when he walked up. The priest prayed in Latin, and Lyman was able to follow some of it. Lyman looked down at the ground, trying to formulate a cogent thought about this girl whose rescuer he was supposed to have been. He had come to bear witness to the passing of this girl, about whom he knew so little. And he thought there might be someone here who would want to know exactly what Lyman knew about her passing.

The ceremony quickly concluded, and Lyman looked up to see he was the only one still standing there. As he turned away, he saw movement through the trees on the other side of the road. The woman who had been killed by her husband was having a real funeral, with weeping, and long, sincere conversations among people who missed her, who might miss her for the rest of their lives.

Near Lyman's car stood a colored man in a chauffeur's uniform. Lyman had the absurd thought that this tall, solemn man was going to open the door of the old heap and drive them home, but the chauffeur pointed to a large blue Buick down the lane, and Lyman understood that he was being summoned by Deborah Boynton yet again.

The rear windows of the car were blocked by curtains. The chauffeur opened the back door and Lyman looked in. Deborah sat in the shadows of the back seat, behind teardrop sunglasses that gave her a comically cross expression.

"Hello." She smiled. "Can you spare me a moment?"

Though strongly tempted to answer no, Lyman nodded and slid in next to her. The chauffeur closed the door. His shoes crunched on the gravel as he walked away.

"Thank you." She gripped his hand in her soft, gloved one. "There's something you need to know."

"No." Lyman shook his head. "No, I'm not here for any more explanations. In fact, no. The more explanations I get, the more responsible I become for everything that has happened. Or is going to."

"Your conduct has been honorable to the extreme. Above and beyond. But I'm here because I have to be," said Deborah. "I am responsible, not you."

"Responsible?" Lyman almost laughed. "You're clean as a whistle, as we all agreed in the stable."

Deborah removed her sunglasses and looked directly at Lyman. "Both Marty and this girl were hurt for my sake, in one way or another. Marty almost certainly deserved it. The girl almost certainly didn't. But in both cases, I was responsible."

If she was going to insist on talking about it, he had to insist that they be very clear about what had happened. "I'll make a distinction. There's nothing you could have done to prevent Lily shooting Nuco. But almost everything you've done since then has been wrong, because of your initial decision to lie for and protect your lover and your reputation."

"My friend and my protégé—not a lover," Deborah replied icily. "I'm the mother of an eleven-year-old child."

"As you wish. I'm not judging. I haven't covered myself in glory, either. I gave your money away before I knew they were safe. To tell you the truth, I was scared to death. I would have done just about anything they told me to."

Deborah fumbled in her purse and pulled out a cigarette and a small gold lighter. She lit the cigarette and blew a thin stream of smoke toward the empty front seat. "That's why you need to know. She was already dead by the time you got there."

This news stunned Lyman. "How do you know that?"

"The police have been to see me."

"So they know the girls were kidnapped?"

"I didn't tell them that." She dropped the lighter into the open purse. "They only came to confirm that Lily had been staying at my house, and that she had been working as an actress. I told them I was helping her get started in the business." She snapped the purse shut and faced Lyman. "As I have helped many other young women. The police were satisfied with that, so I let it drop. They told me what time they arrived at the apartment. It was nine-fifteen. That was about the time you left my house."

"But if they knew about the kidnapping," said Lyman, "they would know who to suspect in the murder."

"And following that trail, they would eventually connect Lily to the shooting of Marty. So she would be cleared of one crime, and arrested for another. I don't see the point of that."

Lyman wanted to grab Deborah by the front of her silk blouse and shake her. "I thought we agreed she had to give herself up for that."

"But she's already been questioned by the police."

"About Nuco?"

She shook her head impatiently. "I don't really know."

Lyman sat back and nudged the window curtain aside with his finger to look out at the quiet, sunny graveyard. Two men in green uniforms were slowly preparing to seal the girl's crypt. Why did he care? What difference could it possibly make?

"But you paid twenty-five-thousand dollars for nothing. Did you get her a lawyer? Did you pay for this?"

Deborah didn't bother to answer.

"You are generous."

"No. I'm afraid."

"Of what?"

"Afraid of my past. Specifically, the Marty Nuco part. Which is now forever linked to the Lily part. Shameful things, done not by me but for me, by misguided people."

"I don't understand. Were you involved with Nuco in some...scandal?" Lyman settled for that word.

"You mean, romantically?" She smiled dimly. "No. We go back. But it was always business."

"Then why are you so afraid of him?"

Deborah opened the curtains on her side. She rolled down the window next to her and tossed the lit cigarette through it. "Because I created him. He got his start as an agent because of me. And his start as a —" Her mouth moved, but for a moment no word came out on her straining breath. "As a blackmailer. As someone who would destroy people for a price."

"You created him? That's hard to believe."

"In nineteen thirty-four I left my husband. Ted was a drunk, and he beat up women sometimes. Like me. He fought me for custody of Andy, who was only a baby at the time. True to his character, Ted went straight to the gutter." She stared straight ahead. "The things he was going to say I'd done. Things of a sexual nature. And he could have sold it to anyone. To my mother. He's a gifted player. He lays on the schmaltz and the heartache like nobody's business."

Lyman knew that the divorce was a well-known scandal. It just wasn't well-known to him. In thirty-four, he was as deep in the bottle as he'd ever gotten. He didn't remember much about *his own* life in that period. "So that could have ruined you."

"Certainly. Marty Nuco offered to do something about it. To convince Ted. I said okay. That was the original, first wrong decision. The one you can't take back, that turns everything after it into a goddamn mess."

Lyman searched for something to say and came up empty.

Deborah was slowly crumpling into herself. "Ted was also a homosexual. I had to know that's what Marty meant. Me, of all people. Marty hired a young actor, a kid new in town, just off the boat. And this young man got Ted drunk and reached for Ted's... Well. You didn't have to do more than that. Ted was a farm animal."

Lyman tried to keep up. She was talking about Ted Hardy, the vaudeville clown?

"And Marty took pictures or got them somehow, and they were very graphic." Deborah gripped the purse. "He told Ted to drop the custody claim, and get out of town for good. And that's exactly what Ted did."

"Don't you think he deserved it? He married you under false pretenses, didn't he?"

"I didn't know enough about him," said Deborah. "That was my fault. His liking boys was the least of it, or anyway not the worst of it. Like I said, he liked to hit. A real bedroom pugilist. But I didn't want to ruin him. I just wanted to be left alone. But I take responsibility for what Marty did. That responsibility has been in the front of my mind at some point every day since."

"So Nuco was actually blackmailing you as well," said Lyman. "He saved you, but he also had the means to destroy you."

"He never had to say a word. I made him my agent and helped him get other clients. He's done some dirty deals, I know. But never for me, after the original one."

"And then one day an avenging angel came to you."

"Lily says Marty was responsible for turning her out. Prostituting her. I don't know." Sorrow and defeat strained her voice. "Not my side of town. The point is, she already hated him. I just inadvertently provided a sort of psychological trigger that pushed her over the edge."

"It would be better for both of you if he just died."

Deborah shook her head. "He has three kids. Who knows if he'll ever see them again."

Lyman wondered how, at the end of this long tunnel of fabrication and deceit, she could care about the guy's kids. But there was something else that had been gnawing at him. "How did Lily know? I mean, how did she know to shoot Nuco that night, after Max pulled the gun on him? It was not self-defense, not like she told us in the stable."

Deborah touched her knee, flicked at a pleat of the skirt. "Lily was following Marty. She had the gun already. She followed him all day. Waiting for a chance. Lily had already made the decision. She must have been there to see what happened at Ciro's. But she was going to shoot him anyway."

"Still, did she intend to frame Max?"

"That was just a coincidence."

Lyman corrected her. "I can see it was a convenience, but a coincidence?"

"I mean, Marty was having an affair with Max's wife."

"While Max was banging his way across town." Lyman didn't bother suppressing a laugh. "Did he really care that much?"

But a persistent cloud in Lyman's understanding of the story suddenly broke up, and he realized he'd been looking past the obvious to the unknowable. "It was because it was Nuco. It was because it was Nuco fouling his nest, not because his wife was unfaithful."

Deborah glanced at him. "There was a particular reason for that. You see, I wasn't the only one Marty knew dirty secrets about. The boy who seduced Ted, who was in the photos, was a young refugee from the Nazis, desperate to make it in the movies."

"Max Beckerman."

Deborah nodded. "He didn't even have a name then. He disappeared afterward, but I knew who he was, always. We became close later on, but we never spoke of it. And Marty knew who he was. Marty never forgot anything, or threw away a picture. I can't imagine what it must have been like for Max."

"Christ, what a mess." That was all Lyman could come up with.

"Yes. Now you know."

They sat in silence for a long moment. This was goodbye, Lyman knew. But he couldn't bring himself to call it good riddance. All he could do was marvel at the destruction around him. She must have signaled the driver somehow, because the door opened. Her absurd teardrop dark glasses were back on her face.

As Lyman got out of the car, he noticed movement around him. The Mexican funeral had broken up. Groups of people in dark suits and dresses walked past on the road, talking, saying hello and goodbye to one another. A Ford V8 pulled around another car and accelerated, the loud cough from its perforated or non-existent muffler warning people out of the way. A pomaded head appeared out of the passenger window, dark commas of hair shaking loose, yelling something angry or just obnoxious in Spanish.

Lyman *tsk-tsked*. Hell of a way to leave a funeral.

A watery-eyed old man appeared before Lyman. He and the portly wife at his side had been at Maria's interment.

"It's a terribly sorry thing," said the man.

"Yes." Lyman tried to be gentle. "Related?"

"No." A wisp of a breeze lifted the old man's thin gray hair. "Just friends. From back home you see."

Lyman smiled reassuringly "Well."

The wife took her husband's arm for support. "Can you tell me?" She smiled hopefully. "Will the apartment be available for rent?"

Chapter Twelve

Max Beckerman fingered the ridges of the scallop shell with his damp, sandy hands. Virginia was ankle-deep in the surf. A breeze blew in from the gray-green sea. Eight thirty in the morning. A ridiculous time to be on the beach. Which was the point. On this isolated scrap of land. Which was also the point. They were in Fort Ross because of the distance from everything, and the foul climate. They were out here with the clams at dawn precisely because it was something they'd never done before. Max had to decide if the marriage was worth saving. Maybe she was doing the same thing. But in the meantime they were going through these exercises.

She'd had an affair. She'd lied. But he'd had affairs, too. Many more. And he'd lied, and manipulated her. In secondary school Max had won a ribbon for his algebra prowess, but this was an unsolvable equation. Pleasure taken, pain given, solve for the value of a heartache.

Virginia squished toward him. "What have you got?"

"Oh." Max gave her the scallop.

"Terrific shell," she said, teasing. Every movement of her head and eyes, every one of the few words she spoke, seemed burdened with some secret meaning.

To hell with this. "My career is not up for negotiation."

Her eyes flared. "That's good to know."

"But my other career. The husband, the… pal."

"What about him?"

Max managed to choke out, "Needs to be better."

She squeezed his wrist.

Max tried to express a warmth he didn't feel. "I've always had the feeling of love. But I've also been selfish. When I'm here with you, I need to be here with you. There with you. Everywhere with you you."

"With *me.*" The squeeze of her hand became a stroke. "Not the girl on your arm. Not the woman in the big house with the beautiful yard. Not the princess, not the prize."

"Yes." He swept out his arm to include the beach, the clouds, the clams. "Here. Now. You yourself."

"*De temps en temps.* And then you can go to work and be that other guy." Her deep blue eyes speared him. "And I can still be the girl on your arm, sometimes. Or even the nude descending a staircase."

Max tried to suppress the warmth that had trapped him before.

* * * *

The hand-printed sign read, "Elevator out of Order." But the stairway was right next to the elevator, and Lyman only had to climb one flight to Tina's room. When he emerged in the second floor hallway, he saw a couple of nurses chirping together in hushed, but excited tones. The nurse Lyman had spoken to before caught his eye. "He's come back to us." She wagged her chin toward Nuco's room. "It's rather amazing."

Lyman smiled and nodded and continued past them into Tina's room. When he had left a few hours earlier, her air mask had been removed, but now it was back in place over her mouth and nose. She lay with eyes closed, struggling to pull air into her lungs. Lyman called her name softly. No answer.

He returned to the hall, hoping to find out if something had happened to Tina in his absence, but the nurses had gathered in Nuco's room to witness the miracle of his revival. "Knuckles" Nuco. The pimp. The extortionist. Lyman did not want to see it, did not want to hear it. He shuffled back into his wife's room.

Tina was awake. She gazed at Lyman placidly. Then he thought she wanted to speak. He unhooked the air mask. "How are you?"

"Okay."

"Really? Why is this thing back on?"

"Need it. Can't breathe. Too hard."

"Then we'd better get it back on." Lyman tried to smile as he hooked the mask back on her face. He was getting quite good at that little operation. Even with the mask, Tina gasped for air, groaning with every breath. Lyman could barely stand it, but he remained by the bedside.

Indeed, where else would he go? Lyman's home was here now. His job was probably kaput. Even though Max had been cleared by the authorities, his future at the studio was far from clear. They certainly weren't going let Max make a movie of *Double Down*, with its seamy, sex-obsessed characters.

So Lyman was somewhat marooned, and at a bad time, because he was bursting to tell his story to someone. He had just been involved in the greatest adventure of his life, and no one really knew about it. Tina had always been his listener, the one to whom he told his tales. She had heard him patiently, even eagerly, all those nights when he had nothing to tell except the made-up adventures of a character in his head.

Now something important and real had happened. Lyman had jousted with actual forces of evil, and survived. He had had a role in two tragic crimes. He had doubts about his performance and his effectiveness, and even his intentions, that he needed to get out. But his longtime listener was out of reach, sailing away, almost lost in the mist.

Lyman read an article about an actor he had barely heard of in an old magazine. The usual folderol. He loves this, and laughs about that; he's a patriot and an outdoorsman and a swell dad just trying to live a normal life. And he fornicates with his gardener, and his wife and daughter follow the 7th Fleet in a cabin cruiser, waving their underthings.

He had to get a cup of coffee. Or a jolt.

But he settled down into the quiet need to simply be there, without waiting, without anticipating. As the day wore on, Tina's breathing eased, and a tinge of color replaced the pallor of her face.

In the late afternoon Lyman walked the hall. The nurse's station was deserted, though Lyman could hear voices from the room behind the desk. Lyman assumed Nuco had been taken elsewhere. He stuck his head in the door expecting to find the room empty, and was surprised to see the man lying there in the twilight. No nurse. No audience. Lyman wondered if the miracle recovery had fallen short.

Here lay the monster who crushed dreams. The family man with children. He wore an air mask just like Tina's. He lay as motionless as a dead man, which frightened Lyman for a moment, as if death was following him around now like a partner, like his straight man. But air rattled in the mask that covered the figure's nose and mouth, and the little bladder fluttered weakly.

Lyman approached the bed. The man had a pale, unlined face with a surprisingly bristly beard making itself known after a week of free growth. Fine blond hair sprouted out of the edges of the thick bandage that covered his head.

As he stood there, it seemed to Lyman that the eyes opened, but in the half-light he would have to bend over to make sure, and he did not want to do that. He decided to get out of there, but felt compelled to say something.

"So you're the one who caused all this trouble?" Lyman spoke softly. "I have heard some terrible things about you." No response, of course. Lyman guessed that the eyes were closed after all. "But I guess I am more afraid of the stories I haven't heard." Lyman walked toward the window, where the nurse's chair and the lamp behind it were in the same place he had seen them before.

"What else have you done?" Lyman said, gazing out the window. "Who else have you hurt that would horrify me, or Tarzan Q. Public, or Jane K. Doe? What about that stunt with, what was his name, Ted Hardy? Deborah's homo husband? You got him good didn't you? When there's no referee, go for the low blow."

Lyman could not claim to be without sin, without evil intent, or malevolent impulse. He did not know what he might stoop to if the motivation was there. The story of Nuco and Max and Ted Hardy had loosed memories long held in cages. One in particular had chased him down and would not leave him alone. Without plan or purpose he began to tell that story to the stranger on the bed.

"I once knew a fellow. This was when I was teaching English for a year at a prep school in Maryland, during my bumming-around period before the war—the first war."

The air machine hissed.

"This fellow became a friend. He was a fag, and he had the misfortune to fall in love with a tennis player—well, that's how I heard him described, but I don't think you could make a living playing tennis back then." Lyman realized he had misspoken. "Yes, of course he did something besides being a tennis player. He was handsome and charming, and he mooched off people. And when he couldn't borrow, he stole."

Lyman stood at the foot of the bed. "He stole from my friend, and borrowed or extorted money. And the bastard cuffed my friend around. And when my friend had enough, he shot the tennis player dead. Then he went to prison, and after a few months he hung himself. My friend was twenty-four. Twenty-goddamn-four years old!" Lyman shook his head, still awed by the tragedy. "Bright, funny, generous, but once you found out he was a fairy—and very few did—you couldn't take him seriously."

Lyman had edged around to the side of the bed, and he leaned over, whispering now. "It is one of the regrets of my life that when he told me of his true nature and his troubles, I essentially stopped being his friend. I told myself that he was only telling me these things to seduce me, because you know how they are. Actually, I knew he was telling me because he thought I was like him. One of them. In the fraternity. Or the sorority." Lyman shook his head slowly. It had been thirty years since that hot, breathless evening, and the memory of his betrayal still pierced him.

"I thought I had put him mostly out of my mind. Then I heard the story of Deborah's husband. And it all came back. I wonder if you ever played tennis." Lyman studied him. "No, you're a big shot. You have a mansion, a pretty young wife you cheat on, and three adorable towheads. You put a dime in the poor box and think yourself a solid citizen." Lyman had a sudden urge to giggle uncontrollably. A titter escaped him, but he tried to control himself.

"But your little shop around the corner is full of bullies and creeps who go out and sell fear and pain and sleazy sex and easy money. And death." Lyman reached out and grasped the air mask on the man's face, and using the mask as a kind of handle, he turned the face toward him. The eyes remained blank, reflecting inward, if at all. Lyman straightened up. "No, I don't think you'll be back." He shook the head slightly, then released his grip on the mask. "And I don't think you should."

"Uuh..." the face whispered.

Lyman jumped back. "Well, well."

The right hand raised a couple of inches off the bed, and quivered. Excited despite himself, Lyman stepped out to the hall, but there was still no one to be seen. He went back into the room. "Are you going to make it, after all? Can you see me?" Lyman leaned over. The eyes seemed now to look at him placidly, but comprehendingly.

"Don't worry." Lyman smiled, again fighting an unholy desire to laugh out loud. "You're not supposed to know me. And I'm not supposed to know you." He looked at the face closely. "You remember the girl? Lily?" Was that a look of recognition in the eyes? Was that a smile beneath the air mask?

"On the other hand, why should you live? I was at a funeral today." Lyman unhooked Nuco's air mask. "I'm thinking it wouldn't take much to do the job, either. Any little thing." He examined the mask. With its neoprene bladder deflated, it resembled a little hot water bottle. "For example..." He gripped the bladder with both hands, and brought it close to the mouth. "About a minute of this, pressed tightly over the mouth."

The eyes closed. A baby would put up more of a fight, Lyman thought. His hands trembled. One way to steady them would be to push the rubber down on the face. Ever since this affair began, Lyman had been running around trying to undo the efforts of everyone else to cover up the shooting and other assorted crimes. But all those crimes traced back to this man, this face in front of him. Many people would benefit from this man's death, including Max and Deborah, who might then understand what they owed Lyman, might then ensure that his career in

Hollywood was long and serene. And the mouth was right there for shutting up.

This time Lyman did laugh out loud. Yes, kill the man. Then he could be the new Marty Nuco. Lyman thought of the girl's funeral—not of the words he had heard, but of how they called up the Latin of his schoolboy years. Something else loomed up suddenly from that time. Shakespeare, and all his unhappy murderers, most of whom ended up mad or avenged. A line—something about how a good deed shines in a naughty world.

A naughty world indeed. He put the mask back on the uncomprehending face, and snapped the straps in place. He patted the man on the shoulder. "Frankly, hearing what you have to say is going to be loads of fun." Lyman let out a gurgling chortle. "It seems like everyone has decided to play along, even the girl. You could turn a nice, simple cover-up into a real pie fight."

* * * *

Lyman stayed with Tina the rest of the evening. She would wake from time to time. He read her little bits from the magazines he had with him. Every once in a while, he would hear little bursts of excitement from the hallway. Once he even heard crying, but happy crying. The pretty young wife?

Around midnight, he took an extra pillow and retired to an empty bed down the hall. Tomorrow he would call his editor in New York. There were several possibilities for a new Archer Daniel mystery that they had been kicking back and forth for a while, and it was time to get serious about that again.

Lyman opened his eyes. Something had awakened him. He heard muffled thunder outside the window of the room. In the dark, he could not read his watch, but the weariness that had dragged him to sleep was gone.

He lay on the bed, waiting for drowsiness to return, but it did not come, and Lyman had an intuition that something was wrong with Tina. He grabbed his shoes and the pillow and hurried toward her room in socks. No nurse at the nurses' station, and that alarmed him.

The door to Nuco's room was closed, which he had never seen before. Despite his anxiety about Tina, he peeked through the little watch window into the room.

All the lights were on. A burly man with black hair bent over the end of the bed doing something. It took Lyman a minute to realize that the man had Nuco's foot in one hand, and a hypodermic needle in the other. He appeared to be injecting something into his toe.

Into his toe? Lyman squinted. The stainless steel and glass of the needle gleamed. And the man holding it did not look like a doctor, to say the least, and even less like a nurse.

A gruesome face suddenly appeared on the other side of the glass, and emitted a muffled grunt. Lyman turned and began to walk. The door opened behind him. He began to run, and dropped the pillow and one of the shoes.

Not toward Tina!

He ran to the stairs, whirled and threw the other shoe. There were two of them, the big ugly-faced one and the black-haired one who'd had the needle. As Lyman shoved the door open and went into the stairwell, the big one—big as a haystack—grabbed him and spun him around. The smaller one with the black hair was there. Lyman saw a fist, and a blinding red light of pain. Then the lights went out.

When he opened his eyes, he was feet-up on the stairs, like diving in a dream, swooping. The black-haired one was on him, pushing his chin over his shoulder, and Lyman, from a distance somehow, thought, it won't go that way!

A roar, like a bomb going off in the close metal space of the stairwell. Another blast, even closer. Lyman was sure he had been shot. But the pressure on his jaw and neck relaxed, thank God, even as a weight crumpled on him, and fell off to the side. The guy with black hair lay next to Lyman and stared at the ceiling.

Lyman looked up. He was there. The sergeant. The roust. The big, pink fist now held a black revolver, pointed at Lyman. The revolver fired. Lyman screamed, or tried to. The man lying next to Lyman quivered, and slid down a step.

The fat cop said, "Come on." He grabbed Lyman under the arms and lifted him up. The other one, the haystack man, lay in the doorway, his arm reaching into space.

"Are you okay?" the sergeant said. Lyman did not answer. "Are you okay?" The face was like granite. Lyman shrugged. The eyes squinted, drilling into him.

* * * *

Lyman closed the door of his aging gray Chrysler. It was a quarter to seven in the a.m. He had seen her as he pulled in, and she waited for him at the end of the row of parked cars. It was his second day back. Tina was out of the hospital, but needed a full-time nurse. And Lyman still had a job. Writing dialogue for Yutzo the Wonder Fern. Or whatever they told him to do.

"How are you?" April smiled, squinting a little in the horizontal sunlight.

"Well." Lyman felt uncertain how to talk to her. "Thank you."

"You had quite an adventure. At least that's what the papers say."

"Yes. Sometimes they get it right. It was more bad luck than anything." Lyman remembered how intense everything had been to him when he started working here at Colosseum Pictures, and how during his investigation of the intrigues spawned by Lily Torrence the sights and smells and sounds of things almost attacked him. Now the sky seemed flat and dead, despite its brightness. All the cars in the parking lot were dull, and filmed with dew and soot. And he looked so bad in the mirror this morning he could barely stand to shave.

He remembered how his imagination, his hunger for life, had been stoked by the mere sight and scent of this young woman. Now even she seemed flat. Her clothes fit poorly, and her hair was clumped rather than curled.

They walked toward the office building. After only a few steps she touched his sleeve. "I was expecting you to call me that Sunday. But I'm glad you didn't."

"Sunday?"

April pulled up. "To go get the girl. But she ended up dead, didn't she? That must have been horrible."

"She ended up dead. For all I know, she started out dead."

April shook her head sadly and sincerely, not noticing Lyman's attempt at hard-boiled patter. "It's a pity."

"Yes." They started walking again. Lyman was limping a little, from where he'd landed hard on the stairs. When he was being beaten by the known gangster Sylvan Koch. Who was shot dead by Sergeant John Shira of the LAPD. Who, like Lyman, arrived too late to prevent the murder of Marty Nuco. Who ran a high class prostitution ring that served some of the most powerful people in Hollywood—none of them named.

Nuco, it could now be revealed, had been shot and seriously wounded ten days earlier by Maria Bielecki, originally of Detroit. Maria met her end last Sunday at the hands of her roommate, Lily Torres, alias Lily Torrence, of Los Angeles, when they fought over, well… attention was slipping. Something about narcotics, and this Lily was apparently just another cathouse whore. No one knew exactly why Koch had executed his colleague in crime by an overdose of morphine, but the rest of the story wrapped up pretty clean.

Deborah Boynton was never mentioned.

The newspaper called Sergeant Shira a "double agent," someone who pretended to be a corrupt cop while feeding information on the Koch ring to his superior. If Shira was acting, he was the best thespian Lyman had ever met.

"Did you get hurt?" Lyman heard real concern in April's voice.

"Bruised hip."

"It must have been terrifying."

"It was."

"You're an interesting man."

Lyman laughed. "No, I'm a very dull man who had an interesting week."

"No. I knew you were different quite a while ago. That story about your daughter, you know. Dying of typhoid fever, wasn't it? I thought, Hmmm, here's something new."

Lyman blushed. "I'm extremely embarrassed about that. I get creative when I'm drunk. And you were right—I'm a big fat hypocrite."

"Listen, I didn't mind. Not at all. Most men just get stupid when they're drunk. And the only time they're tender is when they want to paw you. You know, like King Kong."

They came to the massive mountain of Soundstage Six. Here their paths would separate. She grabbed his hand. "See you."

April Sheffield, or April Showers, walked toward the office where she would sit, bored and beautiful at her desk in the cool, quiet reception room, directing traffic, fending off gorillas, waiting for someone interesting to walk through the door. Safe and simple and useful. It seemed the perfect place for a young woman to be.

About the Author

Fred Andersen has written mysteries and comic fiction, as well as historical books and articles on a broad range of topics, including movies, transportation and the West. He lives in Arizona.

Did you enjoy Lily Torrence?

If so, please help us spread the word about
Fred Andersen and MuseItUp Publishing.

It's as easy as:

•Recommend the book to your family and friends
•Post a review
•Tweet and Facebook about it

Thank you
MuseItUp Publishing

MuseItUp
PUBLISHING

Made in the USA
San Bernardino, CA
26 March 2017